HALO®
EVOLUTIONS
VOLUME II

CW00953479

NOVELS IN THE *NEW YORK TIMES* BESTSELLING
HALO® SERIES

Halo®: The Fall of Reach by Eric Nylund
Halo®: The Flood by William C. Dietz
Halo®: First Strike by Eric Nylund
Halo®: Ghosts of Onyx by Eric Nylund
Halo®: Contact Harvest by Joseph Staten
Halo®: The Cole Protocol by Tobias S. Buckell

EVOLUTIONS

ESSENTIAL TALES OF THE HALO UNIVERSE

VOLUME II

TOR®

A TOM DOHERTY ASSOCIATES BOOK
NEW YORK

NOTE: If you purchased this book without a cover, you should be aware that this book is stolen property. It was reported as "unsold and destroyed" to the publisher, and neither the author nor the publisher has received any payment for this "stripped book."

This is a work of fiction. All of the characters, organizations, and events portrayed in this novel are either products of the author's imagination or are used fictitiously.

HALO®: EVOLUTIONS, VOLUME II

Copyright © 2009, 2010 by Microsoft Corporation

All rights reserved.

Microsoft, Halo, the Halo logo, Xbox, and the Xbox logo are trademarks of the Microsoft group of companies.

A Tor Book
Published by Tom Doherty Associates, LLC
175 Fifth Avenue
New York, NY 10010

www.tor-forge.com

Tor® is a registered trademark of Tom Doherty Associates, LLC.

ISBN 978-0-7653-6695-5

First Edition: November 2009
First Mass Market Edition: December 2010

Printed in the United States of America

0 9 8 7 6 5 4 3 2 1

CONTENTS

INTRODUCTION *Frank O'Connor*   1

BLUNT INSTRUMENTS *Fred Van Lente*
  art by Bryn Casey   5

THE *MONA LISA* *Jeff VanderMeer and
  Tessa Kum
  art by Jami Kubota*   45

ICON *art by Robogabo
  words by Jonathan Goff*   193

PALACE HOTEL *Robt McLees
  art by Michael James Chua*   197

HUMAN WEAKNESS *Karen Traviss
  art by Michael Rookard*   231

CONNECTIVITY *art by Robogabo
  words by Jonathan Goff*   283

WAGES OF SIN   287

THE RETURN *Kevin Grace
  art by Rachel Beaudoin*   303

VI   CONTENTS

FROM THE OFFICE OF DR. WILLIAM
    ARTHUR IQBAL   341

ACKNOWLEDGMENTS   347

ABOUT THE AUTHORS   349

ABOUT THE ARTISTS   353

EVOLUTIONS

VOLUME II

INTRODUCTION:
WHY SHORT STORIES?

Because the Halo universe is almost as vast and boundless as the real thing. And because Halo fans enjoy a broad spectrum of flavors and moments from the games and the extended canon. In fact, no two Halo fans are quite the same. We have hard-core fans who only enjoy one game type, on one map, with one weapon. We have fans who are enthralled by the tactical exploits of UNSC commanders. We have fans who wish to explore the deepest mysteries of a forgotten civilization. We have fans who want to drop from orbit with the ODSTs. We have fans who view the entire canon through the lens of the Master Chief's faceplate.

Moreover, we have fans who can't wait years between novels to get their next fix, that next glistering nugget of data about their favorite part of the worlds Halo has created. Short stories allow us the luxury of sampling those flavors and moments. Like a box of chocolates, to borrow a Gumpian phrase.

We can dive in, visit the bridge of Admiral Cole's latest command, or hide in an abandoned spacecraft with the life ebbing out of us. We can wander the desert of a distant world in the cloven shoes of an Elite. We can explore the ravenous appetites of the Gravemind through Cortana's tortured gaze. And we can do all this in a single book.

The first anthology I ever read was called *Great Space Battles*. It assembled short stories built around completely unrelated illustrations, and wove together a universe from the art it represented. I remember thinking what a wonderful way to read: in bite-size chunks. We have the luxury of an already established fiction and a vast range of characters and worlds at our fingertips.

Some of these stories are short and sweet and will melt in your mouth. Others are heartier fare, but they'll taste like a perfectly cooked chateaubriand. They'll all add ingredients and menu items to the Halo table and they'll all taste remarkably different.

The iron chefs catering this affair are a mixture of masters. We have stories from the Titans of Halo Fiction: Robt McLees and Fred Van Lente. And we have newcomers too: Karen Traviss, who has left an indelible mark on *Star Wars* fiction; Tessa Kum and Jeff Vander-Meer collaborate across an ocean and an international dateline; and Jonathan Goff and Kevin Grace bring some new ingredients. Even I've been in the kitchen, cobbling together something partway edible. I hope.

This anthology is certainly a smorgasbord and may be a lot to consume before we move back to the main course of novels, starting in 2010 with Greg Bear's new Forerunner trilogy. But you guys have the intestinal fortitude.

Bon appétit.

Frank O'Connor
Redmond, Washington
September 2009

BLUNT INSTRUMENTS

FRED VAN LENTE

BRYN CASEY

ONE

Fireteam Spartan: Black's objective was not difficult to locate. All one had to do was look for the enormous pinkish-purple plume of energy spearing out of the horizon on the colony world Verge. They bled silently through ten square kilometers of heavily fortified enemy anti-aircraft positions toward the perpetually shining beam until at last they reached the remains of Ciudad de Arias.

This city had been among the hardest hit in the initial Covenant assault a few months prior. The buildings leaned and listed on their foundations like beaten boxers right before a climactic keel to the mat. It took Black-Four a few minutes to identify an apartment tower that looked stable enough for them to scale without it collapsing beneath their feet.

Once they reached the penthouse, they passed stencils of pandas and koalas still visible on the charred walls as they entered what they assumed had been a child's room. They lay down on their bellies and looked out through the vacant holes where windows once were.

Their massive target drifted about five blocks away, casually knocking over fire-gutted husks into clouds of rubble. Thanks to their untranslatable and unpronounceable Covenant name, FLEETCOM simply dubbed the enormous machines "Beacons." Nearly fifty stories tall and five city blocks wide, the Beacon looked to the Spartans' eyes like a perfectly symmetrical beehive floating atop four antigravity stilts. Out of its gaping lower orifice swarmed a buzzing cloud of Yanme'e, the glittering, winged insectoids humans called Drones. Clicking and screeching and hissing and squealing in a teeth-gritting cacophony, the swarm tore deep below Verge's surface with handheld antigravity grapplers that yanked up great chunks of regolith. The Drones flew back up and deposited the rocks inside the Beacon's hollow, irradiant heart, where the helium-3 inside them would be extracted and converted into pure fusion power. The energy was then projected skyward, focused in the form of a massive purple beam erupting from the Beacon's summit. A weblike constellation of Covenant satellites orbiting Verge transmitted the power to the fleet blockading the colonies on Tribute, in the Epsilon Eridani system.

Like every other colony world's, Verge's helium-3 deposits had been trapped in the second mantle laid down over her original, natural exosphere during the spallation-heavy terraforming process. The Beacon would drift from continent to continent, gathering and extracting all the He-3 it could, until Verge was picked clean, a few weeks from now. Then the machine and its crew would be drawn up into a battle cruiser so the Covenant could glass the planet from space.

Unless, of course, Spartan: Black blew the god-forsaken thing to kingdom come first, cutting off the primary fuel source to the fleet blockading Tribute and giving the colonists there a fighting chance.

Which was exactly what they planned to do.

"What do we see, people?" Black-One asked. Befitting their highly classified status as an unconventional warfare (UW) unit, Spartan: Black's ebony armor had been created as skunkwork prototypes in a top secret parallel development lab in Seongnam, United Korea; as such, MJOLNIR: Black boasted a few variant design elements and enhancements completely different from the standard-issue combat exoskeleton. Its HUD magnification, for example, was much greater than the standard Mark V or VI, with a field of view of nearly five thousand meters. From this distance, Spartan: Black could zoom in on the support troops milling beneath the antigrav "feet" of the Beacon and see them as clearly as if they had been standing across the street.

"Two Hunters per pylon," Black-Two said, noting the stooped, spiny-armored behemoths. Each creature's right arm terminated in a gun barrel studded with luminescent green power rods. "Armed with standard assault cannon."

"Complemented by two—no, three—Jackals at each corner," Black-Three added.

The spiky-crowned, beaked aliens carried, in addition to plasma pistols holstered at their sides, some kind of long pole made of a translucent purple-pink crystalline material. Occasionally, a Drone would flit away from the larger swarm in a confused, almost drunken fashion, and a couple of Jackals would descend on it with a shriek, stabbing the stray in the neck, where it wore a translucent reddish-orange collar. The bugger quaked spasmodically with pain, clutching the collar with its front claws; it could take only a thrust or two from the Jackals and the resulting seizures before it fell dutifully back with the swarm and resumed whatever task it had abandoned.

"Jackals aren't just security," Four said. "They're also management."

"Very nice to meet you," Two said. "I look forward to killing you."

No one said anything for almost five minutes. They just watched the enemy work.

Finally, Three said, "Hunters and Jackals—they're just another day at the office. I mean, I can kill Tree-Turkeys in my sleep. And Can-o'-Worms are something you can sink your teeth into. But the buggers—how many are there?"

"I've got a hundred, a hundred fifty so far," Four said. "But I'm not sure . . . some I may have counted twice. They're moving pretty fast down there."

"One-fifty . . . Jesus," Three said. "How are the buggers going to react when we bring the hammer down? Can they use those grappler things as weapons? What kind of intel do we have on their tactics and behavior?"

"We have jack," said Two, the fireteam's intelligence

officer. "Covenant's rarely deployed them as combatants."

"Jesus," Three muttered again, shaking his head. "I hate surprises."

"If it was easy, they wouldn't call us heroes," One drawled.

"I'd prefer a pat on the back," Three said. "But I gotta be alive for that."

"Two," One said, "find us a room in the interior where we can mull this over and catch some Z's without being seen from the street."

"Copy that, Chief." Black-Two backed out on her stomach until she reached the nursery's doorway, then got up into a crouch and made her way quickly but cautiously through the rest of the penthouse. She determined that what was left of the kitchen had no good sightlines to the perimeter and prepared to return and tell One but was stopped by a fluttering, flapping sound from a doorway on the north side of the room.

She pressed her back against the wall and peered around the doorway. She was looking into a ruined family room, a flatscreen lying facedown and shattered on a carpet littered with tempered glass that once filled floor-to-ceiling windows. On the ground beside a sofa blackened and bloated by fire and the elements, a solitary Yanme'e Drone twitched his wings spasmodically.

Two put both hands on the assault rifle hanging from her shoulder and silently lined up a shot at the crown of the bugger's walnut-shaped head. Something seemed off about the creature, though. She didn't pull the trigger.

Two realized the Drone was on his back, pulsing the hinged armored plates that covered his wings over and over again in a futile attempt to flip himself over onto his belly. Two could now see that all four of his lower legs had been cut off and cauterized at the stumps. His two remaining arms didn't have joints that allowed him to reach behind and push himself upright.

Two watched him struggle for twenty seconds more. Then she emerged from behind the doorway and took several slow strides over to where the Drone lay. His orange, half-egg eyes were fixed at the ceiling and didn't register her approach.

Still covering the insectoid with the rifle, Two tucked one foot under the creature's body and kicked him up and over. He began frantically beating his wings to stay upright while hopping up and down on the end of his abdomen. The bugger was human sized, and they were now practically eye to eye. Two took a step back and made sure the Drone was staring down the barrel of the AR.

Holding the gun steady with one hand, she flexed her other elbow in such a way that a compartment sprang open along the left forearm of the skunkware MJOL-NIR. A wand computer with a microphone, speakers, a digital ink keyboard, and every scrap of linguistics data United Nations Space Command had gathered on the languages of Covenant races popped out of the compartment and slid into her palm.

"Identify yourself and your purpose," Two said sternly, and waited for the Interrogator, as ONI had christened the device, to translate and broadcast the question in Yanme'e.

The icon of a rotating circle appeared on the Interrogator's display, indicating it was working. After only a few seconds, the device emitted a faint series of clicks and screeches in a pitiful attempt to mimic Yanme'e speech. Two had little faith in it succeeding. Sure enough, a moment later, its display flashed: "Untranslatable." Two cursed under her breath. Not enough was known about the damn buggers to make even that simple demand intelligible.

With his head cocked quizzically, the Drone watched as Black-Two tried to rephrase the question a couple of different ways so that the Interrogator might translate, but no avail.

Then the creature made an unmistakable gesture, extending one claw in her direction, then curling his digits rapidly toward himself: *Give.*

Black-Two frowned. What little intel ONI had on the Drones suggested they had an instinctive faculty for technology. Cautiously, she handed the Interrogator over. There seemed little harm in it. A cord attached the device to her forearm to supply it with power and data, as well as ensure that the other half of a conversation couldn't just walk away with it.

The second the Yanme'e wrapped his claws around the device he popped open the access panel on its underside. He rearranged the circuits and microfilament wires in the Interrogator's guts with such speed and precision that one would have thought he had spent every waking moment for the past twenty years working with them.

Two opened her mouth to protest, but found herself just watching, transfixed by the rapidity of the thing's movements, which had a certain kind of flitting grace, like a dragonfly making its evasive way across the surface of a pond. Something in the device clicked.

And the creature started talking.

In the nursery lookout, Black-One was just starting to wonder what was taking Black-Two so long when her subordinate's voice rang out from inside the apartment: "Chief! Better come here! Bring the boys, too!"

The rest of Spartan: Black walked into the living room to find Two tethered to the Drone by the Interrogator's power cord. At first glance it looked like the Yanme'e was holding the Spartan on a leash.

"*Whoa! Whoa! Whoa!*" Instantly, the three other Spartans fell into an attack phalanx, Three and Four both dropping to one knee and raising their ARs while One remained standing, training her own weapon on the Drone's head. "Spartan Black-Two!" she barked. "Step away from the hostile!"

Two held up both hands and made calming gestures. "It's okay," she said. "It's okay. He's not all that hostile. I named him Hopalong. Hopalong, meet the guys. Guys, meet Hopalong."

Hopalong's claws flickered across the translator's digital ink keypad. "*Hello, guys.*" Normally, the Interrogator spoke in the inflectionless nonaccent of the midwestern United States. But whatever the Drone did to the machine's insides had distorted the computer voice so that now it sounded more like a recording of intelligible speech played backward that just happened to also sound like intelligible speech.

"The hell, Two?" Three snapped. "Making friends?"

"He knows an alternate route to the Beacon, an underground one," Two said calmly, but with urgency. "Tunnels that have been completely cleaned out of helium-3 so the buggers don't go in them anymore. We can slip in under the antigrav pylons and take them out before the Covenant knows what hit them."

"How did he know we were after the Beacon in the first place?" Three demanded. "You tell him?"

"Have you looked outside?" Two snapped defensively. "Like there's anything else on this dirtball worth blowing up."

"I can't think of a single reported instance in which Covenant provided aid to human troops against their own kind," One said, pointing her weapon at Hopalong. "We trust this bug . . . why?"

"See that?" Two pointed to the stumps where Hopalong's missing limbs had once been. "The Jackals did that. They work the buggers to death on that thing."

Hopalong's claw flickered across the translator in short, staccato bursts. "*Kig-Yar do this,*" the machine said, using the Jackals' own name for themselves. "*I drop cache twice. Kig-Yar cut legs off. Say I worthless. Let me crawl from Hive. Think I die, but no. Then I see you come. Through city. I follow. I come here. Climb walls. See you. Know you help. You kill Kig-Yar. All Drones help. Hive help.*

"*Covenant conquered us. Jiralhanae and Sangheili. Overthrew our own Hive-Gods. Make Hive worship Prophets instead. Rule through fear and pain. Now they come for you. Together we stop them. Earth Hive and Yanme'e. Just give us freedom. Freedom. Freedom. Freedom.*"

He reached up and touched the red-orange collar around his neck with both claws. He flicked at it, as if wishing to rip it off, but didn't have the power.

"*Freedom. Freedom. Freedom.*"

Hopalong kept repeating the same click-and-whistle combination that presumably meant *freedom* in the Yanme'e language. Two yanked the translator out of the Drone's hand and turned it off.

She pointed at herself, then at the rest of Fireteam Black, then made a "talking" symbol by slapping her thumb and fingers together. "We will get back to you," she said loudly.

Fireteam Black went into the kitchen where they could still see the Drone but he couldn't hear them, Interrogator or not.

The others waited for One to weigh in first. She didn't say anything for a minute, then said, "I can't shake the feeling there's something not quite on the up-and-up about this. But maybe that's because I don't like a roach as big as I am coming up with my battle plans." They couldn't see her face beneath the reflective gray visor of her helmet, of course, but it was obvious to all of them she was wrestling with the idea. "Besides, in-serting ourselves into local intra-Covenant disputes is a little above our pay grade, Two. We're more the blunt-instrument type."

Two glanced back at Hopalong. He lay propped up on the floor on the middle joints of his remaining arms—the elbows, she supposed—and rubbed his claws together in front of his mandibles, back and forth, back and forth, like a housefly, in some kind of hygienic ritual.

"Normally I'd agree, Chief, but the plan he's proposing seems the best way to take the enemy by complete surprise *and* circumvent the Drone threat."

"You can be sure he's not leading us smack-dab into a trap?" The doubt in Three's voice was unmistakable.

"If he wanted us dead all he had to do was whistle for his buddies the minute he laid eyes on us," Four pointed out. "Why contrive some elaborate ambush?"

Black-One said, "I've got to say, the opportunity to hit the ground hot, inside the enemy's defenses, and take out the objective before they even have a chance to mount any kind of a resistance . . ." She stayed silent for a second or two and then announced, "Yeah, that's just too good to pass up. Okay, Two. Tell the bugger he's got a deal."

Two went over to Hopalong to connect him to the translator again and give him the good news.

Once she was out of earshot, Four asked One, "And if it *is* a trap?"

Black-One looked straight at him. "Then we kill them all."

"Now you're talking," Three said.

TWO

Fireteam Black waited until an hour before dawn, which was scheduled to arrive around 0600 hours or so. In the interim they downed some high-protein MREs, then helped Three remove eight medium-sized backpacks from a case he had humped all the way from the drop point by himself. Each Spartan slipped a C-12 "blow pack" over each shoulder. A single pack could punch a hole in the hull of a Covenant Cruiser, as Fireteam Black had had the pleasure of witnessing firsthand. They had little clue what kind of material the Beacon's antigrav pylons were made out of, but the general consensus was that one pack per pylon should do the trick. And they probably only needed to knock out one or two pylons to send the whole thing crashing to the ground.

"And if not?" Four asked.

"Then we try harsh language," One said.

Everyone chuckled. Pre-op gallows humor. Situation: normal.

Hopalong watched them the whole time, hop-hovering in place, glittering head bobbing from one side to the other; whether that was from fascination or boredom no Spartan could say.

They fell in to callsign order and snaked down the stairs and out of the apartment building in single file.

Hopalong chose to crawl face-first down the edifice's side.

On the ground, One insisted that Hopalong point in the direction that he wished them to go; One then sent

Four, with his battle rifle, to scope out the area. It never failed to amaze One, even after all these missions and engagements, how effortlessly Four simply melted into the shadows in his jet-black MJOLNIR, carrying his rifle by its barrel at his hip like it was a lunchbox. She and the others hunkered down behind piles of rubble and waited until the little yellow dot representing Black-Four on the circular motion tracker in the lower-left corner of their helmet displays briefly flashed green. Without giving any verbal commands, One rose to a crouch and sprinted in Four's direction; Three leapt up quickly and followed; Two, a little bit more slowly, so the crippled Hopalong could keep up behind.

They zigzagged through the ruins of Cuidad de Arias like this for twenty minutes, until Four swept, at Hopalong's indication, the basement of another crippled apartment tower via a side stairwell. An entire cellar wall had collapsed, burying a line of washing machines and exposing a rough-hewn tunnel carved in the unnaturally raised mantle of the terraformed planet.

Black-One switched the order of their close alignment at that point, acquiescing to Hopalong taking the lead, Four following, then Two, then Three. She took rear guard. Their sleek train formation was belied by their stumbling progress through the rough tunnel, which had been carved out by insectoids expecting only to fly through it. So the "floor," such as it was, was just as covered in fissures and protrusions and jagged edges as the "walls" or "ceiling." It was more like an esophagus than a tunnel, snaking in cylindrical fashion down, down, down ever deeper into the earth. Hopalong now had the advantage, hastily flitting forward on his translucent wings, disappearing from view until the column of Spartans rounded a bend to find him hovering in place, impatiently beckoning them forward with a claw. Visibility was awful, provided solely by light enhancement in their helmet visors, bathing their environs in a lime-green gloom. The whole experience would have been extremely claustrophobic, had spending days at a time entombed within head-to-toe exoskeletons not cured every Spartan of any possible inclination toward claustrophobia a long, long time ago.

They clambered and crawled through the tunnel until, very faintly, they could hear the unmistakable hum of the Drone swarm at work far in the distance, and the warren walls began to tremble with the looming overhead presence of the Beacon. They were drawing near.

Three stopped abruptly in front of One, and she almost walked right into him.

He turned around, raised his hand before her, and raised an index finger—the UNSC silent signal for *Heads up.*

She peered around Three's shoulder to the front of the line. Four had stopped as well and was turning to pass signs back to Two, who passed them to Three, who passed them to her.

A raised fist: *Hold position.*

Four disappeared into the darkness of the tunnel.

On her motion sensor One could see his yellow dot

move eight, ten, fifteen meters away from their position—then he was out of sensor range.

Nothing happened for what seemed like a very long while.

Then the yellow dot reappeared on her sensor and rejoined the others. Four materialized out of the gloom.

He raised his forearm, clenched his fist, and pumped it up and down, rapid-fire: *Hurry!*

He disappeared back down the tunnel, and the others followed. In a few paces they entered a mammoth, ovular cavern, the top of which was covered with what appeared to be metallic scales, some kind of mineral deposit that caused the ceiling to gleam even in the subterranean nonlight.

Then One's breath caught in her throat.

Spartans were not, as a group, especially well acquainted with fear, but when she spotted one of the "scales" overhead shudder, as if shaking off a dream, One knew exactly what she was looking at.

Sleeping Drones. Hundreds of them, dangling from the ceiling of the cavern, completely carpeting the rock above.

She had only the one chance to glance above before she returned her attention to Three's back. He was in a crouch, weaving a nonlinear path through the cavern. One immediately intuited why: Four had gone out before them to scout the best route through the innumerable loose rocks and ankle-busting crevices in the cave floor so they could make their way through without noise. No need to wake the Yanme'e, no matter how friendly they were supposed to be. She knew for certain now that whatever Hopalong's plan was, it wasn't an ambush. If it were, they'd already be dead.

A distant noise kicked One right in the stomach: She could still hear a different swarm of Drones slaving away in the distance.

There were twice as many Drones here as they had previously counted. The day swarm worked while the night swarm slept, and vice versa.

That meant there had to be three to four hundred Drones all told in the area.

Black-One hoped they all shared Hopalong's democratic sympathies.

After a few twists and turns beyond the large cavern, Hopalong signaled for a stop and the Spartans circled him. They were so close to the work site that the grinding, growling of the excavations drowned out all other sounds, and the tunnel walls shook so violently they were periodically showered by dust and stones from above. A possible cave-in wasn't far from their thoughts.

Hopalong produced a thin broadcast data wafer.

"Hell is that?" Three shouted. In any other circumstances a whisper would have been preferable, but the harsh roar of digging practically prevented them from hearing themselves.

"Hopalong salvaged the broadcast wafer out of the video screen in the penthouse," Two yelled back. "He rejiggered it to show abandoned tunnels that lead toward one of the Beacon's pylons, and avoids ones being used for excavation now."

"I'm not sticking that thing in my head!" Three exploded. "Who knows what kind of enemy worms or viruses Bug Boy stuck on it!"

"I saw him make it myself, while you guys slept."

"Nothing personal, Two, but that doesn't exactly fill me with confidence."

"What's that supposed to mean?"

"You've got some serious Stockholm syndrome going on here with your six-legged boyfriend, that's all I'm saying. Your judgment may be seriously effed up."

"Sorry, I didn't quite catch that." Two got her back up. "You mind saying that again?"

With an explosive sigh that could be heard even over the grinding din surrounding them, Four reached between Two and Three and yanked the data wafer out of Hopalong's claw. He stuffed it into the receiving slot on the side of his helmet.

Three stared at Four. "You're a lot of help. I'm trying to hold an intervention for our sister here."

"In for a penny, in for a pound," Four said.

When a diode on one end flashed, indicating the upload was complete, Four yanked the wafer out and handed it to Two, who stuck it into her helmet too. One was prepared to order Three to do the same but that proved unnecessary. Soon all four of their HUDs featured translucent V-shaped arrows with range meters that indicated the direction of their individual pylons.

"Everybody set countdown timers for . . . T-minus ten minutes," One said. "This spot is Rally Point Alpha. Return here once your blow packs are set. Then we'll have Hopalong give his buggers the good news they've been liberated. We'll evacuate them beyond the blast radius before detonating the C-12."

One pointed at Hopalong, then pointed at the ground. "You stay here and wait 'til we come back. You got me?"

The Drone just cocked his head and wiggled his mandibles in her general direction.

Spartan: Black checked their assault rifles one last time. Locked and loaded.

"Let's get some," One said.

"Universe needs less ugly," Three declared.

Then they headed off, alone, in four different directions.

Black-Two's HUD led her down a wide rabbit hole that snaked several levels deeper into the earth so narrowly that she had to scale down feet-first. At the nadir of the passage, where it began snaking back up again, a fissure in the side of the tunnel faced a much larger cavern beyond.

Two turned on the horizontal lantern over her visor and peered through. The beam illuminated subway tracks, a stalled train, and several signs in Spanish in the human-hewn tunnel on the other side.

She flicked the light off and made her way up the rest of the tunnel in the green gloom of light-enhancement. The range counter in her HUD said she was within fifty meters of her antigrav pylon. The tunnel emptied out into another with a level floor and a ceiling high enough for her to stand up all the way again.

As soon as she did so, a Jackal rounded a bend, his

beak pointed downward at a translucent glowing cube in his hands.

Right before he walked into her, he looked up, sensing an obstruction, and Black-Two unloaded her assault rifle into his face and neck. The deafening digging sounds reverberating off every inch of the warren completely drowned out the burp of the AR and the Kig-Yar dropped without a cry.

Black-Two crouched behind the bend in the tunnel, but no companions of the dead Jackal emerged. Her motion sensor remained clear of red dots. The countdown on her HUD hadn't quite reached eight minutes.

Near the floor, along one wall, she found a crevice big enough to stuff the Jackal's corpse into in case any hostiles decided to come up the tunnel behind her. She scraped gravel to cover the purple bloodstains on the tunnel floor and accidentally kicked the smoky cube the Kig-Yar was holding. As the cube bounced across the floor she thought she could see three-dimensional images in the center of it. She picked it up and turned it over in her hands.

The sides of the cube were perfectly clear, and its interior was filled with a cloudy gel that churned and swirled as if it had its own internal air currents. In the center of the mist stood a slowly rotating three-dimensional image of a Yanme'e male, wings extended. A few Covenant characters floated near its feet. Black-Two had studied her Interrogator enough to recognize these characters as numbers—years, in fact. Two dates about a decade apart.

A trio of buttons appeared beneath Black-Two's fingers on the surface of the cube. She tapped one, and the mist seethed, wiping away the large image of the Drone, and started cycling through a series of images inside an immaculate plasticine honeycomb marred by a spray of Drone legs, abdomens, heads, and splashes of their green-gray blood. Interspersed among these three-dimensional tableaus of slaughter were scenes of smashed eggs, presumably Yanme'e as well, shell shards hurled explosively against the luminescent hive walls, the not-quite-living insides scooped out and oozing across the floor. The same Kig-Yar character floated beside each image, every time.

The countdown on her HUD reached five minutes.

She removed the Interregator from her forearm and waved its optical scanner over the cube until it picked up the Jackal word.

While she waited for the Interrogator's wheel icon to stop rotating, she played with the cube a little bit more, punching other buttons and seeing where they took her. In all cases, the mist wiped away the existing image and replaced it with another 360 degree three-dimensional image of an individual Drone, attached to various scenes of hive carnage, all accompanied by the same Kig-Yar character.

At last, the Interrogator flashed at her. "Untranslatable," it claimed. "Word itself translation from Yanme'e language. Nearest analogue(s): 'Unmutual' (43% accuracy), 'Incapable of Socialization' (51% accuracy)."

Two shrugged, dropped the cube, and made her way to the mouth of the tunnel. One of the Beacon's pylons passed a full story over her head as she peeked just over the ground level. An erupted heap of asphalt four or five paces away momentarily blocked her view from the pylon's guard—three Jackals and two Hunters—but they soon marauded into view. They weren't looking in the direction of the pylon at all, but were fixated on the Drone swarm as it fell like titanium rain into the horizon below the Beacon's massive, pulsating belly, crisscrossing with a second curtain that showered upward, into its bowels.

The counter on Two's HUD ticked down below one minute.

Pre-fight adrenaline slammed into her veins. Her heart rate shot up to a dance-floor drumbeat.

Ten seconds. She flexed her hands around the AR.

"Engage," Black-One whispered across her helmet speakers.

Immediately, the sharp rattle of Black-Four's battle rifle could be heard even over the noise of the excavation. The Hunters turned and began bounding toward the opposite pylon.

Black-Two popped out of her hole and fired three short bursts at the back of the Jackals' heads as they fell in behind the Hunters. Jets of purple spray squirted skyward as they pitched forward.

One of the Hunters instantly spun its spiny head around and pointed its blank gaze at Black-Two. She despised the damn hulks and their completely blank, gray nonfaces, for they had no expressions to read, no way to tell if they had spotted you or not—

Until they started lumbering toward you, swinging

their massive, armored legs with frightening rapidity, as this one did now.

Two leapt all the way out of the hole. She sprinted for the teepee-shaped pile of a collapsed concrete kiosk half a block away.

When she turned to let off a few bursts in the Hunter's direction, the emerald discharge from an assault cannon slammed right into her chest with a deafening roar of static, lifting her off her feet and slamming her onto the ground.

Getting knocked over saved her life, for as she thudded onto her back a second green ray of incendiary plasma blasted directly overhead. With her energy shields completely knocked out and the HUD shield alert honking a furious warning at her, the second blast would have cut her in half.

Two looked up over her chest and saw both Hunters rumbling down on her. She quickly rolled ungracefully behind the rubble cover and willed her shields to recharge, but the Hunter was looming over her before she had a chance to catch her breath. The armored bulk raised its triangle-shaped shield over its head, ready to bring it down on her in a crushing blow.

Instinct took over. The Hunter was tall enough for her to somersault between its legs, and her maneuver caused it to simply further pulverize the pile of concrete when it guillotined its arm down.

Until her shields returned, she didn't stand a chance mano a mano with the Mgalekgolo. But she had an equalizer: the blow pack. She slung one off her shoulder and hung it by its strap onto one of the Hunter's long spines jutting from its back.

She then sprang up, leaping up over the Hunter as it tried to reach back to grab the pack and rip it off—but its armored arms simply wouldn't turn that way. She used his head as a springboard and backflipped over the pile of rubble, remotely detonating the C-12 charge as she landed.

She would have been vaporized if the concrete pile of the kiosk hadn't been between her and the blast. The Hunter disappeared inside an abrupt ballooning mushroom of dust that radiated outward and completely subsumed Two.

When it finally receded, there was nothing left of the Mgalekgolo but a few sizzling bits of chitin fused to the ground and carbonized ropes of blackened worm. The concrete kiosk had been pulverized into powder.

The ground trembled beneath her feet and Black-Two whirled around just in time to see the other Hunter barreling furiously toward her. Her shield bar hummed back to full power. The barrel of the Hunter's assault cannon swirled a fierce emerald green, indicating it had charged for a second blast, but Two threw him off by opening up point-blank with the AR, forcing the thing to throw up its shield to protect itself.

They danced like this for a few seconds—the Hunter recharging, Two sidestepping and firing, the Hunter forced to stop and defend itself. Two knew she couldn't keep this up all day. For one thing, the Mgalekgolo had more armor than she had ammo. She had to maneuver herself into a position to land some shots in the exposed orange flesh between the armored plates around the neck and midriff, but of course the beast was making sure to keep those areas blocked with his shield.

Sudden movement to Two's right drew the barrel of her AR in that direction, but when she saw Hopalong clambering out of the hole she lowered her rifle. He hop-flew in shallow, graceless parabolas toward the underbelly of the Beacon. She looked in that direction and saw that the Yanme'e had stopped working. Instead, they swarmed across the machine's surface in a single glittering curtain. Unnervingly, every one of their amber, half-egg eyes seemed to be fixated on the approaching Hopalong with burning intensity.

Much to her shock, as soon as the Hunter spotted Hopalong too, he swiveled around and lumbered after him, completely forgetting all about Black-Two. He stopped once to aim and fire a concussive green stream at the Drone, but Hopalong managed to get just enough altitude on his membranous wings to levitate out of the way.

It was then that she spotted the smoky cube in Hopalong's claws, the one she had left behind in the tunnel.

It all clicked instantly in her mind at just that moment.

Unmutual.

Incapable of Socialization.

Dead Drones and eggs.

A jolt of fear electrified Black-Two's spine. She found herself running after the Hunter, who continued to fire and miss at Hopalong. She dropped to one knee and let off an AR burst at the Drone, but the gun was spent. Cursing, she snapped in a fresh clip as fast as she could.

Hopalong was far enough away that Two couldn't be sure, but it looked like the cube in his claws flashed as his digits flew across the device's multichromatic controls.

She could see glittering crystalline flashes as, one by one, the collars fell off the necks of the Drones waiting patiently on the Beacon.

The Hunter fired again, and missed again.

"Black-One, this is Black-Two, please come in immediately, Black-One . . ."

"Black-One here. I don't have time to chat. I've got a Hunter with a fuel rod cannon with my name on it pinning me down—"

"We're about to have much bigger problems, Chief. If anyone's placed their packs I say we evac our asses ASAP."

"What? Why? What do you see?"

At that moment the last few collars fell off the Drones' necks.

"We've been tricked," Two said, desperation creeping into her voice. "This is no ordinary collection of Drones—they haven't been 'enslaved' here—"

When the Hunter turned around and started running away, the bottom of Two's stomach fell out.

"*This is a penal colony!*" Two shouted.

Like an explosive cloud of shrapnel, the Drones launched themselves off the Beacon toward Black-Two in a spinning, chittering horde, each mass murderer of their fellow Yanme'e and killer of their young and defiler of their hives clicking and whining out the same word, over and over again, the only Yanme'e word Two had understood as Hopalong had repeated it so urgently back in the penthouse:

"FREEDOM."

THREE

Black-Two's motion sensor became subsumed with red dot after red dot until it looked like someone had cut her cheek open and the blood was seeping over the display, drowning it in crimson.

The cloud of Yanme'e slammed into the Hunter and in the blink of an eye he was covered in dozens of them. He let off an emerald swath from his assault cannon that dismembered any Drones in the path of the blast, but others instantly choked the gap closed. Together, the buggers lifted the Mgalekgolo high in the air. The barrel of the assault cannon was still recharging a flickering green when they ripped the Hunter's limbs and head from its body. The ropy, eellike worms that comprised the creature's true "self" cascaded like grain from a silo out of the ruptured shell. The Drones unthinkingly swooped down on the worms before they hit the ground and tore them into bright orange-red chunks with their claws and mandibles.

Two caught only a few glimpses of this over her shoulder, for almost as immediately the Yanme'e launched themselves in her direction. She turned and sprinted in the direction of the Beacon's antigrav pylon. Once she was within twenty meters she let the second blow pack slide off her shoulder and into her hand. She twirled it twice and hurled it at the pylon, where it hit about three meters up and stuck in place with a magnetic *thunk*.

She turned ninety degrees and ran toward the hole she originally came out of. All around her buggers exploded out of the ground and shot into the air; undoubtedly the hive sleeping below the surface now awakened to a glorious living dream of unbridled mayhem and carnage, no longer held in check by their Covenant wardens.

Two plunged headfirst into the warren just as a horde of Drones dove down to snatch her up as well. The Yanme'e slammed into a pileup, clogging the tunnel's mouth and fighting among each other for the right to pursue her.

Two didn't give them the chance to decide the contest. She primed one of her M9 grenades and underhanded it at the hole. The Drones' shadows wisely flew in retreat as the frag exploded, bringing down the upper wall of the tunnel and sealing Two inside.

The warren maze writhed with the fluttering shadows of rioting Drones in every direction. Two scurried a few meters in the direction of the original rally point then stopped, spotting the fissure leading to the subway system.

Bracing herself against the opposite wall of the tunnel, Two pushed off with her MJOLNIR-enhanced legs and put her shoulder into the fissure. She smashed through to the other side in a cloud of dirt and rocks.

Immediately, she pressed her back against the train tunnel. A few Yanme'e stuck their heads in through the unfamiliar hole to investigate, but not seeing anything moving, and since Two's black armor and gunmetal gray visor perfectly camouflaged her presence among the machinery-covered walls, the buggers moved on with a low, disappointed chatter.

Once her motion sensor cleared of red dots except at the margins, Two walked over to examine the sleek, dust-covered train car. A brief inspection indicated it was intact and straddled a single rail that snaked away into a tunnel unimpeded by any debris or cave-ins she could see.

"Who's dead?" One's voice crackled over her helmet.

"Not Two," she replied.

"Not Four," Four said, calmly, over AR fire. No matter what kind of 110 percent FUBAR situation Spartan: Black found itself in, Four's voice never rose, never wavered; he always sounded like he was shopping for groceries. Two found that both extremely lovable and extremely disturbing about him.

"Black-Three? Black-Three, this is Black-One, come in," One called over the open channel. There was no answer, but Two heard the ragged sounds of what she was sure was breathing.

"Chief? Recommend we change rally points," Two said. She placed a white dot on the team's motion displays to mark the location of the subway tunnel. "I found the Arias transit system. Train looks like standard colonial model, running on internal cell power, and this one is . . ." She popped open the service hatch on the side of the train car to check. "Yeah, it's fully functional. We rev this thing up we can get the hell out of Dodge right under the swarm's noses."

"I'm all for that," One said through what were clearly gritted teeth. Two could hear her firing her AR too. "It's a goddamn bugger convention down here."

"Chief," Two blurted out, "I'm an idiot. I shouldn't have trusted Hopa—that damn bugger. He played me like I was a naïve social worker. I'm so sorry. I—"

"He played all of us, Two," One said. "I fell for it too. No need to beat yourself up about it."

"Yeah," Black-Four said, "particularly when there are so many buggers down here happy to do it for you."

"Shut up, Four," Two said.

One said, "Black-Four. New objective. Shoot your way to Two's choo-choo. It is now Rally Point Beta."

"Copy that," Four responded, then was drowned out by automatic fire.

A pair of blinking yellow dots appeared on the edges of her motion sensor: her fellow Spartans, fighting their way to her.

Just a pair, though.

"What about Three?" Two asked.

"He's not responding," One said.

"I can hear him breathing. He's still alive."

"But unconscious." There was resignation in One's voice.

Two didn't think. "I'm going after him."

"Belay that, Spartan," One said sharply. "I'm not losing half my Fireteam."

But Two was already plunging back into the warren. "I'll be back with him before you're done firing up the train for evac."

The pointer to her Beacon pylon remained active, so despite her grenade's cave-in she was able to circle back through the now largely empty tunnels to her original position. She leapt out onto the surface of Verge and headed to the opposite corner of the Beacon, which still listed in midair, firing its energy beam to the heavens, albeit in a pitiful stream since the Drones had stopped feeding it precious helium-3.

The Drones swirled all around the Beacon—really, as far as Black-Two could see—in a pinwheeling, asymmetrical blur of gray-blue wings. Frequently a pair would collide, then claw at each other with high-pitched clacking and squeaking. Other Yanme'e would hover in midair and stupidly watch them battle until the victor had torn the vanquished limb from limb—literally.

That must have been what the Kig-Yar character "Unmutual" meant: the Yanme'e equivalent of a personality disorder, an inability to relate to others. While in humans such psychopathology could create cunning, hyperaggressive killers, in Drones, with their even more rigid socialization, Unmutuals were incapable of working in concert with the rest of the swarm as a single, coherent unit. The efficient Covenant wasn't about to let those minor details waste a vast source of manpower, however: Unmutual Drones were yoked to Beacons and worked to death by Kig-Yar.

A host of Unmutuals clung to the underside of the Beacon. As she ran underneath it, a few dropped down and attempted to hoist her into the air. She knocked them off her back with the butt of the AR. A solitary Drone plopped down directly in front of her, blocking her path, and she took it out with a short, controlled burst.

Yet they kept dropping down, forcing her to zigzag around them. By the time she emerged on the other side of the Beacon there were dozens of them standing as still as statues facing her, simply watching her with cocked heads, mandibles twitching.

A yellow dot appeared on the edge of her motion sensor.

"Black-Three, come in!" she yelled louder than she needed to. "This is Black-Two. I am closing in on your position. Give me your status."

There was silence for a moment, then Three groaned across her speakers:

"Buggers picked me straight up in the air, and they would have torn me apart like a wishbone if I hadn't let loose with my AR."

She sprinted a beeline for the dot, closing to twenty, then fifteen meters. She was on the edge of the city, and a few skyscrapers loomed before her. The ground was uneven enough that she couldn't see any sign of a Spartan lying before her.

"Can you move?" she asked.

"I don't know . . ." She heard his MJOLNIR shift and creak, and then he cried out. "*Goddamn it!* They dropped me way high up, and I landed right on my

ankle . . . must've broke, even inside my armor . . .
And the biofoam pinned it in the broken shape! Goddamn stupid skunkworks piece of shit . . ."

"Just sit tight," she told him.

She was within ten meters of Three. A Drone landed
in front of her, arms spread, but she didn't slow down.
Instead she barreled right into him, smashing her assault rifle into his face and knocking him over. She put
a foot through the front of his thorax with a crunch
and squish as she ran over him.

A menacing buzz made her look behind. The Unmutuals were falling into a single curtain behind her. Her
dispatch of the last Drone must have overcome their
innate selfishness. They were very slowly, but very deliberately, roiling toward her, a solid wall of flickering
death.

Her motion sensor showed she was practically on
top of the yellow dot, so she stopped.

Looked down.

Black-Three was nowhere to be seen.

"Where the hell are you?" she asked.

"How the hell am I supposed to know, man? They
dropped my ass on some roof somewhere."

"You've gotta be kidding." She scanned the buildings
in front of her and had to guess which one the yellow
motion sensor dot pointed her toward. "Why can't this
goddamn thing be more specific about altitude?"

"Write a letter to the friendly folks at Naval Intelligence," Three groaned.

She could hear the swarm surging forward. She
threw herself through what remained of the plate-glass

windows lining the lobby of an office building and made for the fire stairs, which wound up a reinforced concrete shaft on one side of the building.

Two took the steps five at a time. The building had to be forty stories tall.

She whipped past the sign for the thirtieth floor when the walls of the stairwell began to tremble and an intense, overpowering hum began vibrating through the shaft. She worried the building was about to collapse. She passed a hole punched in the wall and saw five Yanme'e desperately crawling through the exposed, rusting rebars and realized the entire swarm was trying to claw their way inside at once.

She looked behind and saw the shadow of a huge mass of Drones surging up the stairwell right behind her.

"*Aaaaaaaah,*" Three crackled over her speakers. "They found me, Two, they found me! Stay back, you goddamn buggers!" She heard him firing his AR. "*You wanna piece of me, you're gonna have to work for it!*"

She sprinted the rest of the way up to the roof and burst outside to see Black-Three lying on his back struggling with a Drone who was trying to rip his AR out of his hands. The crumpled husks of bullet-ridden Yanme'e lay all around.

There was something about the Drone fighting with Three that looked familiar—the four missing limbs.

Hopalong and Three both turned their heads to look at her at once.

She didn't hesitate.

She unleashed a short, controlled burst at Hopalong,

ripping him away from Three and knocking the Drone off the building.

The swarm poured over the edges of the roof like a cup overflowing and she could hear them on her heels coming out of the stairwell too.

She closed the distance between her and Three in two long strides. She didn't slow down. She scooped up Three, threw him over her shoulder, ran to the edge of the roof . . .

And jumped.

She landed with both feet on the roof of the building opposite and didn't waste any time locating the exit leading down—the door had been blown open by a Covenant raiding force many months ago.

She took the stairs down by leaping from one landing to the next, stopping only once to adjust Three to a more comfortable position across both her shoulders.

As she did so Three said, "For a minute there I didn't know whether you were going to save me or your bugger boyfriend."

"That would be because you are a moron," Two said.

Much of the swarm was waiting for them in the lobby when they burst out of the stairwell. Howling like Sioux warriors on a final charge across the plains, the Spartans unloaded their assault rifles, Three while still draped across Two's back, and cleared a narrow path through the Drones to the exit.

But now came the impossible part—the scenario One had wanted to avoid in the first place: a hundred meters of open ground between the Spartans and the

Beacon with clouds of infuriated Drones swarming overhead, everywhere they looked. Each of their ARs was on its last clip and they wouldn't make it ten paces without expending all their ammo if they tried to fight their way through.

So she just had to run.

The Drones flew down and tried to grab them, or snatch Three off her shoulders, but she was too strong and Three beat them back with the AR, firing off a burst or two when absolutely necessary.

Then Two felt her feet kicking empty air—she was rising off the ground against her will. But no Drones were near them.

"Oh crap," Three said.

She looked up—and saw several Drones floating above them, the antigrav grapplers they used to excavate mantle for the Beacon now trained on the two Spartans.

She saw a familiar form flitting by their side—she had blown off his front arms but he was still alive, limbless but still able to hover-hop on what remained of his tattered wings.

So Unmutuals weren't completely incapable of cooperation.

They just needed the right leadership.

Her helmet headset crackled, "Black-Two, this is Black-One. Come in. Black-Four has powered up the train and we are ready for evac. Return to Rally Point Beta immediately. Over."

"Copy that, Black-One," Two said, "but I'd get that thing moving now."

"Why?"

"Because I am about to drop something extremely heavy on top of it."

And she detonated the blow pack she had attached to the antigrav pylon of the Beacon.

The huge C-12 explosion was so violent that it startled many of the Drones into dropping their grapplers, which in turn dropped Two back onto her feet. She didn't waste any time in dashing for the warren holes. The other three antigrav pylons struggled for a few seconds to keep the unforgiving mass of the Beacon upright on their own, but gravity emerged victorious and yanked the machine downward on one side. The plasma stream still emanating from its top cut an apocalyptic swath through the Yanme'e swarm, vaporizing Hopalong and the dozens of Unmutuals around him. It sliced the buildings Two and Three had just escaped from in half like a giant scythe.

Two dropped underground just as the first pylon hit. The tunnels immediately began collapsing around her and it was a mad dash to stay one step ahead of the flattening ceilings. She barely made it to the subway tunnel and handed Black-Three into Black-One's outstretched arms as she stood on the back of the train car before leaping onboard herself.

The subway disappeared into its tunnel just as the remains of the fallen Beacon crashed through the platform roof.

For a moment, everyone inside the train car paused to catch their breath. The train whined quietly through the absolute darkness of the metro tube. Spartan: Black was too exhausted to celebrate.

"ETA at Pelican in twenty," Four said after a moment, as if nothing had just happened.

Three punched Two playfully in the shoulder. "So what did we learn today, huh? If you see something that looks different from us in any way, kill it immediately and without question."

Two just cocked her head. "We are a hell of a lot more 'Mutual' that's for sure."

"Huh?" Three said.

She watched the tunnel darkness recede back into itself behind them as the train hummed its way to the drop point.

"Nothing," Two said with a smile only she knew was there.

THE *MONA LISA*

JEFF VANDERMEER
AND TESSA KUM

>Lopez 0610 hours

Sergeant Zhao Heng Lopez stood in the cargo bay of the UNSC *Red Horse*, looking at an escape pod. A huge, pitted bullet. About two and a half meters long and thick, pocked and smacked by debris. Around her: Hospital Corpsman Ngoc Benti, Technical Officer Raj Singh, his helpers, the ever-silent, inscrutable Clarence, and a crack pilot named Burgundy who'd just come back from a recon mission. All of them staring at the latest catch. It was so dented the container itself almost looked like something living. Almost expected to see plants growing out of the sides. Was that all it took? Lopez wondered, to make something lifelike? Kick it around enough? Maybe.

James MacCraw joined them. Rookie. Raw. Big-boned, lanky, and freckled. Unimpressive. Maybe if she kicked him around he'd show some life.

"I'm here, Sarge," he said, but not like he meant it. God, she hated indifference in the morning.

"Yeah, you think you're here, MacCraw," Benti said in a half mutter. Next to Benti—who looked so small in combat armor that seemed to eat her up—MacCraw was like another species.

Singh had conscripted Burgundy into helping pry the pod open alongside his assistants. The thing obviously wasn't going to open easily for them—the line revealing the crude little hatch, locked at the side, almost couldn't be seen with the number of impacts it had suffered.

"Not much to look at, is it?" Burgundy said. Lopez knew that the Marines sometimes called her "Sticky-beak" because she was too curious, but she didn't seem to care.

Benti: "Is it, like, old, or a recon pod? Am I here to tranq or treat? I don't get it."

"Is it even ours?" MacCraw asked, ignoring Benti while asking the same question.

"Sure as hell ain't Covenant," Lopez said. "It's human." Just not necessarily military. Serial numbers, but no UNSC markings.

No idea what it was doing out here in uncharted space, floating in the ruins of Halo, a gargantuan alien artifact Lopez hadn't even tried to explain to herself. Hell, Lopez had no real idea what she was doing here, for that matter. They'd popped out of slipspace like a greased egg just three days ago, with no more specific task than "recon and recovery and watch out for Covenant patrols." Lopez wasn't in the mood for more mysteries.

"But—that doesn't mean it's friendly," she added, not wanting them too relaxed. Except for Clarence, who was at his best when he was so relaxed he didn't even seem to be alive; sometimes Lopez wondered if he was a ghost. But it was hard for the rest of them not to be complacent, standing in the bay of their own ship. Lopez knew from experience sometimes you took the worst hits where you lived for that very reason.

They'd seen pods before on this tour—too many. They were plucking them from the void with such tenacity it made her think they *were* looking for something in particular. But almost all of what they'd recovered had been sleeper pods from amid the exploded chunks of continental plate, the almost delicate slices of superstructure: cryotubes ejected from the *Pillar of Autumn* when she was brought down by Covenant fire. All DOA, cracked and ruptured by the wealth of debris out there. Go to sleep expecting to wake, and wind up in a floating coffin instead. There were worse ways to die. There were much better ways, too.

MacCraw might have been slow, but he wasn't that slow. As he helped Benti unsnap a stretcher, he said, "So much for a highly classified top-secret hush-hush location. That's a civilian pod."

Lopez didn't answer because she had no answer. Their mission remained fuzzy, and the rumor mill was surprisingly quiet. All she knew was that even though the *Red Horse* operated under wartime rules, she'd felt like she was signing away her soul when they'd given her additional security documents. *Not to reveal* . . . *Under penalty of* . . .

The oddest thing? Their old smart AI, Chauncey, had been replaced with an AI named Rebecca. Chauncey had been only three years old when they'd yanked him out like an old motor block. No question of his having cracked up. Besides, Chauncey would've dropped her a hint or two. He had taken a real shine to Lopez. Rebecca hadn't.

"Maybe we should tell the commander it's civilian," MacCraw said.

Poor MacCraw. Still so wet behind the ears. She didn't look at him. Didn't need to.

Benti couldn't resist, gave Lopez a cheeky grin as she said: "There are cameras in here, MacCraw."

He frowned, reddened.

Burgundy and Singh's assistants had moved away from the pod.

"Sir!" Singh waved Lopez over. "Life support is still online. We've got a live one in here." An instant quickening of her pulse. This could be something, finally. She was sick of being a funeral director. "Just give the word and we'll have it open."

Lopez motioned to Clarence. "Step on up, Invisible Man. Singh, get your team clear. Sleeping Beauty here is a stranger." Unholstered her pistol, checked the chamber. "Benti, c'mon, get your weapon out and your head out of your ass. Treat as hostile until proven otherwise." Benti had a talent for making friends that served the squad well on leave, especially regarding bartenders, but it wasn't a useful trait here.

The sound of boots behind her as additional Marines filed into the hangar, ranging around the pod at

Clarence's command. Assault rifles raised and ready. She didn't have to check—they knew what they were doing. Lopez had trained most of them herself.

Ever-silent, Clarence drew up beside her, finger on the trigger. A good man to have at her back when faced with the unknown.

Lopez nodded at Singh, who tapped his control pad. The seal on the pod sighed, and the technician stood back.

Three, two, one . . .

She wrenched at the hatch. A hiss of escaping pressure as the hatch rose.

Clarence didn't move. Just stood beside her, watching, calm, even when she started.

"Damn!"

There was a lot of blood. A man, too. But a lot of blood. More than seemed possible. That was what got to her first. The blood sloshed in the creases of the berth. It ran down the floor to pool in the footwell. It had saturated the man's clothes. His face was crusted by blood, his eyes white and bulging in the midst of it. Couldn't at first tell if he really was alive. She and Clarence stared down while he lay there, looking up but not really seeing.

Burgundy grimaced in disgust, mumbled something like "I've got to be going," and fled the hangar. That amused Lopez. Stickybeak'd become unstuck.

Where did the smell come from? Where? It was rank, like the stink she remembered coming off corpses after about three days into a firefight, still pinned down by Covenant at some godforsaken outpost on a planet no one even cared about. But behind that, some sort of infection. She could smell it because she could also smell the antiseptic of whatever the man had used to fight it. The smell reminded her of the nursing home where she'd had to leave her mother a few years back, mumbling prayers and counting her rosary beads.

The man rose up. He rose up like something coming out of darkness into the light, the blood spilling off his chest. Clarence had his gun aimed point-blank between the man's eyes. Those eyes focused as the man cried out, "Don't let them get me!" through a torn mouth. Lopez could see that the blood wasn't just spilling off his chest but *out* of his chest, and that's what made her take a step back, more than anything else. That, and the way he looked at her made Lopez realize the man already understood he was dead.

As dead as any corpse they'd recovered from a cryo-tube.

>Benti 0623 hours

Stabilizing "John Doe" took Benti a few minutes. A thankless task. A pointless task. Not all the bandages in the world would help him now. While a couple of the others lifted him out and onto the stretcher, Clarence kept his gun on the man. Good old Clarence. Other Marines talked behind his back—said he was messed up in the head, said he had his own agenda—but Benti had always liked him. You could depend on Clarence. Who cared about the rest?

With Clarence on the job, Benti kept her calm even

with the guy babbling *don't let them take me, please don't let them take me*. This guy wasn't going anywhere soon. They could have brought a proper bed down; at least Mr. Doe would've been more comfortable.

Mr. Doe had kind eyes. Frightened eyes, but kind. Benti could tell. She was a strong believer in what you could figure out from a person's eyes. It was one reason she trusted Clarence, and why she found MacCraw a waste of space.

Great slashes, vicious and brutal, constituted most of Mr. Doe's wounds. The worst had penetrated his chest, but his feet were a mess too. If only he'd been wearing shoes. Benti *tsk*ed a little at the lack. The left foot had blackened, and it would have to come off. *No, scratch that—chopping his foot off won't save him now.* His left arm had a chunk missing. A shattered shoulder and missing ear were just afterthoughts in her catalog of his problems. The bandages she'd applied were pitiful, the skin around them blue, and a down-and-dirty IV had been hooked up. A waste, but Sarge wanted some quality face time with Mr. Doe, so anything to keep him with them a little longer.

For an instant, Benti had a vision of Mr. Doe encountering some great force. That he'd sustained all this damage in one moment of terrible clarity; of knowing, as they would all know eventually, that the universe was stronger, and meaner, than any one of them. It was something the Marine Corps, after Benti's cushy upbringing in a suburban home on Earth, had been teaching her for five years now.

She depressed the plunger in the syringe. Mr. Doe jerked up, a sudden tension wracking the lines of his body, jaw clenched. Benti noted absurdly that he hadn't been flossing lately: bad gums. That they were gray concerned her more.

"There," Benti said, rising to her feet and wiping her bloody hands. Blood never bothered her, only where it came from. "He's stable. For the moment."

"Good to talk?" the sarge asked her.

Benti twisted her lips, unwilling to commit to a yes or no. "I gave him a cocktail—painkillers, and an upper. He can talk." Yep, he could talk, although it wasn't going to be one of those scintillating discussions you remembered the rest of your life. Besides, the sarge had never been good at polite conversation: one reason Benti liked her.

She caught Lopez's eye, knew the sarge understood. Mr. Doe could leave them at any time.

Benti stood back as Lopez crouched down. "See that?" Lopez pointed to a tattoo and indentation on his right arm, across the edge of Mr. Doe's tricep. Prison barcode, with a scar where they'd implanted the tracking chip.

"Interesting." It didn't really interest Benti, but you had to humor the sarge sometimes.

Mr. Doe spoke up. "Marines. You're UNSC." His voice broke, too long without water and use.

"You're safe," Lopez said.

Benti frowned. Mr. Doe was also at the ass-end of the galaxy, light-years from anything unclassified. *But I guess you don't complicate a dying man's life.*

"Thank God," he wheezed. The tension that had gripped and defined him until then slipped away. "Thank God."

They were attending his funeral, Benti realized. Her, Lopez, Clarence, MacCraw, Singh, and the rest. Forming an honor guard around a man who might or might not deserve it. For once, MacCraw had fallen as silent as Clarence, thank goodness. She'd been about to nickname him "Jackdaw."

"What's your name?" Lopez asked. "Where are you from? What ship?"

Too many questions for Mr. Doe. He coughed, as though clearing his throat, but the cough didn't stop. Blood, dark and fresh, dribbled down his chin. Benti knew what that meant. Everyone did. She shot a glance at Clarence, who met her eye. It wouldn't be long now.

"I don't know," Mr. Doe wheezed, the words hard to utter. Even Clarence, who usually didn't give a crap, was leaning in, trying to hear him. "I don't know where we are, I don't know."

"What ship?" Lopez repeated.

Mr. Doe's reply sounded like "moaning lizard" to Benti. That had to be wrong.

"The what?"

"The *Mona Lisa*." And then: "You don't know, do you? You don't know."

Lopez smiled, which, Benti had told her before, on leave, was grim and not at all reassuring and the main reason men fled at the sight of her, but still she wouldn't give it up. No way Mr. Doe wouldn't see his own death there.

"I don't know because you're not telling me. Tell me, and we'll get you off to the infirmary, and you can sleep."

"I would tell you all kinds of things," Mr. Doe said, stumbling over the words. "If I had anyone left in the world. This is where I'm supposed to say, tell my girl I love her, that sort of thing." A terrible, pitiless laugh from Mr. Doe, then, that contracted his eyes, his chin. A laugh that convulsed him, brought blood fresh through the bandages. "I know I'm dying. I know I'm dying. But that's okay." A clarity in his eyes, despite the kindness of the drugs. "I'm clean. I'm here. I won't come back. It's okay. It's all okay."

It surprised Benti when Lopez took his grime-covered, bloody hand. Somehow Benti thought Lopez would pay for that touch. Benti was used to touching people when they were vulnerable, understood what it meant. Lopez really wasn't. He'd just been this thing that talked before. Now how did Lopez see him?

"What do you mean, you won't come back?" Lopez asked.

Like a thunderbolt, a lightning strike called up un-bidden: the shimmering image of the ship's smart AI, Rebecca, appeared beside them, also kneeling. So sudden that Benti had to suppress a sound of surprise, almost lost her balance, and Lopez pulled away a bit.

Rebecca was in her warrior avatar, looking like half-Athena, half-Ares, with a feathered Greek headdress and ancient armor. Rebecca looked so good that Benti almost clapped.

Rebecca asked, imploring almost: "What do you *mean* you won't come back? Come back from what? *Come back from what*?"

Benti looked through Rebecca to where Lopez knelt, staring wide-eyed at them both. Then realized a moment later, with a fading spike of sadness, that Mr. Doe had gone silent, had become Mr. DOA. Now they'd never learn his name, and all they had was "Mona Lisa," which might be a ship, a painting, or nothing at all.

Rebecca made a sound close to exasperation, and winked out. This new AI wasn't big on niceties like "Hello," "Good-bye," and "Incoming!" Not like Chauncey.

Benti stared down at Mr. Doe. Really, such a waste. Those nice eyes, that strong chin.

"Come on, all you big strong men," Benti said. "Help me get him to forensics." Which was in the infirmary, but Benti didn't like saying that, since it seemed to mix the living and the dead a little too easily. She also didn't like telling people she assisted with autopsies, which Mr. Doe definitely required to write the proper ending to his story.

A slow, sad shuffle then as they took the man's body out of the landing bay. Mr. Doe seemed both heavier and lighter than before. Clarence seemed to take most of the weight, and didn't seem to mind.

When Benti looked back, Lopez was giving a good, hard look to the space that had been occupied by Rebecca's avatar, like the sarge had been trying not to see through her, but into her.

By the time she met with Commander Tobias Foucault and Rebecca, Lopez knew this much: nothing that might identify the dead man, not his prison brand, fingerprints, retina scan, DNA, came up on any of the databases aboard the *Red Horse*. Not that surprising. No way to check against the live databases back home. "Hush-hush," as MacCraw said.

They met in one of those featureless rooms adjoining the bridge that smelled like disinfectant. Lopez had wanted Benti there, too, but she was more valuable sitting in on the postmortem.

Gray walls and plastic chairs that rocked back too far if you tried to slouch. A live image of the empty pod, with MacCraw and some other Marines cleaning up the blood, played across one screen. A video of the Halo artifact prior to Spartan-117 detonating the *Pillar of Autumn*'s reactor and destroying it played across the other. A blue-green place. Like a delicate, inverse cross-section of Earth. Now: a black-and-brown snake with orange cracks raging across its pieces, with the vast bulk of the gas giant Threshold looming behind it, inexorably pulling the debris into its gravity well.

Commander Foucault sat opposite her, as always immaculate. The smell of aftershave. Foucault looked haggard and thin and prematurely graying, not at all the robust man she remembered from before his promotion. When he'd been just another one of them. Something about that soured in her mouth. Now she had to call him "sir." They all respected him, respected the extreme circumstances that such a field promotion called for, but still resented the division of rank.

At the far end of the table, Rebecca manifested in her more usual avatar of a flabby, middle-aged Mediterranean woman in a flower dress. She looked vaguely Italian. Benti had always clucked when she saw Rebecca that way, wondered aloud in their berths why she chose that avatar. But Lopez knew: the same reason off-ship, on leave, she would wear something feminine.

It made people comfortable around Rebecca, took the edge off of their fascination and slight fear of something so seemingly *alive* made out of motes of light, bits and bytes. But, then, Chauncey had never cared whether they were comfortable around him. His actions did the job instead. So why, exactly, did Rebecca want to be disarming?

"Anything new to report, Sergeant Lopez?" Foucault asked. Despite the worn look to his face, the commander's light-blue eyes had a powerful effect. A gaze with a kind of *grip* to it.

"No, sir," she said. Wondering when the shit was going to hit the fan. Because you didn't waste the time of the two most important people on the *Red Horse* by sticking them in a room with a sergeant. It didn't scan. She found herself counting rosary beads in her head, against her will. The image forever anchored to the smell of old wooden pews and her mother as a younger woman, kneeling in church.

"What about you, Rebecca?" Foucault asked, with

the air of someone who already knew the answer. Lopez thought she noted a hint of sarcasm there, too.

A smile from Rebecca that was meant to reassure Lopez, but didn't. Not one bit.

"The pod was launched six hours ago from the *Mona Lisa*, a prison transport. I backtracked and calculated the *Mona Lisa*'s approximate location at the time of launch. The coordinates have been uploaded to the nav system."

"And it didn't show up on our sensors, I'm guessing, because of the debris?"

Rebecca frowned, as if something annoying had just occurred to her. "That's correct." She brought up a schematic on the screen of a freighter with several levels, a docking hangar near the front. Storage bays hung off of it, seeming to weigh it down. To Lopez, it looked ugly. Like, if it were a ship meant for water, it would list heavily. "This is a simulation of the same ship type. They're converted freighters, for transporting prisoners and ore to and from the penal colonies, along with the resources from the mines. The bridge is situated in the top level. The prison cells are down below, close to the hangar. In between you have the usual: kitchen, mess, infirmary, berths, the majority given over to cargo. Most prison ships have minimal defenses and minimal firearms on board—a precaution against an uprising—and rely on an escort for protection. There's no sign of an escort, though."

A thin smile from Foucault as he stared at Rebecca. "What would a prison transport be doing at the most significant alien discovery of the past twenty years?"

he asked, cutting through all the irrelevant details in a way Lopez admired.

Rebecca shrugged. "That, I can't tell you."

Foucault said, "Because you don't know, of course." It wasn't framed as either statement or question.

"Perhaps they encountered Covenant and made a random slipspace jump to escape."

"Quite the coincidence, if they did. They show up here, we show up here." It wasn't directed at Lopez, but in a way it was. Probably the only hint she'd ever get.

Not waiting for a response, he turned to Lopez: "What do you think?"

"I'm not paid to think, sir." Her default answer when she didn't want to get involved.

A smirking laugh. Maybe some residual regret in that look from Foucault. As if, in situations like these, he wished he wasn't paid to think, either.

When they'd first come out of slipspace and seen their destination, seen the alien structure, magnificent even in ruins, Lopez had forgotten herself. "What are we looking for, sir?" she'd asked. Foucault hadn't looked away from the window, but she'd sensed him wince. On that poker face, a "wince" was just a lowered eyebrow. "Whatever there is to find, Sergeant," he'd said finally. Slight pressure on *sergeant*.

"Did either of you intuit anything useful out of what the man said before he died?" Foucault asked. "Anything that gives us more context?"

"He just kept saying he was safe, sir," Lopez said. Maybe death was a form of safety, but not one that appealed much to her.

"Nothing that would be inconsistent with the delusions of a man suffering from dehydration and mortal wounds," Rebecca said.

Foucault did this steepling thing with his hands that was his only affectation. "I'm inclined to finish the postmortem, stow the body, and carry on with our mission."

What mission? In Lopez's opinion, risking their asses for "whatever there is to find" seemed stupid. She knew from talking to some of the noncoms on the bridge that it was near impossible to pilot the Prowler through the debris field. Between Rebecca and the discreet automatic defense firing, they'd avoided any serious collisions. But that risked giving away their position to the Covenant even as the debris helped hide them. Still, if the whispers that came back to her were right, the bulk of the Covenant fleet had left the system in pursuit of a "higher value target"—which supposedly had surprised the commander. Not the kind of thing she could confirm with Foucault, and Lopez didn't know how long ago the Covenant fleet had left. All she cared about: no Covies so far.

Somebody was doing a lot of gambling here, and Lopez still had no idea for what potential gain.

Rebecca turned to Lopez, and said, "What the commander means is he wants you to take a squad in a Pelican and go investigate the *Mona Lisa*'s last known coordinates."

Foucault looked grim. "Is that what I meant? If you say it's what I meant, I guess it must be what I meant." The sarcastic tone had become more pronounced, but, again, tinged with an odd kind of regret.

"Sir?" Confused. She'd never seen an AI contradict a commander in quite that way. "Sir, your orders?"

Foucault stared at Rebecca, as if the force of his gaze might burn two holes in her avatar. Then he said in a clipped cadence, "AI Rebecca is, of course, correct. Take a squad in a Pelican and investigate. Rebecca will coordinate the details. Good luck, Sergeant. Dismissed."

Lopez saluted, rose in confusion, walked out the door. Thinking of John Doe's warm hand. Puzzled. Wondering why neither Foucault nor Rebecca had even asked about the autopsy, or the nature of the man's terrible wounds, or everything else that didn't jive.

Lopez had scars from wounds of her own, collected from long years of making the Covenant pay and keep on paying. Along with a long white reminder on her wrist of why you didn't surprise a sleeping cat.

Every time Lopez was about to go into combat, she was aware of those scars.

They were throbbing now, telling her: *Something bad is coming.*

>Foucault 1003 hours

Foucault sat there after Lopez had left, staring at Rebecca. He was, for all his former exploits, a cautious man who had used extreme tactics when it had seemed the only option for his continued survival. It had made him a hero and given him his command, but he didn't feel like a hero. He'd just been trying to save himself. He wasn't sure he had. Waking from nightmares, from *memories*, awash with sweat to find it was only one in the morning got old fast. So did losing to the Covenant.

Rebecca wasn't helping. He'd had a good relationship with Chauncey. He'd trusted Chauncey. Rebecca, well . . . Theoretically she worked for him, but a directive from ONI's upper echelons had imposed her on him—along with a couple of rookies who acted so raw it made him suspicious—and that was more than sufficient reason for him to be wary.

Foucault'd had a superior once with a prosthetic eye, except that no one knew. This man would call Foucault into his office and, without telling him why he had been summoned, close his good eye and fall asleep, still staring at Foucault. Inevitably, Foucault would lose the waiting contest and be the first to break the silence.

Rebecca was a man with a glass eye. She could outwait him.

So, finally, Foucault sighed, lifted his head, and stated, "You know more than you've told me."

Rebecca didn't quite shake her head. "We have our orders, Commander."

Orders. Strange, simple orders, Foucault had thought upon first receiving them. Jump to coordinates classified higher than top secret, retrieve samples of an alien artifact for study, conduct basic recon, expect *Covenant* trouble. He'd stood on the bridge, staring at the pieces of the Halo, the wealth of such samples before him, and wondered why they'd deploy a Prowler on such a task.

As soon as the pod had come in, Rebecca had shown him the "expanded" orders. Even expanded, they remained strange and simple. Assess the status of the *Mona Lisa*, and if compromised beyond retrieval, destroy. There had been no mention of why the ship was in the area or what it might be compromised by.

The codes were current, the passwords secure. He didn't question their validity. It was the only thing he didn't question.

"Do *you* know what is on that ship?" he asked, knowing he would get no answer, knowing he wouldn't believe any answer she gave. "I don't like being kept in the dark, especially when deploying my troops. We could be sending them to their deaths for all I know."

"Every time you deploy Marines, you could be sending them to their deaths," Rebecca said, talking to him as if he were a child. To add insult to injury, Foucault suspected she was processing some other scene, her attention elsewhere. "It is only recon."

"Our original orders were 'only recon' as well," he said in mild reproach, and steepled his fingers.

Rebecca looked at Foucault then, with her full attention, and her face seemed to soften. A cheap trick he'd seen her pull on others, changing the lighting on her avatar to something less harsh. "We're at war, Commander. Reach has fallen. Our backs are against the wall. Extreme measures are necessary to ensure our survival."

Foucault forced himself to show no reaction and didn't immediately reply. That was quite the overreaction, and it cemented his suspicions that there certainly was more she wasn't telling him, which meant she had orders of her own.

He watched the screen, which showed a real-time view of the space outside the Prowler. A single piece of debris tumbled slowly past. It wasn't a rock, it was a piece of manufactured structure, hard crisp lines and dead cables showing. There was a marvelous logic to its gymnastics, a grace that seemed almost choreographed, even though now it was merely scattered garbage.

How to get Rebecca to share her knowledge?

"Survival," he repeated.

Was that really the only thing they were fighting for now?

>Lopez 1304 hours

As the Pelican headed toward their destination, Lopez found herself marveling at the view, struck by an odd moment of poetic, profound insight, even though she didn't understand it all. Perhaps even because she didn't understand.

Dominating right now was Threshold's ponderous "bloat-belly"; her term, shared with Benti in the mess hall. The vast gas giant so filled the windows it brought the illusion of blue sky to the cockpit up front instead of the empty black of space. Frequent storms raged and died in great cloud-swirls across that surface. From that far away, it looked like a slow, sleepy blossoming. Didn't feel that way on the surface, Lopez knew. The winds blew hundreds of kilometers an hour.

Closer in: the wreckage of the Halo. The massive ring cut through the view like a question mark that'd been fractured to pieces. Thousands of kilometers wide. Great fires still raging, large enough to devour whole continents. Chunks of the superstructure bigger than cities tumbling ponderously in the void. Glowing and flaring as they tore shrieking down through Threshold's atmosphere. Despite the jiggered failures in the structure, the sheer immensity of it made the curve smooth. Constantly tripped her sense of perspective.

Covenant hadn't built it. It was entirely alien, in design and purpose, and she took some strange assurance from that. Here was proof that there was more out there in the big bad universe than just the goddamn Covenant. She had no idea if whoever built this was friend or foe, but the simple idea that there was *another* gave her a strange sense of security. *We're not alone. Again.*

A pinprick next to Threshold, the *Mona Lisa* drifted like a dead thing alongside one of the larger pieces of debris from the Halo ring, on the far side from Basis and distant from the *Red Horse*'s current position. Lopez thought the ship looked lonely, desolate, on the screen as they approached. *Abandoned, even.* Pits like severe acne showed where the escape pods had already been launched into space.

She asked for an update from the pilot, Burgundy, who'd been called up despite being off the clock. Already getting reacclimated to the up-close sweat smell from the Marines in the seats all around her, only MacCraw dumb enough to be wearing cologne in the confines of a spacecraft, like he was on a date.

Rebecca had chosen the squad, pilot included. "The

maximum we can spare," she'd explained. Seventeen personnel in total, including Benti and also Singh's small engineering team, who had received basic training but were technically not combat-ready. Clarence sat next to Lopez like some kind of morose watchdog. He never looked happy, but Lopez thought she could read in his impassive features a distinct *un*happiness now.

"She's not answering on any frequency, Sarge," Burgundy finally replied over Lopez's headset. They were on an open frequency for now. Later, only Lopez would have access, and anyone she designated. "Can't get a peep out of her. No distress beacon. She's cold, and I don't think her engines have been running for a while."

Not if she lay in the same position she'd been in when John Doe had escaped her clutches. So cold and yet hugging so close to the burning shard of a world now lost to them, as if seeking sanctuary.

"Can she zoom in? It just looks like a dark block," Benti muttered to Lopez, not realizing Burgundy could hear her.

A closer view appeared on-screen. "That better?" Burgundy asked. "She ain't that pretty. Not by half. I'd never date her."

A wracked and splintered mountain range formed the backdrop for the *Mona Lisa*, made it difficult to make her out even with the zoom. She had a blunt snout, the five levels Lopez had seen on the schematic, and some definite damage to the left thruster in the back. A few dents. Some bits like barnacles where compartments had been custom-built onto the ship. That was a bit odd, but not unknown. Near the back, Lopez could see where something had left a definite hole. Not enough to scuttle it. Freighters could take a severe pounding. Almost certainly the *Mona Lisa* still had breathable air.

"How'd the postmortem go, Benti?" Lopez asked in a quiet voice. Benti had gotten a peek but Lopez hadn't had a chance to ask her about it yet.

"Why not ask Tsardikos?"

"Huh?"

Benti nodded toward one of the others. "Tsardikos over there did the autopsy. Then they put him on the mission." She shrugged, that *officers move in mysterious ways* look on her face.

That made Lopez's heart do a strange leap. "No," she said. "I want to hear it from you." Didn't want to hear it from a noncom who shouldn't even be on the mission. Tsardikos didn't look comfortable over there, fidgeting in his kit. Why should he?

Benti grimaced. "Nasty wounds. Whatever opened his chest and back wasn't a blade, and took a hell of a lot of force. Don't know what it was, but I suppose when you're busting out of prison you use what you can grab. I brought extra blood bags, though. Just in case. It was a prisoner riot, right? It'd have to be."

"Doesn't matter," Lopez said. "You honestly expect some punk-ass jailbird to get a shiv in one of us? You doubting the Marine Corps, Private?" Didn't mind messing with her people every once in a while.

"It was one hell of a shiv," Benti muttered. "Sir."

"Why bother? I mean, if they're just escapees in a dead ship?" MacCraw piped up. "Just mark her position and come back when things are less hot, Sarge?" Almost like he expected Lopez to say, "You're right, Mac-Craw," and turn the Pelican right around.

Lopez was about to give MacCraw a hell of a reply, one that mentioned his cologne, when Rebecca came over the radio. Closed channel, just for her and Burgundy. "Signal strength is weak, Sergeant. I'm getting the pictures now. We've picked up a Covenant ship in the vicinity. Distant, but we'll have to tread carefully. The commander has ordered the *Red Horse* to maintain radio contact as much as possible in the field, but we mustn't reveal ourselves. Maneuverability is limited. You may be on your own for a while. You have your orders."

"Roger that," Lopez said. "I'll check in with Burgundy once we're on board to see if I can patch you in. If not, I guess it's just me and the pilot." From the forward position, Burgundy gave a thumbs-up over her shoulder. Rebecca signed off.

"And me," Benti said, smiling.

Lopez nodded, said, "Yeah, you too." She caught Clarence staring at her oddly. Jealous? *Yeah, you be jealous, Clarence, you gloomy bastard.*

"The game is always changing," MacCraw said, to the air.

"Give thanks you've got a game on," Lopez said, and almost meant it. Checking on some spooky mystery transport at the ass-end of space wasn't her idea of a good op, but it was better than nothing.

"How'd the ship even get here?" MacCraw asked. He just wouldn't shut up. "They just happened to randomly guess the slipspace coordinates? I mean, we don't even know where we are, and we're *supposed* to be here."

"Don't try to be smart, MacCraw," Lopez said. "That's not what you're paid for."

"No," Benti and a couple of the others chimed in, "you pay us to be pretty." A tired old joke, a necessary one. One MacCraw might not've heard before.

"Damn straight," Lopez said. "How'd that haiku go? 'Something, something, something . . . something, and then comes ice cream.'" Something they'd eaten far too much of, last R & R.

"You missed a 'something.'"

"You kids play your cards right and after this comes ice cream. Don't ever say Mama Lopez does nothing for you."

Some grins, a couple of comments about "Mama" Lopez, and then a near-ritual silence.

Lopez began the count. Not required, but she liked to name each person under her command right before any mission that might turn hot: Benti, Clarence, MacCraw, Percy, Mahmoud, Rakesh, Orlav, Simmons—currently pulling double duty as Burgundy's copilot—Rabbit, Singh, Gersten, Cranker, Sydney, Ayad, Maller, and Tsardikos. Standard equipped with MA5B assault rifles, HE pistols, and ye olde frag grenades. Among flares, food rations, water, medic kits, schematics of the ship, the usual.

A bunch of jokers, lifers, and crazies. Benti, Clarence, Mahmoud, and Orlav were the best of the lot. Mac-Craw was, well, raw, so who knew? A few were average, and she'd deploy them that way. Without remorse. Singh and his engineers Gersten and Sydney were an unknown, really. Two loaners from another squad, Ayad and Maller, she didn't know at all. A lot of the rest of the best had been left back on the *Red Horse*. Because, you know, the ship needed them. Or something like that.

All of them were rosary beads to her now anyway, already counting and hating herself for it. Mystic bullshit. But she did it every time. Had to. It was how she rationalized putting herself in danger. *Perform this ritual and luck will follow. Don't, and it won't.* And that's the difference between life and death. Between a scar and a wound that won't stop bleeding.

"We good, Sarge?" Benti whispered.

"You should have gone before we left, like Mama Lopez told you."

Benti smirked, stopped at the last second from reaching out and smacking Lopez on the shoulder.

The Pelican drew close, the battered and scarred skin of the *Mona Lisa* filling the view. As they all braced for that slight lurching shudder that meant arrival, Lopez tried not to think about the noncoincidence of who had been chosen for the mission and who hadn't.

Because, to a person, her squad consisted of everyone who had come into contact with John Doe on board the *Red Horse*.

>Benti 1315 hours
_____

Benti watched as the soft seal locked on and they had compression. A shiver ran through the Pelican as the hatches disengaged, maw ready to open and disgorge them into the *Mona Lisa*. Benti had never seen a real live pelican except in videos, but it amused her to think of them erupting out of the gullet of a giant bird. A Trojan Pelican, almost.

This silent moment, right before combat, before she had to use any of her bandages and blood bags, this moment always made her regret having given up smoking.

"We're solid, Sarge, and I can go ahead and set you free whenever you want," Burgundy said, voice coming over the headsets now, which somehow made Benti think of Rebecca's *What do you mean, you won't come back?*

Good old Clarence and that dumbass MacCraw knelt to either side of the gangplank, rifles at the ready, the rest of the squad behind them, hunched over, waiting. Clarence was chewing gum ferociously, about as worked up as Benti had ever seen him. Docking a Pelican wasn't a stealthy business. Whoever was on board the *Mona Lisa* would know they were here.

What kind of greeting would they get? A big party celebration, or one candle stuck in a cupcake?

God, she wanted a cigarette *right now*.

Lopez gave Burgundy the order.

"Go forth and plunder," Burgundy said, and somehow Benti could tell old Stickybeak was *glad* to be staying on board the Pelican.

The gangplank lowered in a hiss of hydraulics and fast-fading clang of the plank against ground. Not exactly a red carpet, in Benti's opinion.

A smell came in with the cold air that was both dusty and moist. It almost had texture, a substance. It made Benti wrinkle her nose, and she didn't wrinkle her nose at much.

Beyond the gangplank, the main lights were out. Emergency strip lights threw supply crates, control stations, and loading machinery into murky relief. The oval shape of a small transport ship rose up, too, overlooking the jumbled maze spanning the hangar. Deep, dark, reddish shadows thrown up against the far walls.

Benti looked around. That was *it*? She'd been looking forward to getting off the *Red Horse* and exploring new territory. Even if it was just junk, Benti wanted to *see* it. At least it was different junk.

Nothing moved. Nobody even seemed to breathe.

"Lights," Lopez ordered quietly, and Benti switched hers on.

Suddenly there was a mutual clicking and beams shot out all over the place, temporarily blinding Benti. Crap. You'd think they'd know better. What if they'd been trying to throw a surprise party?

Lopez didn't seem impressed either. "Get your heads on straight, Marines! Move out!"

Benti winked at Clarence, who acknowledged her with a nod, and that was about all. It was enough. Clarence, to her, was like a dolphin or otter or some other creature that seemed to be all muscle and was sleek and functional. What she was to him, Benti had no idea. Comic relief? He hadn't looked amused when she'd told him he was an otter. Off duty they hardly ever saw each other, but they always worked as a team, to the point no one tried to break them up any more. If something works, then don't question it, just work it. Work it to death.

They filed quickly into the hangar in a standard sweep, torchlight raking the crates around them over and over. No matter what you did, regulation boots were never silent, and it was no different this time.

Ten meters out from the Pelican—with Benti hissing Tsardikos back in line, the clueless moron—the surprise party really got started . . .

>Lopez 1317 hours

Trouble came simple, like it always did: a guttural resonance that came from an inhuman throat. A sigh with a texture they knew too well. Sent them diving down behind cover. In the stillness that followed, no repeat of the sound.

"Up periscope," Lopez said to Cranker. He didn't get it, so she said, "Pop yer head up, Private, and take a quick scan around."

Cranker, looking worried, did just that, and then hunkered down even lower. "Looks all clear."

Of course it did. *You didn't get your head blown off.* Wasn't fair, but she always picked the one she liked the least.

Benti, wide-eyed, almost giddy: "That sounded like—"

Don't get jumpy, kid! Lopez raised a finger to her lips.

Scuffling sounds came from about fifteen meters ahead. Multiple contacts.

Lopez gave orders with her hands. Some were quicker on the uptake than others. Percy and Orlav tapped their crew in passing, including Benti, and scurried off between the surrounding cargo containers. That left Lopez with the dregs. She grinned at Singh, who didn't seem to find any of this funny.

"This is Sergeant Lopez of the UNSC Marine Corps! Identify yourself!"

No reply. A flurry of movement. She rose. Rifle butt cozy in her shoulder. Finger on the trigger. The Marines around her rising from cover, too.

"Where—?"

"Two o'clock—"

"It's gonna bolt—"

A rushed patter of sprinting footfalls, flashing across the hangar floor. Darting between storage crates. A glimpse of blue, of familiar backward knees, and formidable shoulders as they came into contact with the corner of someone's flashlight beam.

Covenant Elites.

Tongues of fire from the rifles, that glorious, deafening sound that Lopez knew so well. Sharp shadows danced up in snarling light. Sparks from bullets punched through crates. The target fled between stacked pallets and loaders, not even grazed, no telltale purple glow on the ground. They'd been too eager.

It didn't matter. That one glimpse was all it took. It lit a fire in Lopez. A crazy, irrational fire. Twenty-seven years of war, a war longer than Benti's life, Clarence's life, than most of their lives, so much loss and death and grief and blood and fury—it didn't matter. It didn't need articulating. Not for her, not for any of them.

"Take 'em down!" she roared. "Take 'em all down!"

As if they needed telling.

>Benti 1318 hours
_____

Even though she was just following orders, some small part of Benti thought careening off into the darkness with an unknown number of hostiles in the area added up to a big heaping dose of *crazy*. The larger part of her didn't care.

"To the left!" Orlav shouted, her flashlight beam glancing off the storage containers, breaking off into the distant ceiling. It caught in freeze-frame wide sprays of blood. The floor was sticky with it. They were following drag marks, and over the top, wide stumpy footprints. Fresh.

A bark of gunfire, but no flash, hidden somewhere beyond the containers. Percy and Ayad shouting over the roar of a Covenant Elite. Lopez swearing. Some damn powerful swearing—wouldn't be surprised if some Covie didn't drop dead just from hearing it.

Benti almost fell over a collapsed makeshift barricade, turning too hard around a corner, following the footprints, dimly aware the others weren't around her.

She slipped on the blood-slick floor, caught the impression of movement in front of her, and pulled the trigger without waiting. The bullets punched into the Elite's gut and purple blood splashed down on her face and neck. It doubled over, massive hands cupping its belly. Got a full-on cough of the creature's fetid breath, those four spiny jaws twitching beneath the clenched fist of a head flexed wide in surprise, anger, or some emotion she'd never understand. Especially without their armor, they always looked like they were intensely thinking. But that couldn't be it, and she wasn't going to give it a chance to think.

Her rifle roared until the Elite dropped, collapsing on top of her.

"Crap!" Being crushed seemed a poor reward for doing her job.

But then Clarence was there, grabbing her harness and hauling her from beneath the Elite by the scruff of the neck. Covie blood had soaked her. It glowed in the dark and smelled a bit like armpit mixed with wet cat.

No time to wipe it off: sporadic gunfire throughout the hangar couldn't mask the distinctive footfalls approaching, fast and heavy.

A second Covenant Elite burst out from behind a damaged loader, seeing but ignoring them as they pivoted to face it. The Elite vaulted over an operation console and into the darkness.

"It's going for the Pelican!"

They took off after it.

"Orlav, you back there? One coming your way!"

Benti spat, trying not to think about the alien blood in her mouth and everything she knew about hygiene.

Again she followed the footprints, down one narrow corridor, then another. The container crates formed a kind of maze. Clarence dropped back, checking the corners, not happy about rushing past so many places ripe for more Elites to pop out at them from behind.

The Elite clearly wasn't heading for the Pelican. Instead, it was—

Well, crap. It was *right there*, against the wall of crates.

Crouched, but not hiding, its head tilted, listening. She noticed its muscles were withered and its limbs lined with scars and wounds, not all of them old, and then realized it was naked. No armor at all. How strange, how perfect.

"I'm going to kill you," Benti whispered. "I'm going to—"

It held up one finger. It *shushed* her. Pointed toward the darkness in front of them.

That surprised her so much she shut up, listened with the alien.

Benti heard a last bark of gunfire, the moaning gargle of a dying Elite on the far side of the hangar. Status reports back and forth on the radio. The alien's breathing. Her breathing. Nothing more.

It looked over at her.

Benti was no expert on Covie expressions, but she could tell it was *relieved*.

Nothing more, nothing less.

Even unarmed, a Covenant Elite was more than capable of overpowering any Marine with its bare hands. They never stopped, they never gave up until you put them down. Yet this one remained crouching, unthreatening. Listening.

It wasn't afraid of her. She knew that.

But it was afraid of *something*.

The muzzle of Clarence's rifle entered her peripheral vision, spat fire, and deafened her in one ear. The Covenant Elite smashed back against a container, half its face shorn off.

Face impassive, Clarence looked at her, a faint judgment, a question, only manifesting in the set of shoulders. He'd seen her hesitate. Crap. She stared back at him, reduced to silence, feeling a flare of irritation she knew was her embarrassment eating itself: *Who're you to judge? You could've frozen up a hundred times before in combat for all I know.* But she knew, in her gut, that was a lie. Rumor had it no one had killed more Covies than Clarence.

Lopez, from off to the left: "Marines! Four Covie dead over here. The rest of you, report! Watch for active camo. Keep those flashlights on."

The surprise party was over. A sound-off around the hangar, which didn't seem nearly so big now that their eyes had adjusted to the darkness.

"We're good, Sarge," Benti said, punching Clarence in the shoulder in an attempt to gloss over the awkward strain between them. "Two confirmed kills." She turned her back on the dead, naked alien and followed Clarence to where the flashlights were converging.

"No kills here, just thrills," Gersten said from somewhere off to the right. "That small transport got smashed up good, Sarge. Someone drunk driving, I dunno."

Only one wounded Marine, as it turned out, and that was MacCraw, who had a gash in his shoulder from smashing into a metal hook.

"I think Rakesh wet his pants." MacCraw sounded a little shaky even as he tried to joke.

"Only if you pissed on me, MacCraw."

"No sign of the crew or passengers," Orlav said.

Benti could see that idiot Cranker posing with his boot on a Covie torso, like some kind of conquering hero. That sobered her mood as much as Clarence's look. Bad luck, being not just overconfident but a jerk about it.

Percy crouched by Cranker's leg, examining the body. "Interesting outfit they're running," he said. "No weapons, no gear. Think they're running out of money."

"Maybe we can buy them out!"

"Shut it, MacCraw. Where's Rabbit?"

No answer.

>Lopez 1327 hours

Taking out the second Covie hadn't been as satisfying to Lopez as taking out the first. The third was less satisfying to her than that. She'd just watched by the time her Marines took out the fourth. Mechanically gone through the all-clear and found that Rabbit was missing.

Something was bothering her, even as she ordered a sweep of the hangar just to find Rabbit. It had been too easy. These were Covenant Elites. They'd presumably boarded the *Mona Lisa* and had been hard-core enough to take the ship without too much bungling. But: they'd allowed themselves to be cut down like so many, well, rabbits. She knew her Covies, and they were better than that. Something didn't scan again, and it had her scar itching. Had there been some breakdown in command-and-control? And why hadn't they been able to keep power on in the ship? Had most of them left in the escape pods? If so, you'd think the *Red Horse* would've already picked up a few.

The sweep didn't locate her missing Marine.

"She was with me," Mahmoud said, when they'd regrouped by the main door. "We wasted that dog over there by the messed-up transport, she said she heard something, then another Covie popped up." He shrugged in his armor, dropping his eyes. "Sorry, Sarge, I thought she was with me."

Lopez worried away at a single rosary bead named *Rabbit*, as she opened a channel. "Okay, Burgundy, you've a lovely way with words, talk to me."

"Can't raise the *Red Horse* right now," Burgundy said. "And this ship smells. I mean, it really smells."

"Keep trying. Seal up, sit tight. Don't want no Covies getting in and stinking up your bird even more." Then she turned to the rest of the crew. "Cranker, Maller, Simmons, Sydney, maintain position here. You're base camp. Clean up those bodies you're so fond of standing on. The rest of us are going wabbit hunting. Move out."

She stopped in front of Benti. Looked the little medic down and down. She was practically neon.

"I think this color suits me."

"Yeah, it brings out your eyes," Lopez said with distaste. "Take the rear." Didn't always know what to make of Benti, thought she should take things a little more seriously sometimes.

The corridor beyond was pitch-black, the emergency lighting off, except for one flickering light in the distance. On the wall, a smear of blood where a hand had dragged down to the floor only to join a larger, thicker pool that was red and human and old. Something had then been dragged through the blood, the trail heading aft. Through the drag mark, Lopez could see the telltale marks left by regulation boots.

"There was lots of blood in the hangar, too," Tsardikos ventured hesitantly. "Enough for a few people to have bled out. But I didn't see any bodies."

"No small-arms fire or plasma burns, either," Orlav said.

"Maybe the Covenant really are running out of money."

"MacCraw, one more lame joke out of you and I'll push you out an airlock," Lopez growled, and the chatter shut down. The real Mona Lisa was famed for her enigmatic smile, but Lopez still wasn't in the mood for mysteries.

Rabbit's trail faded, crossed more blood pools, and strengthened again. Fifty meters and still going. Damn fool bunny. Went too far on her own. Lopez ground her teeth, already reaming the soldier out in her head, when a surprised shout barked up the corridor. Cut off abruptly. More Covenant.

Quick hand signals as they hastened up the corridor. Orlav came to a halt by a half-open hatchway. Water flowed over the lip and spilled out into the corridor, lapping around their boots. Shower block. A glimpse of green plastic floor befouled with curling red.

A fetid, wet smell. The sound of gushing water from a shower left on. Near-total darkness except for their flashlights, which illuminated a row of lockers that concealed the space beyond. On her signal they entered, fanned out, swept by rote. Lopez couldn't hear a thing over their progress, the water up to their ankles. Splashing echoed off the walls and bounced from the ceiling, creating confusion with no direction.

Still, she managed to pick out a sound that wasn't water.

Lopez tilted her head at the Marine nearest to her, Mahmoud, who took up a position behind her, along with Ayad. "Rabbit," she breathed into the radio. "Report."

No answer. Then a faint wet burble, which could've been anything. They made their way across the floor, stepping softly in the water. Benti and Clarence watched the door, Percy and Rakesh coming up on their flank to circle in beyond the lockers.

A wet gurgle, followed by a heavy, thick sound, like meat being slapped against the ground.

Rounded the shower wall. The flashlight revealed . . .

"Rabbit!"

Didn't know which of them had said it. Maybe they all had.

Their bunny was dead.

An Elite stood over her. Stood *on* her. No, stomped on her, huge foot pounding down over and over on her chest. Crushed her rib cage into a jagged mess of bone shards. Made a pulp of her lungs and heart. Pulverized her. Flattened a hole through her until it was stomping only on the shower floor, smeared with gore. The lockers were spattered. The Elite's legs were coated with Rabbit's remains.

It saw them, and still it didn't stop. As Lopez yelled something, she didn't know what, and tightened her trigger finger, the Covenant raised its huge foot and slammed down on Rabbit's face, smashing her stunned, vacant expression. Then the rifles roared, and roared, until Lopez shouted for them to stop.

Images of fire in Lopez's eyes. The smell of gunfire and Rabbit's bowels and the Covenant's dead flesh. Rakesh vomiting on Mahmoud's shoes as Mahmoud failed to get out of the way. Putting a hand on Rakesh's shoulder. To comfort him? To steady him? To steady herself?

A commotion from the door, where the gunfire hadn't stopped right away.

Benti yelled, too loud: "Cranker! Two contacts incoming! I hit at least one of them! Cranker, do you copy?"

"Ready and waiting."

Then Benti again: "What was that? Did you hear that?"

"Benti! Were the Covenant armed?" Lopez stepped over Rakesh's vomit to look around the shower wall at the door.

"No," Benti said. "But did you hear—"

Lopez cut her off. "Eyes open. Keep watch at the door."

Benti nodded, mercifully shut up.

"Sir." Cranker again. "Still ready. Still waiting."

"Hold your position, Cranker," Lopez ordered. "You might have some Covie heat coming your way, but they don't appear to be armed, just like the rest. We've got some clean-up here, but we'll be back soon. Over and out."

Lopez crouched down beside what was left of Rabbit. This *really* didn't scan. On any level. It left her a little numb.

She'd been in the war since the beginning. She'd seen far too many friends and comrades and jerks and assholes and people, too many of *her* people, killed; burned up by plasma, run through with swords, crushed by brutes. Too many. And that meant she knew the Covenant by their actions, if nothing else. No single death signaled victory for them. No one Marine stilled gave them pause. Celebration didn't enter into the equation— they just moved on. They did not leave themselves vulnerable, they did not desecrate the dead, they did not pound Marines into jelly. They did not do *this*.

"Sarge?" MacCraw loomed over her. "What're you doing?"

"Give me some light." *Do something useful for a change.*

Rabbit had no eyes left to close.

The bolognese of innards was cooling fast, but was still hot beneath Lopez's fingertips as she felt about tenderly, picking aside fragments of spine, seeking Rabbit's dog tags. This act didn't disturb her, hadn't done so for years. To be repulsed on the battlefield was to be self-ish, put your own distaste over the needs of the dead.

Ah. A glint in the flashlight's beam, and she'd found the dog tags, one of them folded over and flattened. She reached for them, paused, finding something else near her fingertips, half-revealed, half-hidden by the torchlight. MacCraw really couldn't hold a light steady worth a damn.

The universe was a big place and Lopez didn't know it by half, and never would, but what she saw sure as hell didn't come from Rabbit, and didn't look like any Covenant she knew. She stared at it for an instant.

The object was long and thin, and oddly segmented. It looked like a very large spider's leg, but without the stiffness. She only associated it with something living when she saw it ended in a branch of small tentacle-like fingers. The shoulder had been reduced to a pulp of pale sickly goo, veined through with strains of green and purple. Sick, diseased, reeking of the stench Lopez had noticed when they'd first entered the *Mona Lisa*'s hangar.

She reached for it out of some perverse impulse, then paused. The shadow of her hand hid it from the others. *John Doe saying, "I won't come back."*

"Sarge?" MacCraw was getting restless.

Pondered. Decided. Probably nothing. They didn't need to see it.

Apologetically, she nudged a loop of intestine over the thing, then a scrap of uniform over what was left of Rabbit's face. Mama Lopez took care of her own.

Freed the dog tags. Rakesh looked like he was going to be sick again. She got up, cupped his hand with hers, and dropped the bloody tags in his palm.

Did the spider's leg come from Rabbit or from the Covenant? Distracted herself from that thought with the situation at hand: Covenant, headed toward Cranker's position.

"Cranker," she said. "Talk to me."

A puzzled tone from Cranker. "The Covenant never got here. We're still waiting, but they never got here. Did you guys go after them? Because—oh wait. I think that might be—oh crap oh crap oh crap . . ."

A garbled curse. A sound like a muffled rifle discharge, almost an afterthought. A wet sound. Too wet. Then, nothing.

Lopez wondered how much of this Burgundy was hearing.

Did they still have an escape route?

>Burgundy 1349 hours

Burgundy had her pistol out, safety off, even with the Pelican sealed up tight. There'd been too much gunfire out there. The Marines might call her Stickybeak and joke about pilots not seeing any action except on leave, but Burgundy had seen enough to know you didn't wait until you could see the whites of their eyes before turning up the heat. Covenant didn't have whites, for starters.

The feeds from the Pelican's rear cameras didn't help

her mood any. It looked like the Covie action was getting a little too close for comfort.

Lopez pinged her right after she'd heard one last burst of rifle fire that cut off abruptly. The signal was weak, the ship's structure already interfering. Strange static.

"Burgundy, what's happening there? Can you see Cranker? Simmons?"

"Sarge, I'm not sure what I'm seeing." Her throat was dry and she swallowed. "It's dark, and their flashlights are just lying on the floor now. I couldn't really make out what happened. I think I'm seeing dead Covenant and . . . oh shit." The hair on her arms rose, gooseflesh stippling her skin. "Sarge, something just dragged one of the Covenant out of the light."

"Something? Like what?"

"I can't see shit! Something big. I think. I really can't see it. Do they eat their own, Sarge? Because that's what it looks like."

Except she knew Covenant didn't eat their dead any more than Marines ate *their* dead.

She wasn't sure she wanted the lights on anymore.

"Maller, Cranker, Simmons, and Sydney, where are they?" Lopez demanded.

"Sarge, I'm *telling* you, I don't see them, Sarge." She put her finger on the trigger, took it off. She put it on again.

Okay, so she'd seen something earlier, but hesitated to tell Lopez. She *thought* she'd seen them at the beginning of the attack, spinning out of view, hit by something that looked like a handful of pale balls. Twirling and rolling to the ground, rifles abandoned, grappling with them. The feed went to a black box. She couldn't replay it.

"KIA?" came Lopez's calm voice.

"Not sure. Maybe. I'd hate to be wrong," Burgundy said, certain of nothing, and hating that.

Lopez was silent for a moment, then said, "Keep talking to me, pilot."

But there wasn't anything to see any more. Discarded flashlights, fading as the batteries died. The darkness drawing a little closer.

"Nothing. All calm now."

"*Red Horse* there?"

It was hard to look away from the feed, but she scanned the waveband. "Yes! Got her."

"Patch her through."

"Yes, sir." Always good to have a call from home.

"Sergeant Lopez?" If Lopez's voice was weak, Rebecca's was weaker, grainy, but calm. "What have you found?"

"No sign of crew or prisoners. One KIA, four more missing, possible KIA. Unknown number of Covenant forces on board. I don't know how the Covenant got here, and they're acting mighty strange."

"Strange how?" Rebecca asked, echoing what Burgundy was thinking.

"No armor. No weapons. Not really fighting back, most of them."

"That is all you've found?" Rebecca sounded disgruntled, as though she found this report lacking.

A pause from Lopez. "I did mention the Covenant. Acting strangely. On this civilian ship. In an unknown and highly classified location. Right?"

Burgundy bit back a chuckle. She wasn't fond of Rebecca either.

"We heard you, Sergeant," Rebecca said, about as icy as an AI could get.

"Request reinforcements to aid with the mission."

"Request denied."

"I want to talk to the commander."

A false smile entered Rebecca's voice, like the sun rising over an ice field. "The commander and I are of the same mind, Sergeant."

"Requesting—"

"Negative." This time it was Foucault, patched in over Rebecca's feed. Burgundy's stomach churned. "Sorry, Sergeant, but we can't send anyone without alerting the Covenant capitol ship to our presence, and you know we're outmanned and outgunned. I'm invoking the Cole Protocol. The secrecy of Earth's location is paramount, and the *Mona Lisa* does appear to be compromised by Covenant. Stand by for your orders."

"Sir."

"Ascertain if the Covenant have accessed the nav system. If not, destroy it before they do. If so . . ." he stopped, then continued, after what sounded like consultation with Rebecca, ". . . we will inform you when it is safe for you to return."

"Sir." Burgundy could hear Lopez striving and failing to keep frustration out of her voice. "Sir, I'm down five already, as far as I know. We can keep going, shut down the nav and flush out every Covie on this stinking boat, but begging your pardon, it's a big-ass boat. We need some ODST motion sensors happening. Get a Pelican out here on, I don't know, thrusters alone, something!"

Burgundy was thinking it. Lopez was thinking it. She bet even the commander was thinking it. Orders from officers who weren't on the ground weren't worth shit.

"Negative, Sergeant. You have your orders, and I trust you'll see them through in your usual . . . spectacular . . . fashion," he said with a trace of amusement.

"Yes, sir." Said without grace. "Sir, permission to speak freely?"

"Denied."

"You're fading now. You're breaking up," Rebecca said. "*You have your orders*." Said remotely, with finality, her attention already elsewhere.

A beat. And then, "They gone, Burgundy?"

"Yes, Sarge."

Lopez said something really obscene.

"You got that right," Burgundy muttered.

"You cozy?"

"Yeah."

"Alone?"

Nothing had moved on the feed for some time now, the last flashlight flickering on the ground. "I can't see anything."

"Okay. Sit tight. Keep monitoring, let me know

when the *Red Horse* is talking again. We'll come back and mess up your bird and you'll hate us for it."

"And then there'll be ice cream."

"Damn straight. Over and out."

Outside, the last flashlight went dark.

>Lopez 1402 hours

Twelve rosary beads now. Lopez had a burning anger in her guts that had nothing to do with the Covenant. Already blood in the dark. She had her orders. Her lousy orders. She had twelve Marines left, a big-ass ship to clean out, and no support of any kind.

I'll give you "spectacular."

They stood around her, around Rabbit's remains, around the dead Covenant, silent and waiting.

"You heard," she said, looking into each of their faces in turn. Shadowed, murky faces in the flashlight beams, but still those of her Marines. "Change of plan, boys and girls. We got Covies on board, so the good commander has invoked the Cole Protocol. We need to kill the nav system and the backup nav system, that's our primary goal. Ascertaining what the hell is going on here is now a secondary objective. Orlav, you got that rough schematic? See the engine room?"

"Yeah." She didn't sound too enthusiastic.

"All right, Benti, you take Clarence, Orlav, Gersten, and Tsardikos. You're going after the backup down in the engine room. You take care of it, then you get your asses back here. You see any Covies along the way, you kill Covies. I don't care if they're happy to see you or not. None of them get off this ship, got it?" She thought Benti, with Clarence, would be more effective heading things up on that team than Orlav. Orlav did good recon, but she couldn't improvise.

"Yes, sir!" Benti said, already out the door and slinking down the corridor, the others following her.

"I mean it, Private!" she called out after them, not looking at the thing hidden in Rabbit's body. "You shoot anything you see. Don't let anything get close. Nothing, you hear me?"

"Saaaarge, you know me," Benti said. "I don't let anybody get close." Her voice didn't say that at all.

"No gear," Percy said, nudging the Covenant Elite with his boot, ripples spreading in the bloodied water. "Not a one of these bastards has any gear at all."

"All the better for us."

"How'd Covenant get on board this ship, Sarge?" McCraw asked. "How? Just landed here with no weapons and no gear?"

"Maybe they're prisoners," Rakesh said.

Lopez snorted. "Right. Because we take so many Covenant prisoners." Then she stopped, a bead catching in her mind. "Where the hell is Ayad?" she asked.

They had no good answer.

>Benti 1431 hours

Things went wrong almost from the start for Benti and her team. It sure looked easy at first, though, which had Benti humming an old pop song under her breath. They had cut across the ship, passing through processing cells and checkpoints and security stations toward what Orlav assured Benti was a shortcut—a series of access tunnels would lead to B deck. Benti was all about the shortcuts.

But now Clarence was bracing himself, back to the wall and foot on the door they needed to pass through. He grunted, his boot squeaking with the effort, but the door didn't budge. A makeshift barricade on the other side was the culprit. It wasn't the first they'd seen. They'd seen too many, in fact.

The corridor was too straight and dark for her tastes, like being devoured by a throat. Even the continued sight of swatches of blood—across walls, across ceilings—had begun to get to her. Blood still didn't bother her, but she'd never seen so damn much before, over such a long period. She'd run out of jokes about it. Even the dull smell of it was getting to her. She didn't like that she couldn't raise Burgundy, either.

Gersten muscled in beside Clarence, but gave up after a moment.

"No good, not gonna move." Gersten, a great hulk of a man, spoke almost as rarely as Clarence, and with as much authority.

Clarence shook his head in agreement, even as he gave the door another kick.

A high-pitched shriek tore through the corridor, dissolved into a cackle, cut off.

"What the hell was that?" Tsardikos asked.

"Just the ship, probably," Benti said, lying.

"Yeah," he replied, barely heard her. "Right."

"Hang on," Orlav said as she scrolled through the

schematic a lot quicker than she had been. "I'll find us another route."

The tension was thick between them, the muted light shifting imperceptibly across Orlav's face as she traced out paths and access points. Benti could hear the others trying to breathe quietly, trying not to breathe at all.

Benti had a good imagination. She remembered that Elite, unarmed and naked and shushing her so it could listen, and she listened, too. She knew that ships were never silent. They had their own language. Humming ventilation, the drone of the engines, the electronic pitch of a million circuits, the groan of vast plates resisting the vacuum of space. That shriek hadn't been a ship noise, not even close.

As Orlav continued to scroll, a new sound brushed up the corridor and overhead—like an enormous feather sliding across tin foil that then resolved into something soft and sickening and chittering. A sound you'd tell yourself you'd imagined, because you couldn't imagine what would have made it. It didn't repeat. Benti never wanted to hear it again.

Benti held her flashlight steady, deliberately steady, staring into the darkness at nothing, gathering herself. Then she cast a quick eye around the walls. "Ducts?"

"You can get into the damn ducts," Tsardikos said. "I'm not."

"Not enough space for anyone anyway," Gersten said, looking as spooked as Benti felt.

"Okay." Orlav's voice made Benti start. "We need to backtrack. Should be access to the lower level two junctions over from the last intersection. This will take

us through the recycling plant." Orlav sounded triumphant, which bothered Benti a bit. *Don't applaud
work-arounds until they actually work around.*

"Yum," she said, with an enthusiasm she didn't feel.

She cast a last look over the blocked door. None of
them had said it, but the barricade that had stopped
them hadn't held. The wreckage—an unholy flotsam
and jetsam of chairs, couches, smashed up boxes, machine parts, and even a potted plant or two—had been
pushed back and jammed the door after it had been
broken. Just like so many other barricades and blockades they'd passed on their way, as if a frantic siege
had rolled its way through the ship. *Prison riot,* she
thought, trying it on for size. It didn't fit. Not really.

There had been a glimpse, in the narrow sliver of
passage still open, of the corridor beyond. It was
painted purple with Covenant blood. At the edge of the
torch light she thought she'd seen a shape on the floor,
something with dimensions that didn't sit well with her.

They should have found someone by now. Nobody
said that either.

>Lopez 1440 hours

Lopez popped the cap from a bottle of antiseptic and
splashed it liberally on the open gash on MacCraw's
arm. Second time he'd gotten wounded, this time from
tripping over a barricade. He really needed to do a better job of looking where he was going.

"Quit yelping," she ordered, tasting caustic medicine
in her nose and throat. "You a man or a mouse?"

"It burns!"

"Poor mouse," she said, entirely without sympathy. They hadn't found Ayad, might never find Ayad. Lopez would take a gash against being lost in that darkness any day.

When MacCraw kept complaining, she poured the last of the antiseptic in a rush all over the wound. "Be glad Mama Lopez knows what's good for you."

Never expected they'd stop in the infirmary on the way to the bridge, MacCraw's boo-boo notwithstanding, but there were no direct routes left in the *Mona Lisa*. Hatches jammed, barricades erected, some of them still holding, some not. Too many obstacles in unknown terrain, and she'd drastically revised their ETA to the bridge, to the point that she didn't have one any more. Could only hope they could gain access when they got there.

The infirmary itself had remained immune to all of the destruction around it. Did their first aid work on Covenant? Probably not. No reason for the buggers to ransack the joint.

They'd pushed over a pathetic blockade at the entrance with ease. For the first time, Lopez saw graffiti, scrawled in blood across a turned-over chair, and running across the wall: "Tell Ma I didn't do it. I didn't. Not any of it. God bless. —George Crispin." Smaller scritchings across the floor were obscene or devolved into nonsense words.

The place was also surprisingly small, given the size of the ship and the number of cell blocks they'd come across. Maybe the staff hadn't been big on treating prisoners. Just figured they were tough, could take their chances.

MacCraw grunted when she slapped a pad of gauze over the gash. It needed stitches, but that would do for now.

As she put away her medic kit, Lopez noticed a detail that suddenly had her full attention.

"Singh," she said, tilting her head toward the far wall. "What do you make of that?" A sealed chamber, without windows or cameras, the seal around the door so subtle she'd almost missed it. No handle, either.

The technician shouldered his rifle and ran a hand around the seam. "I've seen these before. The opposite of cells. Safe rooms. You can only open them from the inside."

"In case the prisoners get out . . ."

"Exactly."

MacCraw crossed the room—fleeing Mama Lopez's tender ministrations—and put an ear against the surface, like it was a safe he wanted to crack. Now he rapped a knuckle on the door. Da-dada-da-da, da, da.

"MacCraw . . ." A tone she'd used a thousand times before.

But Singh said, "No, let him do that again."

MacCraw obliged.

A concealed speaker clicked on, a muffled hiss speckling the silence. Sounding a lot cleaner and more immediate than the static over their radios.

Lopez grinned at both of them. Good boys. "Anyone

home? This is Sergeant Lopez of the UNSC *Red Horse*."
Remembering John Doe, still the only living person
from the *Mona Lisa* she'd met.

Of course, it might be Covie in there.

A pause, and then a voice: "UNSC?" Male. Nervous.
Dry.

"The one and only." *All five of us. At your service.*
Or not. Depending.

She took a step back and leveled her rifle at the door.
Motioned for the others to do the same.

"How do I know you're really UNSC?"

"You can either take my word for it, or I can prove it
to you. One of these is the fun option, but not for you."

Mahmoud and Percy joined the ring, Rakesh keeping an eye on the corridor. Four rifles on the door, just
waiting for it to open.

Something like confidence entered the voice: "I'd
hate to take away your fun . . ."

Lopez frowned. She didn't find that clever. She'd
been counting her eleven rosary beads nonstop since
Ayad, and she wasn't taking any chances with the rest
of them. Didn't care if a party of gung-ho Spartans was
behind that door. *Well, okay, that's not true.*

"You've got ten seconds," she called out, "and then
I'll huff and I'll puff and I'll—"

The door depressed with a sigh, and slid open. In the
room beyond, cramped living quarters, one pallet and
sink with medical supplies lining cabinets that reached
to the ceiling. Across the ceiling lay a schematic of the
Mona Lisa, but half of it was dark, the rest flickering.

In the middle of the room, behind the pallet, stood

one sweating, thin, sallow man, about five ten, in whites that weren't white any more. Brilliant blue eyes. Looked a bit rodent-ish, like he'd happily gnaw on something, anything, until he'd chewed it all up. But entirely unharmed. Wearing a stink she recognized as fear, mixed with the usual too-long-without-a-shower reek.

He held a small pistol. Aimed at them. Despite the man's poor physical condition, his hands didn't shake. His stance reflected military training: two-handed grip, bent slightly at the knees. Unfazed by the firing squad two feet from him.

"Drop the weapon." Lopez tightened her finger on the trigger.

The man's bright gaze darted from Marine to Marine, assessing them, before he reached some decision. He licked his lips like a gecko. Lowered the pistol, transferred it to his left hand, and set it on the floor while raising his right arm as if in a parody of surrender. Stood there, waiting.

"Identify yourself," Lopez ordered flatly.

A relieved smile, although Lopez thought she'd detected an underlying, undeserved confidence. Already had a growing sense he was putting on a performance for them.

"Doctor John Smith, Chief Medical Officer of the transport ship *Mona Lisa*." When they didn't move, he added, hesitantly, "Er, you can lower your weapons."

Lopez smiled, hoping it came out as grim as Benti claimed. "John Smith" her ass. "You didn't offer us ice cream. You didn't even say 'please.' What's in it for us?"

"Ice cream?" he said, incredulous.

Some guffaws from behind her, but Smith looked at them like he'd entered a room full of crazy people. She could see he wasn't someone who liked playing the fool. Resented her already, even if he came off as polite.

"Yeah, ice cream." Had five dead and wasn't above taking it out on a stranger. "We want ice cream."

Smith backed away a little, said, unsmiling, "I'm not the enemy . . . please?"

Lopez lowered her rifle. The others followed her lead. Smith let out that breath he'd been holding.

Okay, fun was over. Time for business.

"What happened here?" she asked. "How'd you wind up in that room?"

Smith shrugged, gave a helpless little laugh that still seemed like acting to Lopez. He picked at some dead skin on his left palm with his right hand. Worried at it. "What do you think happened? Ship like this, only one thing ever happens. Prisoners got a chance, rioted, overwhelmed the guards, and took over the ship. I was lucky to be in here when it happened."

"Lucky," she echoed, rolling the word between her teeth. Her own scars were itching. Again. "'Prison ship.' That's the story, huh?"

He frowned. "It's not a story. The prisoners escaped, took over the ship."

It wasn't a lie, but it wasn't the truth either. This guy was slick. Lopez liked slick as much as she liked mysteries.

"You know, you're the first person we've found. You might be the only human survivor on this ship." Put all the emphasis on *human*.

Smith bared his teeth, neither smile nor grimace. "The only human—"

"Uh-huh," Lopez said, and gave a nod to her Marines. "Go to it, boys."

MacCraw and Percy pushed past him to investigate the room, MacCraw giving Smith a good knock with his shoulder. They could smell the bullshit too. Good. Mahmoud collected Smith's gun and patted him down roughly, coming up empty.

"Policy on the taking of Covenant prisoners change, Smith?" Lopez asked, prodding. "I don't think we got that memo."

Smith's eyes were slits. "It wasn't a widely circulated memo."

"No fucking kidding," giving herself props for getting him to admit something. More than she'd gotten out of Rebecca or Foucault.

Something made him change tactics; she didn't know what. Saw it in a sudden shift in posture, even.

"Look," he said. "I'm just the medical officer. I don't—didn't—set policy. I just stitched and bandaged, that's all."

Poor pitiful you.

"In this . . . expansive . . . medical bay of yours."

Smith's mouth formed a line like a flat EKG. "I'm not here to help any Covenant bastards. Just us. Just us humans." Had he rehearsed that, too? Sitting in his sealed room, listening to the screams of people dying?

Yet, even if he had rehearsed it, Smith had touched a nerve. Lopez couldn't hold his gaze. She'd had relatives on Reach. Close ones. No longer. Had seen in Smith, for a moment, all the anger, grief, and bitterness that had driven her to take her command, every combat mission, and to give up her life to UNSC. The same she'd seen in each of her soldiers. *It was always us against them.* Always.

Balanced against that: taking prisoners. That left a sour taste in her mouth. *Leave none alive.*

Did he really think she was going to let down her guard? She hadn't let down her guard in twenty-seven years. "Tell me about the Covenant prisoners, Smith."

Smith, exasperated: "For intelligence. Research and development. Know your enemy. It's a war. You know that—you're a soldier, right? I *don't know*, I'm just the medical officer."

Her fingers flexed. The memory of John Doe's hand. "Research and development, huh?"

He held his hands out as if he had a peace offering for her, but there was only air. "I'm just the medical officer." An echo. A shield.

"What's the *Mona Lisa* doing here?"

Frustration on Smith's face. "Where's here? I've been in this room since the outbreak. It's a black box, nothing in or out. I have no idea where we are. Where are we?"

"Why don't you tell me the last place you were, then, and I'll tell you if you're still there?"

That got Mahmoud's and MacCraw's attention. That gave Smith pause.

"In chess, they call that 'check,'" Mahmoud muttered.

Gears and wheels were turning in Smith's head. Lopez could see them.

"Didn't you come here to rescue us?" Smith said. "Am I under arrest or something?" Face gone completely blank.

So you're going to play it that way. Well, she had time to play, too. All the way up until they got to the bridge.

Countered with: "You would have access codes to the bridge, right?"

Smith nodded reluctantly.

And, finally, she did relent. She might not like him, but that didn't make him the enemy. "We're off of a planet called Threshold and we've got Covenant loose on a ship capable of making a slipspace jump. We're following the Cole Protocol. We need to get to the bridge and take out the nav system. I hope the bridge isn't locked down, but if it is . . ."

Smith had blanched as soon as she said Cole Protocol. "No. No, no, we need to get off the ship. You came here somehow, a Pelican? We need to get off the ship."

Knew instinctively Burgundy would hate this guy as much as she did. "Sorry, but that's not an option. You're coming with us."

"No, no—"

"*Please*," she added, with another dazzling smile.

>**Burgundy 1445 hours**

At least Marines got to go out and do something, even if "something" meant getting into trouble. Not long after the last communication with the *Red Horse*, Lopez and her crew had dropped off the radio, their clichéd bravado and lame jokes slowly swallowed by static and interference. She thought she'd heard a crackle of contact from Benti, but that'd been snuffed out immediately.

Burgundy worked her way through a pack of gum. Her jaw ached something fierce. A book lay unattended on her lap. She'd tried reading, but couldn't stop checking the cameras, and had given up after she'd read the same paragraph for twenty minutes.

There wasn't anything to see. Just the barricades in the shadows. Once, she thought she'd glimpsed a silhouette with two heads, one head pale and veiny, which was a pretty ridiculous thing to think you'd seen. Nothing came out of the darkness to confirm that glimpse, so she'd put it down to nerves.

Her aft running lights were still on, so with the cameras she could still see about ten meters past the Pelican's rear. She'd thought about turning the lights off, but nixed that idea. If something was out there, she'd be as good as putting out a flashing holographic sign that read "Burgundy's Home—Just Come Right In."

So she waited.

And she waited.

And she waited.

She took the latest wad of gum from her mouth, thumbed it on the dash, and froze when two figures lurched into the light on the feed. Her thumb sticking to the gum, she yanked free and gripped her pistol.

*Don't you lay a hand on my bird, Covie scum. I'll hole
you, I'll hole you a hundred times over.*

Then she looked closer. It was Cranker and Maller.
They were stumbling, injured. Head wounds, it looked
like, dark patches running down their faces, torn clothing, and they were leaning into each other, but they
were *walking*. Alive!

The relief that washed over Burgundy was so intense
she almost cried.

"Oh thank Christ."

They clearly needed help. She'd not thought much of
them—loud and rowdy and pushy in the mess line—
but here, now, it didn't matter, they were the most ex-
cellent human beings in the universe. She wouldn't be
alone now.

She slapped the controls for the gangplank and
vaulted out of the cockpit, snatching up an assault rifle
from the locker as she passed. The ramp opened too
damn slow. She ran to the lip as it lowered, checking
the nearby barricades and containers for any other
movement.

"Guys!" she hissed. "Get on in here! Now!"

Up close they were worse than they looked on the
cameras, Cranker listing badly now, Maller pivoting
toward the sound of her voice, the ramp dropping,
dropping.

"You're—"

Much worse. Much, much worse.

Skin mottled and bruised and sunken, veined
through with dark tendrils. Eyes white and unseeing.

Some growth fastened to Cranker's neck, an enormous pustule that shivered and twitched. Maller, what had been Maller, opened his mouth, and howled, a sound no human could make.

Burgundy scrambled back, opened fire.

But it was too late.

>Benti 1450 hours

When they found that the hatch to the lower deck was also locked, Benti let loose with a stunning stream of curses that left them all looking at her like they didn't know her anymore. Except for Orlav.

"We got a Plan B?" is all Orlav asked.

This being-in-charge thing was wearing thin. Benti wished, not for the first time, that she was back on the *Red Horse* taking a nice bath.

"This *was* Plan B," Benti said. And Plan C, if you wanted to be precise. They'd lost contact with Lopez, and Benti wasn't sure they'd get it back any time soon. Hailing the Pelican had become a kind of personal joke that gave her the giggles. Didn't know if she really found it funny or was just becoming hysterical. Hellooo Pelican, come in, come in? No? Okay. You just be that way, you petulant bird.

Clarence shrugged and started back down the corridor.

"Hang on, just wait, I'll find another way." Orlav's frown deepened, clearly sick of peering at the tiny screen.

Benti shouldered her rifle and knelt by the hatch. The

access panel wasn't secured. She flipped the panel open, gave it a once-over, and pulled a knife from her boot. Being a medic wasn't all she was good at.

"Shine your light down here. Thanks." It wasn't so complicated. A little tricky, but nothing she hadn't done before. Just expose this wire, strip back this one and put a bridge here, and—

The hatchway unlocked with a sharp clack and she hauled it open. Triumphant.

But only for a second.

"Pheeeooooow!" They cringed away from the stench that came billowing out, the air thicker and moist in the worst possible way. "Bilges. They're the same in every ship."

"Foucault would be pissed to hear you say that about the *Red Horse*."

"Yeah, well, he ain't here," Gersten said, and swung himself onto the ladder, Orlav and Clarence leaning into the hatchway to provide cover.

"See anything?"

"Yep. Looks like bilges, smells like bilges . . . I think it's bilges!"

Benti hadn't expected Gersten to turn into a comedian. She rolled her eyes and dropped down after Gersten. "No shit."

"Oh, we got shit a-plenty here. Special price for you."

Wow. It wasn't going to stop.

The space was tight and cramped, full of tanks holding clean water, gray water, and sewage, and yet more tanks for the processing as it was all recycled and made ready to go back into the mix again. Moisture beaded across the ceiling and dripped onto them irregularly, leaving oily marks on the walls and residue across every surface.

"It's in this direction." Orlav gestured at a passage leading through the tanks.

"Lots of spaces to hide in there," Benti said.

Clarence gave her a look like *Who would want to?*

"Lots." Orlav agreed. "So we'll do it real carefullike."

Moving in stages, creeping, darting into new territory, their backs only to each other, they moved deeper into the bowels of the ship.

Benti wished she could get used to the smell, but it was impossible. Even keeping her hand over her nose didn't help. The smell had a taste, a texture, that got around any defense. Benti wanted that bath more than ever—and ice cream, damn the sarge for putting the idea in her head. But more than anything, she wanted someplace with a blue sky and no ceiling. She wondered, not for the first time, if Lopez was already waiting for them on the bridge.

"I've been in the shit before," Gersten said, "but this is ridiculous."

"Shut it," Benti said. Mouthy Gersten was ruining silent Gersten's rep. But also her ears had pricked up at the hint of an echo.

"Let Gersten wallow in it, for once," Orlav said straightfaced. Even Tsardikos, who had been almost as silent as Clarence, couldn't suppress a chuckle at that.

But Benti shushed them again. "I'm serious. Clarence, you hear that?"

Clarence nodded. It was impossible to miss. A voice that rose stark above the muted hubbub of the recycling system. A voice that spoke no words, that didn't try to, that didn't know how.

They knew the wide array of Covenant sounds, and this was not one of them.

"Keep moving," Benti said through gritted teeth. Boy, she wished now they hadn't split up. The sarge would've had a much better plan. But right now the sarge might as well be on a beach in Cozumel.

"Where'd it come from?" Orlav asked. "I can't tell."

Another sound, containing a depth and jaggedness that tripped Benti's pulse.

"What the hell was that?" Gersten asked, spinning about. "Covenant bastards, what the hell is it?"

"Shut up and keep moving," Benti insisted. She couldn't shed the image of the Covenant Elite Clarence had killed for her, listening for something that frightened it more than a bunch of Marines.

Shedding caution, they sped up into a jog, a glance at each corner, knocking into the holding tanks because they looked behind them so much. Tsardikos was lagging. Benti hissed at him to go faster, but he couldn't keep up.

Another roar, a bellow not even really animal in nature—too ragged and discordant. It echoed off the tanks and pipes, hiding its source. Moaning, eerie changes in the timbre, like someone tuning in a messed-up radio channel. More and more voices—no, they couldn't be voices—joined in, as if alerted to a hunt. Just discernable above the coalescing howl, something that chittered and scuttled.

"They're behind us, I think," Gersten said, not trying to be funny any more, as he swiveled to jog backward, flashlight spasming across the pipes behind them. Benti turned, couldn't see anything. Not even Tsardikos.

"And they're gaining," Orlav added. Unnecessarily.

They broke, running so fast now that anything could ambush them, but needing to take that risk. Running felt good to Benti's tense muscles.

"Where are we going, Orlav?" Benti shouted. "Come on, where are we going?"

"Maintenance storage room, with access back upstairs beyond!"

"How far?"

"Fifty meters!"

"They're gaining," Gersten said, rising strain in his voice. There was more than one voice in the growing growl behind them, multiple footfalls, heavy, far too heavy. They turned a corner, kept going.

"Grenade?"

Orlav: "Too close to the hull!"

"Here!" Benti splashed to a halt by a narrow passage that led through the last of the tanks. A quick scan indicated that the space beyond was clear, nothing lurking in the corners. She dropped to a knee, checking the ammo remaining in her rifle as Clarence took up a position behind and over her.

"How many you make out, Gersten?"

"Lots," he said, wide-eyed.

Great help that was . . .

The noises reaching to them through the darkness swelled, sometimes familiar, yet also utterly warped, alien, broken. Benti couldn't slow her breathing, her hands cold on her rifle.

Tsardikos came running toward them in a final burst of speed, terrified and swearing. He jumped over her, spun into position behind and fumbled with his weapon.

"Took your damn time," growled Orlav. Tsardikos ignored her.

"I don't think they're Covenant," Benti said. Behind her, Clarence shifted, his calf against her hip. He had her back. Again.

Orlav smacked a flare and tossed it out into the passageway. They waited, stinking of shit, like a group of cowering sanitation workers. With guns.

The first of their pursuers staggered into the spluttering light.

They weren't Covenant.

>Lopez 1501 hours
_____

At last they'd found a body. Never thought she'd sound a silent huzzah for that. Never thought evidence of death could be such a relief.

Security stations and checkpoints were choked with furniture, the doors themselves jammed. Sometimes on purpose. Most of the blockades had been torn apart, great gouges left in the steel walls and floor. In the process of finding a path through the debris, they'd been funneled into one of the crew's rec rooms. Archaic ceiling fans. Pool tables. Bar stools and a TV. One wall with a blown-up photograph of the beach on some tropical island. An honest-to-god facsimile of a tiki bar in another corner. Something about it made Lopez think of the words *in denial*. Even down to the plastic tiki glasses still sitting on the counter.

Nothing disturbed; no one had fled here.

It almost looked normal.

Except for the body.

Or two.

Honestly, it was hard to tell.

Right about then, looking at the pieces, Lopez could have done with some answers. Real answers, not the extra mysteries she was being offered by Smith. Remembering Rabbit, the last conversation with Burgundy, Ayad still gone.

Too many more unknowns and her soldiers were going to start to fray. No matter how she tried to stop that from happening. She'd seen it before. It had damn near happened to Foucault before he'd turned the situation around. Become a hero.

So there was Mahmoud muttering under his breath while Rakesh and Singh focused on the tiki bar. Only Percy, at her side, seemed unable to look away.

"I get the feeling this wasn't a very happy place," Percy said.

This wasn't the battlefield. This wasn't what they'd signed on for.

The storage cupboard at the far end of the room had been wrenched open so hard the hinges had spun off and the door lay crumpled to the side. Inside, pieces. Leftovers. She couldn't think of it as anything else. Flesh she knew to be Covenant. Skin she knew to be human. And something half grown across them, *inside* these pieces, bulging the muscle and mottling the skin. They couldn't have been here long enough to look that rotten. Something in the physiology had altered, shifted, from the inside. A massive protrusion from what should have been a shoulder, but it wasn't an arm. It looked like a growth of bone, grotesque and huge, with strips of flesh gripping it tenuously.

Savage. Brutal. Made her remember John Doe's wounds. Had he ever been in this room? Guard or prisoner?

"Sarge, what the fuck is that?" MacCraw pointed, as if she hadn't noticed.

"Well, MacCraw, that there," she said grimly, slipping into a drawl, "that's a hand." Death had not relaxed it. The fingers didn't curl, the palm didn't fold. Flat, with the fingers straight, rigid and stiff.

"What the hell is that other thing, Sarge?" MacCraw again. Was he never going to stop cataloging?

"Almost looks like they got fused or something hiding in the cupboard," Rakesh said in a distant voice. "Together," he added, more distant. Clearly not believing it for an instant.

But none of that really got to Lopez. What got to her was the carefully tended bonsai tree sitting right next to the cubby. Had a terrible image of someone tossing the body parts in there and then doing a bit of gardening.

Lopez took a step back, and another, and draped an arm over Smith's shoulders. She pulled him companionably close, seemingly oblivious to the way the muzzle of her rifle drifted back and forth across his face.

"John," she said. "Can I call you John?"

He leaned away. Not from her, no. From the bodies, the bits of bodies she was dragging him near. He really was a little man. There wasn't much muscle on him.

"I think you know what this is."

Smith glanced at each of them again, *assessing* them again. Seeing no escape.

"And I think you're going to damn well *tell me what this is*."

>Benti 1502 hours

As Benti grimly fired and fired, rifle hot in her hands, she had one small satisfaction: no room to miss, no distance to interfere with accuracy. The first figure jumped and spun with the concentrated fire from the five of them, falling back into the second and third, who didn't pause. They just shoved their comrade aside, climbing over each other to get through the gap. They tripped and stumbled too as they pushed their way into the line of fire, even as the first was, oh god, Benti could make out the first thrashing its way back up. She knew she'd dropped a good line of hot lead straight in its belly, but it was *getting back up*.

Clarence threw another flare.

Most were human, some were actually Covenant. All of them so misshapen and shambly you could hardly tell. Branching fungi tumbled and poured from their limbs. Their eyes were glazed and vacant. The stink of them overpowered the shit smell. There was a low mumble coming from them, almost in concert, that unnerved Benti.

"They're not staying down!" Gersten yelled. "Reloading!" Popped a clip and slapped in a new one as Orlav covered his zone. "What the hell are they?"

She concentrated her fire on the frontmost, and it dropped, and she shifted her aim to the next, and oh god, it was getting to its feet too, and she saw shoes on those feet, slippers, and a distinctive orange color.

They'd found the prisoners, and apparently they didn't like the bilges, either.

Tsardikos wasn't even firing. Just watching, mouth open. Benti elbowed him in the thigh. "Snap out of it, soldier!" she screamed at him. And he did. Miraculously. Started firing again.

Still, there was no way they could hold this position. No way.

"Fall back to the maintenance room!" Benti rose from her crouch, sliding up against Clarence, who stepped back, and she with him, moving like practiced dance partners.

"We lose this spot, they're going to swamp us!" Orlav shouted.

"We stay here, they'll swamp us sooner!" Benti shouted back.

The flares showed a swarm of pale globes, like living snotbags, scuttling up the ceiling from behind the shambling mob, toward them.

The passageway behind them was an unknown quantity. No time to look at the map. No telling what they'd find there.

No avoiding that. No time for caution.

She yanked a grenade from her belt, ripping the pin out in the same motion. "No more jabber! Get going!"

A raised eyebrow from Clarence, a look of panic from Gersten.

She tossed it as they broke and ran.

Not far enough.

The force of it slammed into her, slammed through her, throwing her forward into Clarence. Her bones shrieked in protest. All the air fled her lungs. She rolled over the top of Clarence, heat at her back and then on her face.

None of that mattered.

"Keep moving!" she screamed, before she'd even opened her eyes, crawling to her knees. *Don't ever stop moving. Unless you want to die.*

Her ears rang like wineglasses. She couldn't hear anything, hardly could see anything. Slapped a hand on Clarence's helmet as he pushed himself from the floor. Cast about, Orlav and Gersten scrambling to their feet. *Where was Tsardikos?*

Aftershock: A wash of warm water came tumbling down the passageway and swept her legs out from under her just as she'd gotten all the way up. It was murky, it was rank, and swept along with it was one of *them*, flailing and thrashing, and a trailing arm—no, it wasn't an arm, it was a whip of bone, it was a blade of *body*— slashed Orlav across the back, arcing a wide spray of blood across Benti and Clarence, peppering blood through the filthy water and across the pipes, and slamming her down again, her mouth an "O" of shock as Benti, who had never released her rifle, they were all better than that, drew a bead and fired a hole through the thing's chest until she could see the other wall, and watched as, truly dead, it smacked up against a tank and lay there.

Thought she saw something else, too, near Orlav—one of those snot creatures—but, no, nothing when she spun, it must've just been something bobbing in the water. Part of the thing she'd just killed.

A glance down the passageway brought her a small measure of relief. Patchy fires singed churning sewage around a new barricade of ceiling and caved-in tanks. It'd worked for now—there was no other movement. The smell of mingled crap and the stench of the enemy made her cough. It'd gag her if she let it.

But so would the memory of them, those things, rising up despite being blasted full of bullet holes. They wouldn't—couldn't—be stopped for long. She could already feel the vibration of digging. The shit wouldn't hold.

She surged to her feet, too fast, off balance, shook her head angrily—she needed clarity now more than ever.

A quick check, Clarence was okay, Gersten okay, just cursing a lot as he tried to lift Orlav.

Her hearing had started to return. Over the cursing, she could hear Orlav shrieking with agony. There was another sound, too, another kind of shrieking, like a man being devoured alive. It almost froze Benti, until she realized it came from the other side of the barricade.

Tsardikos, screaming as those things took him apart. Nothing Benti could do about it. Nothing that wouldn't put the rest of them in danger.

She shook it off. She shook it off, even as it damaged her, and scrambled over to Orlav, shit bouncing from her shins.

"She's bleeding bad," Gersten said, supporting nearly all of Orlav's weight.

That was the least of Orlav's worries. This tainted water in her wounds would kill her anyway. It would just take a little longer. Benti leaned down for a quick inspection, and froze. The injury itself was long but not deep. She could see the blue curves in the dark muscle of her back, but the spine didn't shine through. What kind of a victory was it when the medic in her leapt for joy that she couldn't see bone? But fastened to the lower back was a quivering bulb of pus, finger-like tendrils digging into the open wound ecstatically. Holy crap. It looked like a parasite of some kind. She reached for it, and stopped. Not here, not in this water.

"We have to get her out of here!" She threw one of Orlav's arms over her shoulder, the other around her waist, taking some of the burden off of Gersten. "Head for maintenance. Clarence, come on, let's go!"

They fled, dragging Orlav between them. Clarence staggered in their wake, watching the darkness behind them. He didn't have any more flares. Their flashlights would have to do.

Benti flinched as she thought she heard something in the air ducts above them.

"Orlav," Benti raised her voice, turned to yell in her ear, "Orlav! Report!"

"'s fadin' . . ." she slurred, and her head dropped, eyes wide open, not even pretending to walk now, feet dragging in the water. ". . . where . . ."

"There's the door!"

A burst of speed and they collapsed against it. Locked. They were trapped outside. Benti propped Orlav against the door, Gersten shouldering her weight again. "She's bad," he moaned.

Benti ripped the faceplate from the control panel, straightforward wiring again. She walked her fingers along the wires.

"Oh god, she's bad, look at her face, look at her face, look—"

Benti yanked a wire, and looked.

What looked back at her was not Orlav.

>Lopez 1503 hours

Lopez had her orders. *Find out what the hell is up with this damn ship* was down at the bottom of her priorities. *Get to the bridge* was at the top. But the more time she spent on *this damn ship*, the harder it was to ignore that she might not achieve the first without knowing the last. Couldn't help thinking of the intel blackout. Found herself rather taken with the idea of knowing something Rebecca didn't want her to know.

"So tell me," she nudged. "Tell me what I'm looking at." Knew whatever came out of Smith's mouth would come out sideways, but that was okay. She could make it honest.

"Covenant get sick too," Smith said haltingly. "We noticed it in some of them. Any of the prisoners displaying the symptoms we kept in isolation. Just in case." He wiped his mouth, still resisting Lopez's grip. "We took every precaution against it. Every precaution."

He stopped. Lopez jabbed him in the side with her rifle. She was pretty sure Smith was going to give her another scar eventually.

"It made them aggressive. Savage." Smith worked his mouth, clearly thinking about the words before he said them. "We did some tests. Managed to isolate it." Now he couldn't look away from the bodies. "An alien virus."

Percy raised his head, raised his eyebrows, as Mac-Craw covered his mouth and leapt back.

"We've been standing here breathing around this thing!"

Smith smiled, no humor in it. Mostly disdain. "It doesn't work like that."

"Did it jump from Covenant to human?" Percy asked.

A dull boom reverberated through the floor, the walls shuddering slightly. "Grenade?" Mahmoud mouthed. Not good. Like the explosion had jump-started his urgency again.

Smith relaxed, stopped pulling away from Lopez. Accepting his fate, finally?

"It did."

>Benti 1507 hours

Get moving again, soldier!

"Get—" The words stuck in her throat, wouldn't come out, not fast enough.

Orlav—the thing staring out from behind Orlav's eyes—opened its mouth, lips already purple and cheeks veined with green. In control now, it turned Orlav's head, drew Gersten into an embrace using Orlav's arm thrown over Gersten's shoulder.

What used to be Orlav bit into Gersten's cheek.

The words still wouldn't leave her mouth. They were stuck. As Gersten shrieked, she couldn't look away, the teeth sinking into the cheek and worrying it. Blood washed down Gersten's throat to soak his collar. Orlav's other arm was already writhing and changing right in front of Benti, becoming something bulbous that had nothing to do with the Marine she'd known.

That arm, that club, that infernal claw, rose, about to become a weapon crashing down on her skull.

Clarence shoved her aside, fired point-blank into Orlav's temple, ripping a tunnel through the skull. As the body slumped, Clarence matter-of-factly put another burst through the heart.

It dropped, Gersten screaming and flailing to be free.

Staggering back, holding one hand against his torn cheek. "Jesus, Jesus . . ."

Clarence popped the empty clip. It hissed in the water at his feet, Benti watching in the flashlight's glow, trying to adjust to what had just happened.

He slapped another in, turned, grabbed Benti's shirt and hauled her to her feet, which brought her out of it. A once-over to confirm she was uninjured, and he tipped his chin at the wires she'd left exposed, then stared at the grenade-created wreckage behind them as it shuddered and shifted, pushed from the other side. The water was rising around their knees.

She got back to it.

"Benti, my face," Gersten moaned.

"I know," she said, shaking fingers stripping this wire, then that wire, "just let me get this. Then I'll take care of you." She needed a moment so her hands were steady before she did anything medical for Gersten. Clarence had his hand on his pistol. Most people wouldn't have noticed, but she knew Clarence. *Just in case?* Was this what it came down to? Knew, too, Gersten, and not sure she could do it. Any of it. But knowing she'd have to, somehow.

A crash and tumble behind them. Something was breaking through the wreckage. A spike of tension in Clarence's posture. Her hands were wet, the wires were slippery. She twisted the two and the lock clacked open.

She spun the lever, shoulder to the door, and pushed. It stuck.

A dragging sound from behind them. A hiss like static. A moaning.

"Oh for Christ's sake come on!" Another shove, and it gave suddenly, sewage spilling into the opening, and her tumbling after it. Gersten sagged in after her. Clarence backed in and shoved the hatch closed quick as thought.

Benti looked up, into the light.

A Covenant Elite stood there, looking down at her.

Holding a cricket bat in one alien hand.

>Lopez 1507 hours

Smith looked at Lopez at last, motioning to the rifle she now held none too nonchalantly by his head.

"Sergeant, please. I am not the enemy."

"You said that already." But she released him. "So I guess you're trying to tell me one of your plague-carriers got out, grabbed one of the crew, and dragged them into this here cupboard to—" *Burgundy asking if the Covenant ate their dead.*

"I guess," Smith said, edging toward the far door. He might be trying to get away from her, but he was right. They'd lingered long enough. Didn't know if Smith would give her anything else anyway. Maybe, too, she'd wanted a tiny window of respite for her team before they went back into the thick of it.

"Rakesh, get the door. MacCraw, get your damn act together." He gave the jumbled bodies a wide berth, hand clamped over his nose and mouth.

"It's locked, Sarge. Security coded."

Lopez gestured to Smith. "Be my guest." The lying bastard.

Clearly glad the interrogation had ended for the moment, Smith rushed over, pushed his way in front of Lopez's unhelpful boys, and punched in his code. The door slid open.

A pulsing white sack of flesh with gnarled green outgrowths and tentacles for legs stared up at them. The fugliest thing Lopez had ever seen.

In that instant, trying to figure out what the hell they were looking at, it leapt, snapping out its tendrils. Rakesh was closest, had been the most eager to leave. The thing caught him around the torso like an overeager dance partner. No time for Rakesh to react.

"Shoot it!" Smith shouted, stumbling back.

Rakesh yelped. Beat at the sac that clung to his chest. Its grip too tight for him to wrench off. Lopez took aim, but Rakesh wouldn't keep still, cries rising into a shriek. His shirt darkening and soaking, oh god, the thing was eating into his chest, and she could hear more coming toward the door—

"Shut it!" Lopez screamed to Singh. He slapped the controls. No code. Percy lunged for Rakesh. Tried to get a grip on the creature. Knocked aside by his thrashing. Mahmoud firing past them at something else coming fast from beyond the door.

Smith shoved Rakesh out the door, and the pale sac with him. Hammered the controls. The door shut.

Rakesh still shrieking.

MacCraw reached for the door, but Lopez stepped in front of him, a firm hand on his chest. "No."

"We can't just leave him out there!" *Yeah, we can. If you want to live.*

Singh pale. Percy and Mahmoud weren't protesting. Only the new guy.

Rakesh stopped screaming.

MacCraw's shoulders slumped. Moved away from the pressure of her hand on his chest. "Sorry, Sarge," MacCraw murmured.

"It's okay," she said. "It's okay."

But it wasn't.

She turned, and put all her weight into that turn.

Smashed Smith across the face with her fist.

>Benti 1510 hours

A tall man jumped between Benti and the Elite with the cricket bat. "Don't shoot!" He wore the torn orange jumpsuit of a prisoner. He hadn't shaved in days. One eye sagged a little in its socket.

Despite herself, Benti didn't shoot. Maybe because the cricket bat, a narrow but solid slab of wood, puzzled her as much as the man.

They'd tumbled into what looked like a storeroom or a transition space between rooms. Just the door and racks of tools and parts. A ladder at the rear that might lead up somewhere or might not. The white walls were covered with tiny black marks, like some kind of design.

"He's not infected, it's okay, don't shoot!" the man said. "My name's Patrick Rimmer. I'm a prisoner, but I wasn't in for anything serious, I swear!"

"That's a Covenant you're protecting," Benti said. "Why the crap should we care if he's infected or not?"

She got up off the floor, rifle at the ready. *The naked Covie looking up at her, shushing her.*

Rimmer just kept his tall, lanky body in front of the Covenant, looking nervously from one to the other. Ready to die for a Covie.

"Please, guys, please, *don't kill him,*" Rimmer pleaded. "You gotta understand. He's cool. We're cool. He's my friend. He's the only one I've had to talk to. The only one. He's cool. He's clean. Please. You gotta understand. You've gotta understand it isn't the Covenant's fault. Not this time. We're cool, really." Rimmer looked so lonely, so lost, that it almost got to Benti.

Beside Benti, Clarence glared down the line of his rifle, finger tense on the trigger. Crap. Things could get ugly fast, even if the Covie only had a cricket bat. Something told Benti they could afford to suss out the situation before shooting. Making noise didn't seem like a wise move right then anyway.

Benti put her hand on Clarence's rifle, gave him a long look, and stood between him and Rimmer, her own gun aimed at the Elite. Gersten had slouched up against a wall and could wait until they'd resolved this standoff.

"If that Covie makes one wrong move, looks at us the wrong way even, it's dead, you got me?" Benti said it staring back at Clarence, trying to put extra weight behind the words. Let it be *her* decision. Clarence had made a lot of decisions on his own already today. Some of them she hadn't liked.

Clarence stared at her a second, and then nodded.

But she couldn't read the intent in his eyes at all anymore, and that scared her.

Rimmer relaxed a little bit, although sweat beaded his forehead. He nodded. "Yeah, cool, then. He's okay, Henry's clean, he's cool, he's okay. You're Marines, right? You're going to get us out of here, right?"

"Henry?" Benti tried the name out. "*Henry*." A Covie with a name other than "bastard" or "asshole" or "shithead." A Covie named Henry who carried a cricket bat. That left her speechless.

The man was jumpy, twitchy, couldn't stay still. Benti didn't know if she blamed him. "Yeah, I mean, I don't know his name, can't understand a thing he says, I just call him Henry—and he calls me Rimmer, of course, 'cause that's my name, although he doesn't really pronounce it right, or say much of anything, 'cause he can't speak our language—but he's cool, seriously, he's cool. There's more of you, right? You can get us back out, right?"

"Those aren't my orders—no, wait, you tell me, what were those things? We're not going anywhere until you tell me what they are."

But Rimmer no longer cared about her answer. He was looking beyond her, over her left shoulder. "He's . . . he's been infected."

Henry was raising his cricket bat. Rimmer looked around like he wanted a weapon too.

For a second, Benti didn't understand. "Infected?"

She turned, just as Gersten lowered his hands from his face.

"I don't, I don't feel so good . . ."

A mottled patch of yellow dust encrusted his torn cheek and a stagnant green tint ran through his skin. At the base of his neck, another quivering globe of pus, one soft tendril resting tenderly on his throat.

Benti reached for a pouch at her hip, automatically going for sterilizers, knowing she had nothing powerful enough, stupid stupid stupid, should have gone for her weapon, but unable to stop the reflex.

Clarence stepped up, pressed the mouth of his rifle against Gersten's forehead. Gersten stared at him, marshalled his energy to say with utter shock, "What the hell, Clarence, you—"

Clarence pulled the trigger and jumped back as Gersten went flying up against the wall. Blood sprayed out into the water, missing Clarence and smacking up against the wall with its weird black marks.

None of it hit Benti, shielded as she was by her partner.

Gersten slid down the wall. A torn cheek was the least of his worries now.

The extra blood bags Benti had brought seemed like a quaint affectation, and had for a while. There was no lack of blood here.

Clarence turned, checking her for wounds. He looked in her eyes, made her look in his eyes so she could see there was no threat there. *For now.* Clarence kept his rifle down and away from her.

Still, she had to say it. "You killed Gersten." *You killed Gersten real casual-like. You killed him.*

He nodded, impassive.

"His dog tags—"

"Forget the dog tags. You gotta rip the bodies up," Rimmer said, like he was telling her how to heat noodle soup properly. "That's not dead enough. Gotta destroy the body or they just come back."

"Don't be stupid." Benti couldn't keep her voice from cracking. "He's dead. He's *dead*." But the fact was, even if her heart couldn't accept it, she knew what *they* were now. She had an idea of just how right Rimmer could be.

"He ain't! He's infected!" Rimmer stepped forward. He'd found a chisel. "We gotta take him apart, he's going to come back!"

Benti had her rifle pointed at him before she knew it. A mistake, seeing the Elite's posture change, and Clarence's hand coming down heavy on her shoulder. Clarence had her back. Always. And he'd just shot Gersten.

She'd just about lost control of the situation, but then, she thought with an odd kind of relief, there was hardly anyone left under her "command" anyway.

"Clarence," she said, her voice steadier than her thoughts. His hand slid up her arm and with light pressure lowered her rifle. She couldn't resist. "You're not—"

Rimmer lurched back again, chisel held out pathetically. In the water pooled on the floor, ripples . . .

Clarence pivoted, shot Gersten, and killed him a second time.

Benti didn't turn around. She'd seen her fill, enough for the rest of her life. She wanted to sit, but didn't. She wouldn't have the strength to get back up.

"You see?" Rimmer said. "You *see*? They come back. You leave them enough, all the important body bits, and they all come back. Me and Henry here, we're the last ones. They didn't know we were here. But now you've *let* them know. I mean, I'm not blaming you, not really. But they'll try to get in. We have to move. There are more of you coming, right?"

"Right," she said without feeling. *No, wrong.* The radio had been silent for too long. Too much interference. Benti knew that if more were coming, it wouldn't be to help them.

Henry looked at her, then Clarence, and the Elite's shoulders sagged in a universal sign of disappointment. It read Benti's expression just fine. Its shoulders sagged further when, beyond the door, came a crash and rumble.

"There's another way out of here?" Benti asked.

"Yeah," the prisoner said reluctantly, "but we've heard them things outside that hatch too."

"Just show us the way out," Benti said impatiently.

Cricket bat resting up against his shoulder, Henry pointed without enthusiasm to a ladder and hatch leading up to the next deck.

"We'll have to chance it. You're on a prison transport, you must be badass." *Despite befriending a Covie.* "Get Gersten's gun and use it."

Rimmer shook his head emphatically. "Not that badass. Nobody's that badass. He touched it, I'm not touching it. I'm not going near it." She wasn't going near it either, which was the point.

Clarence retrieved Gersten's rifle, took a wipe from

the pouch Benti had half opened, cleaned the weapon, and thrust it at Rimmer. Benti he might argue with, but under Clarence's glare, Rimmer took the rifle. Reluctantly.

"What about Henry?" Rimmer asked. "Henry deserves a better weapon."

Clarence gave the two of them a look like, *Isn't it enough we haven't blasted him to hell?* Benti just gave a humorless laugh. Even with the odds stacked against them, no way would she willingly hand a rifle to a Covenant.

"Let him keep his cricket bat," Benti said. "And he can be the one on point. If he doesn't like it, tough."

Henry didn't seem surprised. Rimmer seemed about to argue, then thought better of it.

"Henry, Rimmer, me, and Clarence, that order. One of us drops—"

"We leave them," Rimmer said. "Or make sure they don't come back."

She put her foot on the bottom rung of the ladder. If there was anything up there, she couldn't hear it over the din back in the recycling plant.

"Covenant are not in charge of this ship." It wasn't framed as a question.

Rimmer snorted. "The Flood got out. There's no one in charge of this ship any more."

>Lopez 1510 hours

Lopez shook the pain out of her hand. Her knuckles stung. "Never hit someone in the jaw, MacCraw." But, damn, on some level, it had felt good. She'd wanted to do it for a while.

He gaped at her. "But you just did! Sarge!"

"Silly of me," she said, turning to Smith, who'd staggered to the floor, holding his face, blood on his chin. "Very silly." She slammed one regulation navy boot into his gut so hard he curled around her foot, the force exploding saliva from his mouth.

"Sarge!" What outfit did MacCraw think he'd joined? The Lady's Auxiliary Gardening Society?

"You know what that thing was, you lying son of a bitch." Lopez ignored MacCraw. "Virus my ass. Mahmoud, search him again."

Four rosary beads in her mind, possibly six more hanging in the balance. She flexed her fingers. Yeah, never hit someone in the jaw, unless it was utterly necessary.

"Still nothing," Mahmoud reported.

Smith looked a little too smug about that. She was beginning to think he couldn't help himself.

"Take off his shoes. Check his tighty whities, if you have to. Check his damn body cavities!"

"Sarge!" Mahmoud looked as mortified as Smith.

Lopez curled her lip in a snarl. Didn't need to say anything further.

Nothing on Smith's body, who flinched away from the rough hands on him. But then:

"Sarge," Mahmoud couldn't conceal the relief in his voice. He rose, Smith's shoes in one hand, an identity pass in the other. "I found this."

Lopez read it. "Office of Naval Intelligence, Section

3, Major John Smith, Research and Development."
The foulest tasting title she'd ever uttered. "Lovely."

ONI. *Spooks*. *Wraiths*. The mystery was suddenly a
whole lot less mysterious, and Lopez found that didn't
make her any happier.

Smith wheezed suddenly, sucking in a huge gulp of
air, face beet-red and not just from the punch.

"Officer on deck, soldiers," Lopez said to the others
as she crouched down beside Smith, if that was even really his name. "Why didn't you identify yourself?" She
thought she had a good idea why. Whatever Smith's
mission had been, that mission had gone belly-up. Not
just failed, but failed in a spectacular, amazing, epic way.

He choked and coughed, curled up to protect his
belly.

"Why didn't you identify yourself, *sir*?" Lopez
asked.

Percy spat on the ground. MacCraw still just stood
there, stunned by the way events had broken.

Smith uncurled, up on one elbow. Now Lopez could
see he was furious. "Let's cut the bull-crap, Sergeant. I
outrank you. It doesn't matter why I didn't give you
my rank to begin with. Effective immediately, we abandon ship." He stopped, coughed again. "I cannot be
infected. I am privy to highly classified intelligence—I
can*not* be allowed to be infected. We abandon ship,
return to the *Red Horse*, and destroy the *Mona Lisa*
from a safe distance."

When she didn't answer, Smith said, "I know you
had to come on a Pelican. Probably in the hangar right
now, waiting for you."

They stared at each other.

"That's an order, *Sergeant.*" Quietly. In control of himself now.

A whole new game now, and Lopez didn't have the right of it. Or did she? Smith could've told her men to arrest her, but he hadn't.

"I have soldiers aboard I cannot contact. Sir," she said.

The others looked on with a kind of fascination, witnessing something she knew they'd never seen before. Smith outranked her, but these were extenuating, extraordinary circumstances. Lopez was their Mama. Smith wanted to retreat to a safe place. Command was a privilege those under you had to grant. You assumed it, but you couldn't *assume* it.

"There have been many casualties in this war," Smith said. "There will be many more."

Well. That sealed it. She bent at the knees and landed a punch from above. Damn, that *hurt*. Grabbed his collar and hauled him to his feet, shoving him back at Mahmoud and Singh.

"Sarge?" Percy said.

She nursed her hand. "Shit, ouch, shit. We're going to the bridge. No spook is going to leave my kids in the dark and then scuttle the ship on them. Shit. Benti would haunt us if we did, and she'd be a real annoying ghost. Damn, that stings. Any questions?" Said it casual, but knew this was the break point. If they were going to break.

Met their eyes, relieved to see no argument there. You didn't leave your own in the dark. Not even if there were big bad "viruses" out there. Especially not then.

"Um."

Except for Percy, apparently. Was she going to have a problem with Percy?

"Private?"

"Can I hit him too, Sarge?"

>Foucault 1515 hours

Foucault stood on the bridge beneath the light of the images brought back from the ship's remote cameras. They'd displayed the same thing for hours: the *Mona Lisa* dark and tiny against the backdrop of broken Halo, the endlessly shifting cloud of debris, brief flares in Threshold's atmosphere as pieces of Halo plummeted into the gas giant, and one Covenant capitol ship, on the very edge of the sensors, nearly masked by the planet. The Covenant ship hadn't picked up on them, and some part of him—the reckless part—wanted to sneak up and lay down a few well-placed mines.

A timer, nestled in to one corner of the main screen, counted the seconds since last contact with Sergeant Lopez and her team.

It had been running a long time.

Rebecca stood on a holopad in her war avatar. Foucault had insisted on it. It seemed disrespectful of her to show up on the bridge looking like a dumpy Italian woman. It offended his sense of decorum. Besides, he often underestimated Rebecca when she took on that avatar. He didn't want to do that, not now.

He knew: there were Covenant on board the *Mona Lisa*.

He knew: there were ONI personnel on board the *Mona Lisa*.

He knew . . . well, not much else.

He knew his options were limited.

The timer flicked over, another minute gone.

A new context, a new paradigm. A new something.

"Helm," he said, determined to break the spell of inertia. "Bring us up on the *Mona Lisa*. Quietly. I want Sergeant Fugazi and two squads prepped and ready for dust off as soon as we're alongside."

"Yes, sir! New heading—"

"Commander," Rebecca cut in over the top. "What are you doing? Our orders specifically state that if recon, or a loss of recon, indicates the *Mona Lisa* has been compromised beyond retrieval, the *Red Horse* is authorized to fire a Shiva missile and destroy the ship, regardless of passengers and regardless of revealing our position."

Foucault turned, caught the eye of the helmsman, who was hesitating, and nodded. "Yes, Rebecca. I am aware of our orders."

Sometimes he'd much rather be a private than a commander. Sometimes he'd much rather be lowered down into the middle of a firefight than have to make overarching high-level and *distant* decisions. Field combat came more naturally to him than this posturing and fencing.

Rebecca crossed her arms, tilting her head toward

the timer. "That indicates a 'loss of recon,' Commander. It is time to reassess the situation."

Intimidation tactics were wasted on an AI, but he leaned down, close to the Ghost Who Must Be Obeyed, and whispered. "I have been given my orders, but I have not been granted any information with which to assess the situation. We are to destroy the *Mona Lisa* if it is 'compromised,' but by *what* I do not know."

"Covenant," Rebecca replied succinctly.

"Sergeant Lopez and her team are more than capable of handling the Covenant presence on board that ship. No, I say again: I have not been given any information that would warrant firing on one of our own ships with my own soldiers aboard. Prep a Pelican, bring up the *Red Horse*. I suspect you could tell me what I need to know, and I suspect you will not. Thus, I see no alternative but to conduct further recon." Perfectly aware he was beginning to sound like his prissy schoolteacher of a father. "You were right. We do send our soldiers to their deaths, but we do not willingly abandon our own, Rebecca. We do not turn and leave them."

"You're getting spittle on my projector," Rebecca said.

Foucault straightened, turning away. He really missed Chauncey.

"Once I have all the facts, then I shall reassess the situation. And part of that reassessment will be to determine if you are fit for duty, given your current conduct. Your activation date was, as I recall, more than six years ago." He did not use the word *rampancy*, but knew she damn well understood his meaning. A dirty tactic, but these were dirty times.

Silence between them. Foucault thinking of his superior officer with the glass eye.

This time, Rebecca broke first.

"Okay."

Foucault struggled not to raise an eyebrow in surprise.

This time it was the AI's turn to lean in and whisper. "Somewhere private, Commander. I have something to show you. Something you won't want your crew to see."

>Burgundy 1520 hours

Hands and claws and deformed bodies and the stink of something so foul she'd vomited. Forming a living conveyor belt, passing her along the passageways. Always the roar of their anger to drown out her screams.

She'd gone down fighting, but she'd gone down. The mistake had been thinking Cranker had still been Cranker, Maller still Maller. A shot through the heart didn't do it. A shot in the leg didn't do it. By the time she'd figured that out, they'd had her. Maller had broken one of her legs as she'd tried to get to the pilot's seat. Cranker had knifed her in the side.

As she'd lain there trying to get up, Cranker had kicked her, and Maller had reared up with fist and claw held high, like he was going to finish her off. But then a whole bunch of the small ones, the ones like bouncing beach balls—that's what her mind made them into so she could handle it—had come surging up the gang-plank. Cranker had stopped, and Maller with him.

They'd stood there, heads held like they were sniffing the air, or like they were receiving information. *Plants reaching for the light.*

By then, Burgundy had begun to go into shock, the pain draining away. She couldn't get over the strange-ness of those living beach balls, which made her mind flash to images of the ocean when she was on leave. A strange, quick glimpse of Benti drinking a piña colada, Clarence alone in the distance like a lost soul, wander-ing through the surf, looking for seashells. Surely Lo-pez had to be somewhere. The sarge would come and save her.

She'd tried to resume her epic journey to the pilot's seat, but Cranker and Maller had come to some kind of decision.

Suddenly, Cranker was picking her up and slinging her over his shoulder, growling as he did it. The pain of that cut through the shock, her leg a burning plank of wood. She screamed, beat at him with her good arm, only realizing in that second that her right arm hung useless across Cranker's back. Across the horrible nod-ule of a passenger he'd picked up. There was a wetness that clung to her that she realized must be blood.

Maller brought up the rear, followed by the beach balls. She closed her eyes against that sight, and most of the time since she'd tried to keep them shut. It was her only defense against what was happening.

Because now, slowly, laboriously, with starts and

stops where Cranker carried her again, she was being passed along by a great community of the horribly transformed—down corridors, pushed through airducts, sometimes dropped as Cranker and Maller fought with some new monstrosity that apparently hadn't gotten with the program. Whatever the program was.

Sometimes now she tried to reason with the two Marines. "Cranker," she'd say, "please take me back to the Pelican. I know you're still in there. I know you can hear me." Or she'd say, mumbling it a bit because she felt so weak, "Maller, I know you don't want to do this. I know you want to help me. Please, please help me." Once she even said, "If you'd just put me down, I could do the rest. I can find the sarge. I can explain it was a mistake." She laughed bitterly at that one, knowing everything was past repair, and her laughter dissolved into panicked sobs again. She was alone.

Cranker and Maller never answered. Cranker and Maller had their marching orders, and they didn't come from the sarge.

>Lopez 1527 hours

"Hell of a big virus," Lopez said, pushing Smith ahead of her. He'd pleaded his case for a while, told her he'd launched the empty escape pods to avoid anything getting off-ship as soon as he realized the situation. Told her he'd tried to sabotage the bridge but hadn't been able to get close enough. And, then, apparently, decided to wait it out in his little blind room. None of it really made Lopez see him in a better light.

Backtracking, now that their path through the rec room had been cut off, looking for any way forward. Any way backward. Any way at all. "Hell of a big virus," Lopez said again. "Looked more like a giant angry testicle to me."

No one laughed. "Not a virus, no. More of an . . . infestation." Smith was hunched over, hadn't stopped cradling his stomach. "It came with the Covenant prisoners and just spread. The more bodies they took over, the more—"

"Taking over bodies?!" MacCraw near tripped at the words.

"It was a Flood infection form that took your friend," Smith said. He had an enormous shiner swelling his cheek that made his words come out a little soft. "They get under the skin. It will take him over and assimilate him entirely. It'll wipe his memories but retain his knowledge. Then the Flood will control his body—all of his body, down to the cellular level. Then mutate— like you saw with those bodies—to make a better weapon of him."

Lopez hastened her steps, hearing the words "retain his knowledge."

Smith couldn't seem to stop now that he'd started, like it was a relief to talk to someone about it. "A form infected by Flood is difficult to stop. They don't register pain, don't require all organs functioning, are fueled by such rage that even when disabled they are extremely dangerous. Mindless as animals. Less than animals. Destroy the core, the head, or the infection form."

Or, maybe, Smith was spreading a different kind of infection. That information had to be classified, and now they'd heard it. Lopez had to fight the urge to tell him to shut up now.

But he was done. "Stop here." Smith put a hand up against a wall that looked no different from anything else and flinched when Lopez reached for him.

"Concealed door," he said, coughing. "There's a scanner at eye level here. There's no other way out, Sergeant." When she hesitated, added: "All passages are blocked."

"So helpful all of a sudden," Lopez said dryly.

Smith shrugged. "The sooner you get to the bridge, the sooner I get off this ship." Smith pressed his hand to the wall.

The wall sank back, slid aside, revealing another black box of a room.

"It leads to the labs," Smith said. "We can get through from there." He didn't look happy about that.

A crash and roar bounced up the corridor. Somewhere close, something was trampling a barricade. A tremor through her kids. A shudder they couldn't hide.

"Mahmoud?" Lopez said out the side of her mouth, shining her flashlight down one way, as Percy looked the other.

"I'm looking, I'm looking." He scrolled too fast through their schematic. "Okay here. It looks like ventilation shafts. Leading . . . yeah, there are a couple of other access points, we can get to the bridge through here. Theoretically. Maybe even back to the hangar."

Another crash, more final, and then the thunder of

heavy footsteps. Just around the corner. *Okay, boys, time to go.*

Lopez shoved MacCraw into the room, catching Percy's harness and dragging him back in as Smith scanned his hand again and sealed the door.

"Quiet," Smith murmured. "It may go straight past us."

Lopez held her breath, and counted rosary beads in her mind, in time to the *thumpthump-thumpthump* of uneven running, drawing closer, closer, flying right past.

Waited until the sound died away, until it had been silent for some time, before exhaling.

"Your friend is looking for you," Smith said with a kind of gallows humor, cringing when Lopez raised her hand. He hadn't earned the right to joke with them.

"Another black bloody box," she muttered. "What's the point of a black box you can't see out of? Masterminds at work."

"Masterminds at work, *sir.*"

She ignored the ONI agent. Let him waste energy on sarcasm. "Ready?" A round of nods. "Smith, the door, and keep your mouth shut."

Whatever had happened in the lab, it was over now.

No lighting, no emergency lighting. Their flashlights bit out pieces of the room, little snippets of chaotic destruction. Glass smashed to hell and back, crunchy on the hard floor. The walls dented, with a sickly green fuzz growing in patches. Benches and cupboards overturned. Blood drying and tacky on the walls and ceiling. She'd become jaded. It didn't really register as any different from the decor in the rest of the ship. The *Mona Lisa* had been turned into a vast garbage pit, a nightmare for insurance adjusters.

But: the smell hit like a fist, a shudder and cringe running through them on that first inhale. Where did that smell come from? Lopez had never experienced it before the *Mona Lisa*. Ever. It combined the bitterness of the inside of a walnut shell with, as far as Lopez could tell, something from way up inside a dog's ass.

"Geez, Sarge," MacCraw groaned, as if she were somehow responsible.

"Buck up, Private," Lopez said. "The rest of us have had to smell your cologne all day."

He had no answer to that.

As they fanned out, Lopez barking out the usual refrain—secure the doors, don't let your guard down—she realized this must've been ground zero. Whatever Smith had done, whatever he'd *really* done, it had happened here. The remains of scientific equipment, so broken, so mixed together, resembled the mixed bag of wares available at some infernal flea market. Nothing she could put a name or purpose to.

Outbreak, but not a Covenant outbreak.

But the room was empty, just the aftermath and their trembling shadows, big and bold against the walls. Whatever had been here had moved on.

"The way to the bridge looks clear," Mahmoud said, coming back to them.

Could it be that easy? No, it couldn't. But still she told Mahmoud, good work. Sent Percy and Singh to check the other exits. MacCraw stared at a thick growth of green pus on the wall.

"What were you doing here?" Kept her voice low, as if the ghosts of whatever had trashed the lab might hear her otherwise. Left boot prints in the congealed blood as she shifted her stance.

Smith slumped on a data bank, running his hand over it almost sadly, the smashed casing and shattered circuits.

"I told you, research and development," Smith said, with a touch of scorn. "Like ONI's always done. You should be thanking me. We came up with some interesting data that will help us maximize the damage inflicted by our weapons on the Covenant. They've developed a natural resistance to the radiation put out by their plasma weapons—a forced evolution, from the look of it. With further research, we'll be able to use it against them, and to help us treat plasma burns, too."

Mahmoud listened to this answer with what seemed to Lopez like derision. They all knew how long it took for any "development" to reach the people on the ground. "Yeah. Right. What about your 'Flood'?"

The glimmer of pride Smith had displayed, listing his accomplishments, vanished. "We could have solved one of the greatest threats to the human species since the Covenant."

Mahmoud, disbelieving. "'Since the Covenant'? Why didn't you just focus on them, sir? They're kicking our asses all over the galaxy."

Smith smiled, or tried to, swollen face barely moving. "The Flood is pure of intent. Relentless. Almost primordial. And it *is* a virus, spreads as fast as one. I had to study it. *We* had to study it. So we used Covenant."

"You didn't *have* to do anything," Mahmoud said. "If the Covenant knew we were taking prisoners, can you imagine—"

Lopez noticed the death stare Smith gave Mahmoud.

Smith still wasn't telling the truth, but he wasn't lying either. Misdirection, misinformation, she didn't trust any of it. She stepped up to the smashed viewing pane of a small cell. Human skin and flesh caught on the jagged glass.

"Keep talking," she said, as she shone her flashlight inside. Stared at a leg in the small cell. Forgotten, like it was a dog's chew toy. Human. A slipper had ended up against the opposite wall. Around the ankle and shin the now familiar orange fabric, half an ID number visible through the gore.

"We were looking for weaknesses, a cure, an antibody, anything. We only had one infected Covenant, but we needed to see how it worked, how it spread. Just . . . it's strong. So strong." He trailed off. Suddenly tired, defeated by something larger than any of them. And yet, was that the barest hint of respect for the Flood creeping into his tone?

"You were testing on prisoners."

"It may be abhorrent to you," Smith said, "but such measures will be what wins us the war. Don't tell me you're getting soft for an alien race now, Sergeant."

No. She had no problem with anyone torturing Covenant. That wasn't the point.

"We face extinction," he said, almost like a politician. "We have to win this war. No matter what the cost."

No matter what the cost.

"You weren't trying to cure Covies of your Flood," she said, unable to look at him. "This is a prison ship. A civilian prison ship. *You were testing on prisoners.*"

Something in her tone must have let him know exactly what she meant. Written in the set of her shoulders, the cords standing out on her jaw.

Smith gave Lopez the half-embarrassed cringe-grin people with no integrity gave you when you caught them doing something wrong and they weren't really sorry. But wanted to pretend they were.

"It's a big, bad universe, Sergeant. Covenant aren't the worst of it."

Lopez raised her head, shifting her balance to her heel.

"You've done what you thought was necessary," Smith said. "And so have I."

God, he was fast. Faster than she would've thought. Missed it in the pat down? Hidden in the lab? A knife in his hand, and Mahmoud's throat slit, his rifle sliding naturally into Smith's hands, he got a burst off just as Lopez raised her weapon. She grunted with the impact as the bullets smacked into the armor on her left side. Went down on one knee. Could feel the bruising. Could feel she'd live. *Another scar.*

Was already reaching for Mahmoud, even though it

was too late for him. There was a curve of new blood spattered on the floor, as emphatic as a scimitar.

By then, Smith was through the hatch, sealing it behind him.

>Benti 1530 hours

"Where are we?" Benti asked Rimmer.

"Guard's tea room. God's waiting room?" He peeked up over the window. "Didn't really get a tour of the ship, you know."

They'd been lucky, nothing had been on the other side of the ladder. Without the schematic Orlav had carried, they were running blind, but the engine room was back here somewhere. They'd passed one very helpful sign, directing them on their way—the only time she'd felt like they were someplace even halfway civilized.

She wasn't sure how she was going to explain Henry to the sarge when they met up. Henry kept close to Rimmer, for all the good it did the Covenant. Rimmer kept looking around and starting at shadows.

"You said 'Flood,' before. What did you mean?"

Rimmer pitched his voice low. Henry craned to listen, even if he couldn't understand. "Some uniform came on board. He was with ONI. After that, we weren't allowed out of our cells. Sponge baths, if we were lucky. I think they brought the Covies on board then. We could hear them talking. Could smell them, too. Sorry, Henry." He gave the Elite an apologetic pat on the arm, which seemed to surprise the alien. "No one told us anything. Not even the guards knew what was going on. We made some slipspace jump, to here. Wherever here is. Could hear them bringing stuff on board all the time, and tossing it back out, like they were looking for something. Guess they found it. Started taking people, you know. And Covies. They didn't seem to care if we saw the Covies, then." He stopped. "Think they figured we weren't going anywhere, and it didn't matter what we knew." He kept patting Henry's arm. In his words, in the flat lack of emotion in his voice, there was an absence of dread that was louder than anything he could have screamed. And he kept patting Henry's arm like he'd developed a nervous tic.

"The air con on this ship, you know how it is. It carries the noise funny. We heard things. No one they took ever came back. None of them. "

Something small and hard crystallized in Benti's mind. "Nothing good ever comes from ONI," she said low, with vehemence that surprised even her.

Clarence was paying attention, she noticed, but trying hard to act like he wasn't. *What the heck is that about?*

"There was a guard, fat asshole called Murray; he found out about the Flood. Some new biological weapon, I dunno, something. He said, he said," a tremor entered his voice, "he said they were studying it. Here. With us." He stopped moving, hand not quite on Henry's arm.

Henry's head drooped, and Rimmer patted him again. Henry flinched.

Rimmer took his hand away, embarrassed. "Sorry," he mumbled.

"——," Henry said, with poor grace, and looked at Benti expectantly.

That brought Benti up short. She stared at the four jaws of his mouth, curled meek against his face now, little teeth fitting into the grooves of his gums. She'd never had the opportunity to watch a Covenant Elite speak before. It was one of the grossest things she had ever seen, and she'd seen plenty of gross. She could still see down his throat. It wasn't pretty, either.

Clarence shifted slightly, bemused, and raised an eyebrow at her. She raised both eyebrows helplessly, looked at Rimmer.

"Um. What did he just say?"

Rimmer stared back at them like they were asking the impossible. "How should I know? But maybe he's trying to tell his side of the story. All that black stuff on the walls of the room you found us in? That was him writing down words. I couldn't read any of it."

Henry slumped, clearly fed up, the tip of his cricket bat thumping into the floor, and muttered something that didn't require translation.

Rimmer gave Henry a pointed look that said *don't interrupt again*, and continued: "Something happened, I don't know, I think the Covies made a break for it or something. And in all the chaos, I guess . . . the Flood got out. Covies let some of us out, too, which might surprise you but by then we'd all been through the same stuff. All got the same fate on this ship. 'Course, it didn't help at first, because the guards didn't like it, and they started on us, all of us prisoners, and some of the Covies didn't like that and started on anything human. But me and Henry, we're cool. We knew. Bigger problems on board."

"And you've been hiding ever since."

"A day, I think. Maybe two. You lose track of time real fast around here."

"So fast?"

Rimmer nodded. "We gotta get off this ship. Soon, you know?"

Benti couldn't disagree. She also couldn't tell him Henry would be shot on sight once they reached the hangar, that she'd do it herself if she had to. Because the sarge wasn't going to like this, not at all. But Henry would be useful getting back to the Pelican, even if only to provide another target for the Flood. Besides, Clarence, hanging back, always had his rifle pointed vaguely in Henry's direction.

"Do you know where this leads?" She pointed out the door. Henry shivered faintly.

"Yeah," Rimmer said. "D cell block. I think the engines are behind them. We should . . . we should find a different way."

"Why?"

"That's where they took all the dead. That'd be like going into an angry beehive right about now."

>Lopez 1537 hours

Lopez wasn't sure, but she thought Mahmoud might've mumbled " . . . *and then comes ice cream*" as he'd bled out onto the floor in her arms, his blood mingling with all the rest. His hand had been warm, just like John Doe's had been, and she'd been just about as much help.

Another bead down. It wore on her, and never stopped wearing. But at least she could take his dog tags. Tell everyone back on the ship how well he'd served. They were in her pocket along with Smith's security pass.

"That's on me, not you guys," she'd said as Singh and MacCraw had wordlessly bandaged her up, with a kind of care she guessed meant respect. Even standoff-ish Percy helped.

Now she hardly even felt it, except as a sting if she bent or turned suddenly. Just the four of them now, heading toward the bridge down the longest corridor in the world. The only point of interest, an intersection about thirty-five meters down. Didn't like turning corners any more. Didn't like it one bit.

Trying to give up on the weird taste in her mouth from losing Smith, from letting him take Mahmoud out. She could see him, in her mind's eye, popping out of some secret door somewhere, trying to make his way by secret spook passages and guile, to the Pelican. No, he wouldn't make it. Wouldn't last long on his own. Even gladder now that she'd beaten him up. A small victory, but still. He'd feel it for the rest of his short life. He'd remember her.

The corridor was so long that Percy had been toss-ing flares down toward the end of it like he was playing in some weird shuffleboard tournament. Reached farther than their flashlights. Flares they had plenty of, bullets not so much any more. They'd taken a break to wolf down some MREs, but still she was hungry.

MacCraw'd acquitted himself well, too, despite his bitching. When they'd made it back to the *Red Horse*, she'd tell Foucault that. He scooped up the flares they reached, squinting and handing them back to Percy to throw again. Wished they could do the same with bullets.

Singh came to a sudden halt.

"Talk to me," Lopez said.

"I heard something."

Lopez studied him a moment. Singh was holding it together. Barely. *Don't get jumpy.*

"Flare, Percy."

He obliged. Flung it as far as he could, until it came to a hissing stop at the far edge of their vision.

Right at the feet of a silhouette, the figure of a Marine.

MacCraw frowned. Singh held a hand up to his eyes to shield them from the glare.

The figure came out of the flaming mandala of the flare, roughly fifty meters away.

"Is that . . . ?" MacCraw began and then trailed off. "That can't be . . ."

"It's Ayad," Singh said. "It's definitely Ayad."

Lopez could see him clearly now, running toward them. Loping almost. Trying to make a sound in the back of his throat, but it was coming out like *thnnnnnn* or *thmmmmmm*. Should've been a hum, more like a moan. Holding out a hand as if in greeting. A huge smile on his face.

MacCraw let out a whoop. "Ayad!"

"It's not Ayad," Lopez warned.

"What do you mean it's not Ayad?" Singh said. "Of course it is. It's Ayad."

Ayad hadn't had a smile that went from ear to ear. Or something growing out of the back of his head. Ayad hadn't had an extra arm with a claw, held a little back behind him, as if to disguise it. Ayad hadn't been preceded by a smell that made Lopez's eyes water.

But MacCraw kept babbling on, like he didn't want to believe it, and Singh just fed into that, almost manic. Percy backed up until he was level with her, would've slipped back farther if she'd let him.

This wasn't the way Lopez wanted it to end.

When Ayad was about forty meters away, she put a bullet through his left shoulder. It knocked him off his feet. Which brought MacCraw and Singh out of their trance or whatever the hell it had been. A lot harder for them not to see the problem.

Ayad rose with a howl, and kept coming, running now on all fours like something born to it, with Mac-Craw babbling in a different way now.

"Don't fire until he's closer," Lopez ordered. "Right after he's cleared that intersection."

Ayad reached the intersection—and something with all the speed and weight of a freight train smashed into him and splattered him up against the opposite wall. Ayad fell as the creature howled at him, then picked him up and held him with one monstrous hand out in front, turning toward them. The other arm weighed down with what could almost have been antlers coming out of its palm.

The suddenness of the act, the viciousness of it, shocked Lopez. Threw her for a second. Just a second.

"That's an Elite, " Percy said. "Look at the size of it!"

Lopez had never seen one bigger, either. Its head almost bumped against the ceiling. As it came toward them down the corridor, she could see the striations of infection running up and down its legs, the suggestion of an outline on the Elite's chest of the same fungal-jellyfish thing that'd taken Rakesh.

The infected Elite turned this way and that, sniffing, as it ran. Some perversion of a howl tore up through the torso. Out through what was left of the mouth. One of the jaw hinges hung, snapped and loose. A single tendon kept it attached.

"We're not outrunning *that*," Lopez said calmly. "Singh, kneel and go low, for the legs. MacCraw, keep your cool and aim for Ayad. Make it drop Ayad before it gets to us. Percy, heart. I'll go for the head. Now . . . fire!"

It lost its Ayad shield first, dropped it. MacCraw made a lucky shot and hit the muscle and bone in its wrist. It stumbled as the bullets hit it, each one more precious than the last. Slamming into its body over and over again. It might be Elite, but it didn't bleed. A sigh of something green and dandelion-seedlike puffed out from the wounds opening on its skin. Strangely beautiful, those wounds, in the hissing light of the flares. Wounds that should've stopped and dropped it, but it kept coming. Kept howling.

Staggered onward on tottering balance, pressing against the storm of bullets as if they were toxic raindrops. Until, finally, Lopez managed to take out its knees.

It crashed down, not seven meters from them.

But it didn't stop. Didn't even pause, clawing and crawling its way across the floor, on its belly, a smear of dark green behind it.

No one hesitated. No one waited for another order.

When it was done, the corridor reeked of gunsmoke, the smell acrid in their mouths and the backs of their throats. Lopez's eyes stung, unable to handle the swamp-gas smell of the dead Elite.

Lopez thought of the bodies in the cupboard. Thought of the Elite stomping on Rabbit's chest, *on the infection form*. She walked up to it, this thing, and pressed the muzzle of her rifle into the suggestion of a giant angry goiter clinging to its chest. Let off another quick burst. Realized she'd forgotten something, something important.

Ayad rose up from the darkness beside Singh.

Singh hadn't the reflexes, hadn't the training. Enough time for the technician's face to change. Knowing. Not wanting to know. Then he was smashed into the far wall with one terrifying blow, so hard his skull shattered in the helmet, face flattened to a pulp as he dropped.

Percy, cursing, a burst from his rifle going wide, caught by the backswing. Lopez heard his neck crack.

Turned too fast. Sudden pain where Smith had shot her.

And MacCraw, like he'd done it a million times, brought his rifle up and shot what was Ayad right through the head.

The flare light painted everything red and gold, made beautiful what should've been ghastly. MacCraw stood there, staring at that tableau like a painter who didn't know what to make of the paints on his canvas.

Lopez put a hand on MacCraw's shoulder, her one remaining bead. That shoulder heaved under her touch, and then steadied.

"Where to, Sarge?" MacCraw asked in an empty voice.

Lopez gave him a smile, knowing it was grim and making it brief. "Objective hasn't changed, kid," and as she said it, it became true. They were Marines. The job kept getting harder, but they got the job done, and that meant they had to keep getting better. They'd faced the worst and best the Covenant could throw at them, and now the worst the universe could throw at them, and survived treachery by their own kind. And they were still walking. Still breathing. That was a hell of a thing.

A *hell* of a thing.

>Benti 1544 hours

Rimmer told them Henry had found the cricket bat in the guard's locker room. Who knew when the guards had the chance to play cricket, or where, but the Elite was a natural with it. A rabid white slug thing had dropped from one of the overhead lights, moving too fast for any of them to shoot, and he'd splatted it against the far wall with one easy swing.

Clarence examined the green goop falling in clumps and nodded his approval. Yet Benti knew Clarence could turn around and kill Henry in an instant.

Benti hadn't been able to speak to him since Gersten's death. She'd found it hard to even acknowledge his presence. The fact was, it had cost him nothing to pull the trigger. That was what bothered her the most.

Beneath that, another, deeper, layer of unease.

He'd seemed to know. Before Rimmer had said anything about infections and coming back. *How did he know?*

Rimmer: "Henry was the one who sprung me out. There was a . . . one of the guards, she'd been, she wasn't, but he took her out. Saved me. He's a good guy, really." Rimmer couldn't stop talking, which set Benti's teeth on edge—thought maybe he'd been imprisoned because he'd talked someone to death. He couldn't stop touching Henry either, like a frightened puppy, and she was sure she wasn't imagining the distaste on the Elite's face at that.

A stairwell branched in the hallway. She didn't mind at all the sudden convenience of a sign pointing up that indicated engine room access. She crept up, peeking over the lip of the landing, the others crowding at her back.

"They learn," Rimmer whispered. "They take what you know and learn."

Something small and pale leapt out of the darkness. She threw herself back only to stop flat against Henry, who pulled her aside with one arm, the other swinging that cricket bat and hitting another ball sac down the length of the hall.

Benti scrambled up, away from the Covenant, with undue haste. He looked at her, lower jaw hinges flexing subtly. You could tell a lot from someone's eyes. Had to remind herself he wasn't a "someone." She could still feel the impression of his hand—not human, not at all human—on her shoulder, knew the hair on the back of her neck was up, and it took all her willpower not to pump his gut full of hot lead.

"Thanks," she managed, as more Flood bugs came bouncing out of the hall.

It was like a fairground game, shooting ducks. Only, not really.

Funny how you adjusted to the situation, no matter how messed up. She felt relief that these weren't the great ravening horrors that had chased them through recycling. They weren't going to slash them open and crush them. They were small, these little infectors. One bullet, one hit, and they would burst.

Just, there were so many of them.

And Rimmer couldn't shoot for shit.

"Stop!" Benti yelled. "You're just wasting ammo! Swap, and reload mine."

Even Clarence switched to his pistol, single shots popping white pods there, there, and there. A good sharpshooter, on top of everything else. Not too many of those in the Marines, not at private level.

"Where are they *coming from*?" It was like a machine full of half-chewed gumballs had broken all over the floor.

One slipped in close, and Henry smashed it flat.

Benti could've sworn the Elite looked a little gleeful.

>Foucault 1559 hours

The video ended, and the loop began again.

Foucault knuckled his eyes, taking the moment to collect his thoughts. After what he had been shown and told, he was inclined to think maybe Rebecca had indeed gone rampant. Found himself hoping that were true, because if forced to choose between the story she had spun and a rampant AI embedded in his ship, the latter seemed the lesser trial.

On the monitor: a wide, high room of unfamiliar architecture, and a ravening horror leapt at the camera, decayed and misshapen and still unfortunately recognizable as a human, UNSC logo just visible on the remains of the uniform. A shotgun blast floored it, but there was another to take its place, and another, and another. In the background, on the floor, a recently killed Marine convulsed, and came back. Footage of what Spartan-117 and the Marines who preceded him had found on Halo.

He picked his words precisely. "We have not been able to defeat the Covenant in nearly three decades, and yet, here we are, returned here for the sole purpose of seeking this out." He felt tired, more than sleep-deprived. "This greater threat."

An infected Marine ignored the bullets striking its torso and leapt at a healthy, live, uninfected Marine. Foucault had turned the volume off, but the screams still sounded in his mind.

"I don't believe it was in the original brief," Rebecca said. "The ONI agent heading the research project aboard the *Mona Lisa* seems to have exceeded his parameters. Significantly. And we still don't know *for sure*."

Foucault shook his head at the insanity of it all. "Is there more?"

"No," she replied. He didn't believe her, and didn't not believe her. Almost didn't care. "But now you understand, we cannot deploy any more Marines, not without explicit confirmation. We cannot risk the *Red Horse*."

He watched a small white pod of a creature latch onto a Marine's chest, watched the life leave those eyes, watched something else take over. A cold worm of dread coiled in his belly.

"We do not willingly abandon our own," he said, to himself, and knew right then and there that statement was close to becoming a lie.

>Lopez 1602 hours

What had once been Rakesh chased them toward the bridge, howling and gibbering and raising a chorus of answering growls. Lopez had caught sight of him stumbling on a derailed security door and bolted. Didn't look back. Hadn't wanted to see what he'd become, and definitely didn't want to see if they were, in fact, being pursued by more than one. Couldn't waste ammo if they could possibly help it, even though they'd taken all Singh and Percy had left.

"Sarge! The door!" MacCraw pointed, looking back at her, then beyond her. Only to look forward again. Fast. Didn't make her any more curious about what was behind them.

"I see it!" The bridge up ahead, a giant arrow on the wall confirming it, and the door to the bridge sitting back from the wall a hand span, an overturned chair stopping it from sealing. Oh, small mercies. Crashed up against the door, lighting a fire where Smith had shot her, and kicked at the chair. "Get in there!"

MacCraw turned to face Rakesh, backing toward her and fumbling for his weapon. Lopez cursed. Without the obstacle the door began to slide shut. Shoved her shoulder in the gap. "Dammit, MacCraw, I said—"

Caught a glimpse over MacCraw's shoulder. Oh shit.

MacCraw added his own weight to the door. Rakesh was fast, way too fast, oh shit oh shit ohshi—

The door shifted, and they fell through. Scrambled back, MacCraw landing an elbow in Lopez's injury. All the air left her; she couldn't even grunt. The door closed slowly, and Rakesh was so fast, footfalls so heavy, ravening shout loud in her ears. But: cut off cleanly. The door sealed with a sigh, and locked, as it had been trying to do for hours.

MacCraw scrambled to his feet, flashlight on the door, then the room beyond, then back to the door.

"He knows we're in here," he said, voice shaking. A muffled but insistent thudding began on the hatch.

"It," Lopez corrected him, clamping down on the pain in her side. "It's an *it*, now."

MacCraw nodded, mouth moving as if trying to convince himself. He flinched at every knock on the door.

Lopez stood. She pursed her lips, stepped past him, making a slow pan of the bridge with her flashlight, her hand steady, that small show of calm enough to reach him.

"Sensing a pattern here," she said, noting the arcs of blood on the walls and floor. The drag marks that almost didn't register with her anymore. Nothing moved except drifts of green dust, growing in little crests here and there. Someone had holed a beastie before going down. Good to see. Most of the displays had been wrenched from their stands and smashed, but some still showed readouts, broken through the cracks. *The bridge must have a separate power source.*

They ran their lights across the ceiling, shone them into every corner and under every station, until Lopez dared to believe they might be safe. Let out a deep breath. They might actually have some time to *think* for a change.

"Don't think anyone is gonna use the nav system." MacCraw stood over the ruined console. "Guess we can go home now?"

"Soon," Lopez promised. "Soon." Smith's voice echoed in her mind. *Retain their knowledge.* Didn't like the implications. Wondered if any of the crew had been infected. Didn't like *that* thought, either.

"We came here for the nav system, didn't we? What else is in here?" MacCraw glanced nervously over his shoulder at the door. The assault showed no signs of waning. The infected Rakesh was going to pummel itself into a pulp trying to get at them.

"We can use the ship's system. Get me radio contact. I don't care how, and I don't care who: Benti, Burgundy, raise the *Red Horse*, hell, raise that damn Covenant ship. Just get me someone to talk to."

MacCraw spun suddenly, taking aim at a corner in the ceiling, jerked to check another corner, looking for giant angry boils, snotbags, infection forms.

Lopez couldn't blame him, but they didn't have time for it. "Private! Get to it!"

"Yessir." Training overrode his fear. He brushed broken plastic and green dust off the glass atop an undamaged console. "What are you gonna do, Sarge?"

Lopez righted a chair, ignoring the foam bulging from the slashed seat. She'd been counting rosary beads again. So many lost. Thinking about that thing wailing on the door, that had been one of her Marines. Thinking about *why*.

"I ever tell you I can touch-type?" She pulled Smith's security pass from her pocket and waved it at him as she sat. "Old school, I am. Now get cracking."

>Benti 1608 hours
_____

Somehow, against the odds, they'd reached the engine room.

Now what? Benti hadn't a clue.

They were crouched down, peering over dead consoles on the control platform mounted two flights up, and they had a fine view of the main engine deck below.

The space engines dominated, sinking beneath the floor and looming high above them, the shielding around the thrusters looking to Benti like giant centipedes, stretching back through the rear of the ship. Nestled between them, oddly innocuous, the slipspace engine, a standard Shaw-Fujikawa translight, nothing more than a six-pack of boxes propped against each other. A melange of grease and oil and rancid hydraulic fluid mostly snuffed out the pervasive mold smell.

The floor was crowded. It was busy. It was Flood Party Central. No surprise there.

Details began to leap out at her. Covenant strode huge among the turned humans, most of them trailing scraps of prison garb, some in official uniform, and there, in the middle of them, Maller still in Marine armor. He was warped out of shape, limping, dragging an appendage of gristle behind him. Maller crossed paths with a Covenant Elite ruptured like a huge septic bruise, and they almost seemed to nod at each other. All of them, the prisoners and guards, humans and Covenant, united, in total harmony. *Of one mind.*

Better to think of it as a party, and they were the rogue DJs who'd crashed it.

But, no, that didn't really help. She had to look away, up at Henry, who was checking, kept checking, the catwalk behind them. He met her eyes, unhappy but in control, too much the warrior.

Clarence swallowed, his lips parted, gaze fixated on something below, and swallowed again. The muscles in his jaw worked as he clenched his teeth. He looked a question at her. Their orders didn't seem to apply anymore.

Rimmer had been partly right. This wasn't all the ship's dead. On the slipspace engine, the Flood had fixed a giant clot of mucus. Not mucus, Benti corrected herself, some sickly membrane, throbbing and quivering, odd shapes distorting its skin, half caught in it, as if something were moving within, and suddenly the picture resolved itself, and those odd shapes against the membrane became arms and legs dressed in uniform, the crew caught and suspended in the glob. Struggling. *Alive.*

Benti raised a numb hand and covered her mouth, not sure if she was holding in a sob or vomit.

A squeak that might've become something louder and Benti snapped around. Clarence was faster, one arm around Rimmer's head, the other hand clamped firmly over his mouth, expression dour. Rimmer gripped the arm around him, not struggling but holding on like a drowning man to a life preserver. Benti bit her lip and hoped he wouldn't release Rimmer until they were well out of here. There was too much terror in Rimmer's eyes.

A new sound cut above the shuffle and murmur and held the full attention of all the Flood below. As one they turned blindly toward the sound, a horrible synchronicity in the way they raised their heads to sniff, claws and nails flexed, ready to attack. Benti could almost taste the mindless rage that swelled and peaked, and then suddenly dissipated.

An infected person, a human, came into view, carrying a body. No, an infected Marine. Cranker. Carrying someone alive. Someone badly wounded, dripping blood, but alive and struggling, wailing, sobbing, thrashing and kicking as they neared the mucus glob.

"Don't let them take me!"

Benti's heart thumped. She put her other hand over her mouth, recoiled, sagged back against Henry's leg. A sour smell and trickle. Rimmer had pissed himself.

Burgundy.

>Lopez 1613 hours

What are we fighting for? The question rang loud in Lopez's mind. She couldn't think around it. *What are we fighting for?* She took a data crystal from the console, tucking it firmly in her vest pocket. She had only skimmed some of the files Smith's pass had granted her access to, but there would be time to read the rest later. She'd read enough for now. Too much. There was no mystery left in this ship, their mission for even being here. *What are we fighting for?* It took conscious effort to keep everything she'd learned from rasping in her voice.

"I think . . . yeah, I got a signal, Sarge! Booyah!" MacCraw pumped his fists in the air.

"You raised the *Red Horse*?"

Neither of them paid any attention to the dull booming any more. The infected Rakesh was a lot more aggressive and annoying than the real Rakesh.

MacCraw couldn't and didn't try to dampen the goofy grin on his face. "She's talking, oh yeah, she's talking!"

"What about Benti and Burgundy?" she said, crossing over to him.

MacCraw jittered in his seat, too excited by the sound of home. "I couldn't raise either of them, but the intercom is online in most of the ship."

"Patch this through, then." Hooked her chair over, but didn't sit. Couldn't sit. "Maybe someone will hear."

"—is the UNSC *Red Horse* to the *Mona Lisa*, come in *Mona Lisa*. Anyone hear me?"

A deeper echo as every speaker in the ship broadcast Rebecca's hail. Lopez never thought she'd be happy to hear that voice.

"Never a sweeter sound, AI Rebecca. Is the commander there?"

Foucault's voice entered. "I am. The situation here—"

Didn't want to cut him off, but also wanted to deliver her information fast, and in as calm and professional a manner as possible.

"Sir, I got all the recon you'll ever need. This ship is ONI, with a certain Major John Smith most recently in charge. Section 3 sent it here, to experiment with the Flood Spartan-117 encountered on Halo, although ONI might not have known about all of Major Smith's project "enhancements." But at the very least they came to secure a sample, so they could 'study' it, and they brought guinea pigs with them too. Under the orders of Major Smith, they've been deliberately infecting human prisoners and"—she paused for a second, unable to believe she was saying this—"*Covenant* prisoners too. Covies and civilians. Our own. Infecting them and turning them into these damn monsters, these zombies! And no one *told us*!" *You never told us, Commander.* MacCraw was staring at her, his grin gone. "I found a passenger manifest here and some of the people, they were ours, sir, Navy, they were *soldiers* who'd served during the insurrection—"

"I know, Sergeant."

That brought Lopez up short. Something in his tone had turned her stomach to ice. She put a hand on MacCraw's arm, not sure who she was reassuring.

"Sir?"

"The Major Smith you refer to is en route to the *Red Horse*, in your Pelican. He has informed us of the situation."

Damn. Her stomach roiled, and something in her plummeted. How had the evil little spook even made it to the hangar?

"Sir," Lopez said, gritting her teeth. She couldn't think of anything else to say. "Sir."

"Major Smith did fail to mention that any of you had survived."

"Bastard," MacCraw said, but without emotion, gaze uncharacteristically distant.

Lopez swallowed. "He's a liar and a traitor and a *war criminal*." Reduced almost to incoherence. "Everyone who died on this ship, my kids, the crew. If not for him, they might be alive." Couldn't even begin to articulate her rage at Smith. Her disappointment in herself for letting him escape.

"Rebecca has verified his story."

It wasn't a lie. It wasn't the truth, either.

"I'm going to kill him," she whispered. "I'm going to—"

Foucault ignored her. "Having witnessed this 'Flood' firsthand, Sergeant, what is your assessment? If it were to reach one of the outer colonies, for example?"

"I'm not paid to think, sir. Remember?" Bitter. Furious. Knew what Foucault was driving at, knew that the coward wanted her to have to say it. To have to accept it.

The pounding on the door increased. Rakesh wasn't alone anymore. Now he had friends.

"Nevertheless."

Officers. *Officers.* Making decisions from a distance.

"We have no defense against such a foe," Rebecca said, sparing Foucault from uttering the words. "Any planet infected by the Flood would be overrun in a matter of days. More food for the Flood. More knowledge of where to find food. They retain all useful information. Outpost coordinates, more pilots, increased numbers with which to commandeer ships, to reach more colonies. You know this to be true."

Lopez found herself quoting Smith. "'It's a big, bad universe, Commander. Covenant aren't the worst of it.'" Found herself agreeing with him, as he'd wanted her to.

Rebecca again, in a soothing tone that didn't soothe

at all: "The Flood represents the greatest threat to humanity since the Covenant. A cure must be sought—"

"A cure?!" Realized she was digging her nails into MacCraw's arm. Couldn't let go. Served him right for elbowing her before. "There is no goddamn cure! According to the files, this was never about a cure, this was about *control*, about creating mindless monster soldiers you could *control*. Who knows what Smith was doing that isn't in the record. But a cure? If you'd seen what we've seen . . ."

"We have, Sergeant," Foucault said. "We have . . ."

Lopez loosened her grip on MacCraw's arm. He put his hand over hers, palm sweaty. "I guess I thought we were better than the Covenant. Not just a little better. Really better."

"Research is always necessary, Sergeant." Rebecca was calm, assured, implacable. But she hadn't had the worst day in the history of worst days.

"The research was useless," Lopez said. "Totally useless. We've known about this thing for weeks and all we've done in that time is expose ourselves to more risk. That gas giant was drawing in the debris, crushing it. It would have vacuumed up everything. And what did we do? We sent a goddamned cab."

MacCraw's silence grew heavier beside her.

A pause, and Foucault again: "Our orders are to destroy the *Mona Lisa*. We cannot allow any of the Flood to survive. Rebecca has informed me that there are two remaining escape pods on the lower deck. The launching mechanisms appear disabled, so they may need manual releasing. Once Major Smith is on board, you will have until we are in position and the Shiva is armed, and then we will open fire. We cannot delay any further. The major has brought the attention of the Covenant capitol ship upon us."

"*You knew.*" Those two words saturated with grief, fury, betrayal. Betrayed twice, three times over. For nothing. Didn't want to come close to acknowledging the hope Foucault had held out in the form of the two pods.

A force rippled through the ship, made the bridge almost flip for a second. Lopez went flying, righted herself before she crashed into the wall. Saw that McCraw tried to hold onto the console before falling. The ship settled, but Lopez could hear tearing sounds in the metal, a booming through the air ducts like a giant smashing something with a huge hammer.

"What was that?" Foucault asked, urgent.

"I don't know. But it's gone and passed," said Lopez. "And we're still here." Making it sound accusatory.

A moment of silence. For all of them. She hoped that was Foucault's conscience knifing him.

"Eight, maybe ten minutes, Sergeant," he said finally, and she could hear the shame in his voice. Hoped even harder it knifed him for the rest of his life.

Lopez pulled MacCraw to his feet.

"Good luck," Foucault said, already becoming distant.

"You know what you can do with your luck," she snarled, and kicked the mic. Turned to MacCraw, who looked close to being sick. "That went out over the ship?"

MacCraw nodded dumbly. "At least, the part the explosion didn't cover up. Do you think that was Benti?"

"Could've been. Could've been something else. We don't have time to worry about it, so long as we're still breathing air."

Nothing on the remaining consoles indicated a drop in air pressure, just a sudden surge of energy near the engines.

Eight to ten minutes. Knew what MacCraw was thinking. They'd survived nightmares only to get shot down by their own commander. He'd already given up, tears glistening in his eyes.

Couldn't have that. She was still his sergeant.

She slapped his chest. "Let's hope someone was alive to hear it. Now hustle! We blow through some space zombies, get cozy in a pod, and we're gonna live, you hear? We're gonna live." She grinned suddenly, fiercely. "And we're gonna get back home to the *Red Horse*, and then we're gonna tear the commander a new a-hole. Two new assholes, one for you and one for me. And then we're gonna find Smith, and we're gonna take our time with him, I think." Couldn't even pick one of the many things she wanted to do to the spook, saw the same violent yearning lift MacCraw's chin. "And then, when we're done with him, then what?"

MacCraw sniffed and blinked his tears away.

"And then there's ice cream, Sarge."

Their grins were hollow. Voices breaking. The Flood still hammering on the door, the door they had to go through.

"Damn straight."

>Benti 1613 hours

Benti raised her rifle, Burgundy in her sights, but both
Clarence and Henry reached out, with expressions that
said, *No, don't, you'll let them know we're here, and
there are too many of them.* Benti bit her lip bloody,
couldn't block her ears; Burgundy wouldn't stop screaming, even though her voice was ripped to shreds she
shrieked and screeched, begged and pleaded, all her
terror and desperation echoing around the cold engine,
ringing in Benti's ears as they lifted the pilot and
pressed her against the mucus glob with the rest of the
Mona Lisa's crew.

And then she really started screaming.

Benti couldn't look any more. She screwed her eyes
shut, but that wasn't enough. Turned, pressed her forehead against Henry's knee. She had to do something,
but didn't know what to do. Henry looked over his
shoulder, then dipped his head down to peer at her. His
breath reeked. He stank of Covenant, a smell that
never failed to get her blood up, and she leaned back.
But he had intelligent eyes. Kind eyes. Something like
recognition in them. He could hear all she could hear,
could understand it all.

She had to do something.

But.

A thunk and crackle tripped their attention, disorienting the Flood on the deck below. The ship's PA was
waking up.

"—is the UNSC *Red Horse*—"

Rebecca.

Benti's delight was drowned out by the crashing, raucous cacophony that exploded from the Flood.

"What's going on?" she hissed, leaning close to Rimmer. Clarence lifted his hand from Rimmer's mouth just enough.

"You gotta find some way to turn it off, it'll enrage them, they go crazy when they hear something, might be food, they go crazy, they'll look for where it's coming from—" Clarence clamped his hand over Rimmer's mouth again, the prisoner already too worked up. He shook his head, indicated with his eyes. There was a speaker way too close to them.

Down below, great spasms of rage gripped the Flood. The voices over the PA, Foucault's, Sarge's—*oh, Mama Lopez, what the hell is going on?*—sent them into a mad frenzy, howling and throwing themselves about, pouring in doors, out doors. An infected prisoner smashed a speaker down on the deck with a single blow, denting the wall. Benti saw Cranker turning this way and that like a drunk puppy trying to do a trick for its master.

Just audible over the din, the sarge listing all of ONI's sins. Rebecca spelling out the doom of the human race, should the Flood be allowed to spread.

The more she heard, the more Benti began to think she understood what the Flood might be doing in the engine room. It stank of insanity. It stank of processes and alien know-how that messed with her mind—but what if it was true?

What if they were collecting pilots?

Benti ducked down near Clarence's ear. "We have to

destroy it. That thing they just shoved Burgundy into, I think, I dunno, I think they're trying to somehow hot-wire the slipspace engine without bridge control. We have to destroy it."

Clarence looked at her like she was crazy.

"And even if not, that engine is important to them somehow," Benti said. "We have to take care of it."

Clarence looked around, skeptical. Their options were limited, and the smell of Rimmer's piss was getting to Benti. She checked the engines again. Henry put a hand on her shoulder, steady and strong.

If they damaged the slipspace engine, things could go bad. Very bad.

But . . .

"To heck with it." She was in charge.

Benti leapt to her feet, grabbed her remaining grenades, pulled a pin, and hurled it at the mucus glob. Clarence lunged at her. Too late. Pulled another pin and lobbed it. Watched it bounce off the glob as she threw the last. Henry surged up beside her, over her, cricket bat at the ready. He stooped and grabbed a handful of Rimmer's jumpsuit, Clarence's vest, and jerked them upright.

"Let's go, now now now!" Benti didn't wait to see where the final grenade had landed. She grabbed Rimmer's sleeve, dragged him into a run, running from the howling Flood, from the first detonation booming behind them, running for the hatch they'd come through, shoving Rimmer before her, Henry, Clarence, hauling the hatch shut behind them with a solid clang.

Burgundy had stopped screaming, at last.

>Foucault 1616 hours

"Major Smith is secure on board," Rebecca announced to Foucault, and part of him wanted to say, "So what?" The screens showed the Covenant ship readjusting its course to intercept them and the *Mona Lisa* still wallowing there, dead, but with all sorts of life aboard it. About to be extinguished.

Foucault inclined his head slightly, his only acknowledgment of her words. He had no wish to meet Smith at the moment. Or any other moment.

"What should we do with him?"

"Let's keep him in solitary for a while," he said. *A good long while.*

Rebecca seemed as if she might leave it at that, and then ventured, "Doesn't it help to know the major may have acted on his own? ONI isn't responsible for this. This was never meant to happen, and the very fact we're here shows that ONI is acting in good faith. He'll be court-martialed. Maybe even worse."

Foucault wondered if she was right, if he should take some comfort from that fact. Someone would pay. At some point in the future.

Then he thought of the two pods and of all the Marines who might be alive and heading for them, the only chance for survival.

"No. No, it doesn't." A new kind of hell. A fresh bout of nightmares to keep him up. He wondered in a distant kind of way if it'd all fade in time, or if eventually he'd have to give up his command. "Smith may have acted on his own, as you say. Or he may have been following orders, and Section 3 will now use him as a scapegoat and wash their hands of the matter. It doesn't matter. It doesn't change a thing."

A moment, and then Rebecca said, "Telling them about the pods was a pointless gesture. Under the circumstances."

Pointless? Her tone told him she was giving him a warning. She'd told Foucault about the Section 3 operative she'd sent with Lopez's squad. The one tasked with cleaning up any messes. Perhaps she envisioned the same terrible dilemmas. Or perhaps not. Anyway, she'd sent an operative and he'd fought back by opening a narrow line of retreat for Lopez. Whatever happened, it was beyond their control now.

"Politics. Survival." He said the words like curses.

Rebecca watched him. Who knew what she was thinking, this copy of a person?

"The survival of humanity is paramount, Commander."

Rebecca needed a better speechwriter. Lopez would never forgive him, not for the rest of her life, be it eight minutes or eighty years. Neither would he.

The timer since last contact was now replaced with a status feed on the loading of the Shiva missile. Another monitor tracked the Covenant capitol ship bearing down on them.

A voice from the bridge: "Commander, picking up a detonation within the transport. Slipspace splinters. I think the slipspace engine has been ruptured. We need to withdraw before it goes completely."

When he didn't respond: "Sir, we need to withdraw to a safe distance."

"No. Not yet."

"Sir—"

He felt old. Tired.

But still.

"No. We stay." He was aware of the attention of the bridge crew on him, on the monitors, waiting, their own fate in the balance. "We stay until the last second. We don't abandon our own."

Until we have to.

>Benti 1616 hours

In the aftermath of throwing the grenade, Benti thought she'd heard Foucault on the intercom saying *good luck*. Had he? Really?

Those words echoed in Benti's ears. In her bones. In her feet pounding the corridor floor. She'd always defended the commander when the others were poking fun at him in the mess. All she had to show for it now was "good luck, so long, nice knowing you." She felt sick to her stomach.

"The important thing," she said, panting, the sound of pursuit on their heels, "is the pods. At least we have somewhere to run to." Her legs were tired, were heavy, but she couldn't stop, had to keep going; knowing what was behind them, didn't even want to stop.

Rimmer clung to Henry's arm as he ran, like a child to a parent. The hand on Henry's arm was white-knuckled with strain, fingernails digging. "They did that to us. *To us.* I mean—we were never meant to—how could they—" Even out of breath he didn't stop talking. "I'm not even on death row." Henry growled and shook his arm, but Rimmer didn't let go, didn't shut up. "I only sold stolen goods. That was all. I never—"

Benti tossed a look over her shoulder. Clarence behind her, stone-faced and focused, unflinching as the walls groaned beside him and at the rumble and explosion they left behind.

"Which way—?" Intersections and junctions flashing by. She had no map, but now there was no useful map of the ship. *Just keep your head down and cross your fingers.* Lots of graffiti scrawled in blood now. Some of it by prisoners before they'd become part of the Flood, some of it after, all of it unreadable at that pace.

Henry looked at Benti expectantly, loping alongside with ease. He could have left them all behind, but hadn't. She couldn't help thinking of him as a big dog, forgetting the intelligence and awareness in those eyes.

The Elite dipped his head, and said something. A question.

Given the circumstances, there were only a few things he could've been saying.

Benti slowed a moment, took the rifle from Rimmer and put it in Henry's waiting hands.

"Hey, what are you—"

His hands were almost too big. He could barely fit a finger to the trigger. Nodded at her, lower jaws quivering, but kept his cricket bat.

"You're a lousy shot," she answered Rimmer. "Keep moving!"

Clarence drew up beside her as she sped up again, and the look he gave her made her glad, suddenly, that she had Henry at her back.

>Lopez 1620 hours

"Is this a hull?"

"No, sir!"

Lopez pulled her last grenade and tossed it down the hall at a cluster of forms shifting in the darkness. In her mind, the forms were Rebecca and Foucault.

"Place is gonna get trashed anyway—"

The explosion blew out the rest of her words.

>Benti 1620 hours

The unmistakable sound of grenade detonation reverberated through the dying ship, the deck shivering beneath Benti's feet, distinct from the rumbles of the disintegrating engine. The sarge, she thought. Had to be. Remembering the others might be alive added a sudden spring to her step. They weren't the only ones left. If they could just get to Mama Lopez, everything would be okay. She knew it, had to at least make herself believe it.

A figure lumbered out of a room and she ripped a short burst through it, taking out the knees while Clarence, in sync, shot out the chest, and Henry clubbed it with his bat as they fled past. They had no time to be more thorough. They dropped down ladders and slammed hatches shut behind them, seeking only to delay what was following. No time to sneak. All the noise they made, they were getting a lot of attention. A huge following. Benti had never been so popular in her life. *Is it my birthday or something?*

"Reload!"

The voice in her headset made her start. They were in radio range, oh at last!

"MacCraw!"

"Benti!" A pause and gunfire before the sarge spoke again. "Who you got?"

"Clarence." She didn't look at him or Henry. "And a couple of survivors. One deck to go."

"Get your butt into gear; that ice cream isn't gonna wait."

"Yes, sir!" She'd never been so happy to be told to hustle. She turned to grin at Clarence.

It leapt out of the corridor before she could check. Something rabid smashed into her shoulder and threw her against the wall, so fast, all the air knocked out of her, head flung back knocked hard, the shock not enough to crowd out a terrible waft of rank decay and a moan that came from no human throat. Keep your eyes open, always keep your eyes open, her medic training kicking in, and her eyes were open, and she recognized Sydney, what was Sydney, before Clarence stepped between it and her, shot it, kept shooting it, never lifted his finger from the trigger, not even when it stopped moving.

Sydney. How could you do that to me?

She drew a breath in. Let it out. In. Out.

When Clarence looked at her, she knew it was bad.

She could see it in his eyes. She couldn't feel her arm; it hung too low on her lap, sleeve already saturated. Her eyes focused on the rifle in his hands. Orlav. Gersten.

You wouldn't, she thought. *You might.*

Henry scooped her up in one arm, tucked her up against his chest, pushed past Clarence, and kept going.

>Lopez 1622 hours

Benti, alive. The voice had conjured up such relief for Lopez, adding a bead or two back onto the rosary. Conjured up images from a world that seemed so distant. The *Red Horse*. On leave, singing in a karaoke bar, getting blind drunk, picking up men, telling her how to smile properly. Did any of that exist anymore? Had it ever existed?

The airlock was miraculously vacant, but it wouldn't be for long. Benti and Clarence were approaching from aft. They'd jammed the forward hatch behind them, using pieces of shelving from a barricade that hadn't held the first time. Only one direction to watch now. Then jiggered the manual controls. Both were ready to go.

"Two pods," MacCraw said, checking the time. "Two of us, some of them. What are we going to do?"

Lopez didn't answer. What could she answer? *Yeah, kid, we've still got some tough decisions.*

Instead she said, "Benti's taking her sweet time."

"It's those short legs." MacCraw checked the time again. "Sarge . . ." The strain in his voice said everything. *Let's get the hell out already.*

"Sarge!" Benti gasped over the radio, the signal good and strong. "Sarge, we're coming, don't shoot, oh please don't—"

A flashlight jagged about, coming down the corridor, the figures behind it resolving.

"Covenant!" MacCraw shouted, down on one knee and finger tightening on the trigger.

"Don't shoot!" Benti's voice.

There, suddenly: a Covenant Elite sprinting down the corridor, assault rifle in one hand, *cricket bat* in the other, and Benti slung over his arm like an errant child.

Not even the craziest thing Lopez had seen all day. Didn't register at first that Benti might be hurt.

"It's okay! Sarge!" The panic in Benti's voice didn't make sense. "Henry's okay! Don't shoot!"

Henry? Lopez didn't lower her weapon. "MacCraw, do *not* take your finger off that trigger!"

The Elite Benti had called Henry slowed, eyeing them warily. Closer now, she could see Benti's shirt and pants soaked red, her arm tucked into her vest, bone jutting from her shoulder. Benti's other hand gripping this Henry's thumb for dear life. Behind the Elite, Clarence and one human survivor in prison clothes.

Somewhere behind them, not yet visible, the deep unnatural choir of the Flood, like a physical presence. Sounded like they'd brought the whole ship in their wake.

"What's this Covie bastard doing here?" Lopez demanded. "You said survivors, Private!"

Benti blinked groggily, a frown of concentration, yet still not fully there.

"She didn't mean it," Clarence said, glancing back at the corridor, mindful of the Flood, and then reached out with his pistol and shot the human prisoner in the head. The man didn't have time to look startled, just dropped, a small and surprisingly neat puncture in his skull.

Lopez had no time to react. Everything happened real fast after that.

Henry spun, Benti crying out with the sudden movement. The Elite saw the dead prisoner, roared in unmistakable grief, and raised its rifle. Clarence jerked his own rifle up, staring down the barrel at the Elite.

Benti slapped its arm, pleading: "Don't shoot! Nobody shoot!" But staring at Clarence. Lopez was staring at Clarence, too, stunned. *A good man. A good shot.* Someone she wasn't sure she knew now.

And the Flood. Louder, closer, relentless, unstoppable.

Lopez's rifle wavering between her Marine and the Covie: "Clarence, what the hell?"

Henry bellowed, a terrible accusation in that alien voice. She couldn't get a clear shot with Benti there, just as Clarence couldn't get off a shot at them without Lopez dropping him. Except she had MacCraw.

"MacCraw, shoot that—MacCraw?"

He wasn't at her side. Behind her, one of the escape pods clicked shut.

"Fuck!"

The pod ejected.

From the bridge of the *Red Horse*: "Three minutes to launch sequence."

>Benti 1623 hours

Benti stared at Clarence, her partner blurring in and out of focus. She really couldn't see much of anything anymore. Knew her pulse was thready, that she'd lost too much blood, medic training both a blessing and a curse. Henry's embrace felt like a warm bed around her body, a bed she was falling into.

"You're ONI," she said at last. "You've got to be." She could see it in his eyes.

From off to their left, the voice of Lopez, coming through gauze: "ONI? I'm not surprised."

Knew the good old sarge still had them in her sights or Clarence would've blown her away. She realized every sympathetic quality she'd found in him had come from her. Just because he never said. Anything that. Would change her opinion. Realized she was floating a bit now.

"It's nothing personal. There were never meant to be any survivors," Clarence said. "Benti, get down. Come on, you can walk." He narrowed his eyes at Henry. "Put her down."

The sounds of the Flood, coming closer. But muffled, like she had headphones on or something.

"You're Section 3," Benti said, quieter. A softness entered Clarence's mouth and eyes. "I'm sorry," he said, but Benti didn't think he was sorry.

"Clarence, drop your rifle," Lopez said fuzzily. Except Benti knew Lopez had said it sharp. The sarge. Always said it sharp. "It's two against one."

Benti squirmed and made Henry set her down. She was almost there. She could almost see the end.

"Henry can have my ice cream," Benti said.

She pushed off Henry and staggered into Clarence, legs so unsteady, and he was farther away than she thought. But still got too close-in for him to shoot her, inside his guard. She collapsed against him, with her one good arm around his neck in a hug.

As the Flood surged around the last corner and came toward them. A slavering mass of rage and violence and nightmares they never knew they had. Her vision blurred, but she caught glimpses of what once were faces, moving with singularity of mind. They seemed to crawl on disembodied human hands and Covenant hands.

Pushed, then. Used all of her weight to push the two of them back toward the Flood. She had just enough strength to hold him there for the second necessary for Lopez to shoot him in the leg, the shoulder, send his rifle flying. Send him flying back into the corridor. Benti followed, to keep him out there, with *them*. The farther back into the darkness the better. Clarence was too wounded to stop her.

Lopez and Henry were shooting—at them, at the Flood. It didn't make a difference now.

Clarence was shouting something. At her, but it sounded so far away. His eyes were wild and scared, and part of her felt proud to be scary and part of her had never wanted to see Clarence scared.

She was losing her grip on him, and a bullet had

found her side, just pumped in there like it belonged, took more energy out of her.

Clarence had just about managed to put his pistol to her head to get her off of him, when she tripped him.

And the Flood washed over him, over her.

Found them.

Suddenly they were pulled back. A sensation of flight, then. A blessed numbness and strange alertness. Looking up for a moment to see that she'd done it— that Henry and Lopez, framed by the doorway, firing away, were far enough away to close the door on both them and the Flood. Yeah, they were shooting her and Clarence, but they didn't mean any harm. They would never mean her any harm.

Clarence writhed in the embrace of what looked like part of Simmons, screaming, "Don't let them take me!" It was too late for that. She wanted to say, "Relax, Clarence. You've got my back," but her mouth didn't work quite right. *Don't want to wake up. Not now. Not for this sad party.*

Last thing she remembered: Lopez's face clenched in concentration, standing in Henry's shadow, as Henry fired point-blank into the Flood and into her. Thought she saw Lopez raising an arm in a gesture of good-bye.

Tried to hold onto that image as the Flood repurposed her.

>Lopez, 1624 hours

Lopez, tired as hell, blinked, and . . .

Henry roared, deep and eternally Covenant, and

next to the discord of the Flood, something welcome and familiar to Lopez's ears. He fired into the mob that had taken Benti, ammunition spent in an instant. Hurled the rifle hard enough to knock an infected prisoner off its feet. Raised his cricket bat. Lopez opened fire, taking no specific aim. A glance at her ammo counter.

"Benti!" Brought back only to be taken away.

The ammo counter ran down.

"Clarence!"

All her beads gone. All her kids gone.

She couldn't see them in the throng anymore. Couldn't pick them out. Couldn't spare . . . anyone. A handful of infection forms scuttled across the ceiling. She lifted her sights. Shot them as they launched at Henry. Small pops. Puffs of green powder.

She dropped and Henry swung his bat, smashing an infection form she hadn't seen away from her. She rolled back into the airlock. Slapped the controls as Henry joined her, beating away at a transformed Elite. Beating it into a green froth before the airlock sealed.

With infection forms on the inside.

She twisted, firing a crazy line around the airlock, chasing the zoomy little maggots. Had no swearwords left to use on them. One popped. Two popped. Henry pushed her aside. Swung his bat. Four popped. Punched the last so hard against the wall the panel dented, green sludge on his fist. He reeled back from the puff of spores, waving them from his face.

Safe.

They looked at each other. The small room thundered with the pounding at the door.

The ship's PA crackled again.

"Shiva armed. Targeting lasers online. Initiating launch sequence in forty-five seconds—"

The airlock door dented inward, and both flinched, taking a step away from it. A step toward the last pod. Henry was big. There was only room for one. This alien, this enemy, had carried Benti to safety. On this ship of messed-up humans.

Finally understood how this was all going to go down. Some little backwater side action, maybe a footnote in some ONI operative's field report.

And beyond the door, something bigger and badder than all of them.

It's a big, bad universe, Sergeant.

Henry's four jaws flexed. Lopez narrowed her eyes. Put her finger on the trigger. Noticed Henry's grip on the cricket bat tighten.

Covenant aren't the worst of it.

No.

But they were pretty damn hideous.

"Sorry, Henry," she said, "but there's only one pod."

She pulled the trigger.

Click.

No ammo.

Lobbed the last curse she had in her, and hefted the rifle like a club.

". . . thirty seconds—"

The Covenant Elite snarled, jaws spread, and raised his bat.

And they went at it.

ICON

ICON

Soldiers forged from youth to serve as tools of war—weapons of direct and conclusive destruction—the men and women of the classified military project known as the SPARTAN-II program will live on in legend following their exploits during the Human-Covenant War.

Prepared for the harsh realities of combat against known enemies, but thrust into battle with forces unimaginable—and terrifyingly alien—the Spartan-IIs, and later the Spartan-IIIs, delivered numerous decisive victories against the overwhelming might of the Covenant.

Altered to a level far beyond that of normal humans, the warriors of the Spartan-II program were humanity's best, and possibly only, hope when faced with the threat of extinction from an advanced alien collective bent on our eradication in the name of false prophecies and hidden agendas.

Rising through the flames of war, echoing through the silent vacuum of space, word of the Spartans' deeds spread throughout the human colonies—offering salvation, offering a faint glimpse of ultimate victory.

Thus came a "Demon"—a hero, a soldier, a man. One Spartan above all others; equal, but for one defining factor—one immeasurable advantage. Like his brothers and sisters, he was trained to fight, to win, a master of the latest weapons of war. But Spartan-117, the Master Chief, had one intangible asset few others possessed—luck.

Added to an unmatched drive to win—whether it be a simple game, or heated combat— Spartan-117's uncanny combination of finely honed skills and unprecedented good fortune made for the ultimate warrior in a battle against impossible odds.

Never one to give in, never one to relent, the Master Chief, and each of his fellow Spartans, did more than engage the enemy; they delivered hope—with each burst of gunfire, with every battle won.

PALACE HOTEL

ROBT McLEES

The hastily concocted mission to board the Covenant carrier that dominated the sky over New Mombasa ended almost as soon as it had begun. A single Scarab— one of the Covenant's ultra-heavy ground-based weapons platforms—had knocked the entire assault group out of the air, leaving Master Chief Petty Officer "John" Spartan-117 to pull himself out of the burning wreckage.

"Aside from the Covenant discovering the location of Earth and our being on the ground with no viable means of transportation to our objective, I'd say we're in pretty good shape." Cortana's voice seemed to come from just over the Spartan's shoulder. The AI had been put in his care a little over a month ago and he still wasn't used to the intimacy of its communication.

"How's that?" John said, glancing over his left shoulder, half expecting to see her.

"We have one of the top-ranking members of the Covenant leadership within our reach—there's a Prophet Hierarch on that ship. On top of that? We're still alive, Chief. And while there isn't anything I can do about the Covenant being here, I am working diligently to devise a viable solution to our other problem at hand."

John moved between what meager cover the few abandoned vehicles littering the toll plaza afforded him. As he closed in on a row of toll booths, he found his eyes drawn to the mouth of the outbound tunnel of the Mtangwe Underpass. It looked like a kiln—exhaling heat and light. Cutting across the plaza was a smear of molten glassiness three feet wide leading to the tunnel mouth and then up away from it along the face of the city's famous sea wall. Curiously, the inbound tunnel was undamaged. A dull smile crossed his lips behind his visor as he considered his options. He thought back. The correct choices have always been this obvious. He had always been able to see the tiger and the lady—doors had never factored into the equation.

A thin whine from above signaled the arrival of Banshees. John dashed beneath the canopy of concrete that sheltered the island of toll booths—he was less concerned about the Banshees' effectiveness as attack aircraft and more about remaining out of sight. He flattened himself out against one of the booths momentarily and looked through its clouded and sagging polycarbonate window. The attendant, still seated within, wasn't much more than a partially articulated skeleton hung with the charred remains of a uniform and fused to an ergonomic seat bolted to the floor.

"His name was Carlos Wambua, age fifty-two, widower, three adult children. The oldest still—" Cortana rattled off before John cut in.

"He just sat there—the position of his feet," John pointed at the man's smoldering shoes with his chin for emphasis. "He didn't even try to get away. From his position he would've been able to see the *tee forty-seven* even before it crested the bridge—that's a little over eight hundred meters out." He gave his gear a shake test then moved to the corner of the structure.

"Your point being?" Cortana challenged. "Do the words 'transfixed with terror' mean anything to you? You may find this hard to believe, but most people find Scarabs to be rather unsettling."

With a barely noticeable shrug he began looking for a path to the mouth of the inbound tunnel—moving along the line of booths until he found a straight shot with no obstructions. It was seventy-three meters to the entrance. That meant he would be out in the open for about four and a half seconds—enough time for one of the Banshees in the air overhead to make a positive ID. He slung his rifle and hunkered down.

Kelly had always been the fastest in their class—easily making her the fastest human being who had ever lived—but as he tore across the plaza, he was certain that his performance would have made even her take notice.

Once he was within the tunnel, John slid to a stop against a burnt-out sedan. He unlimbered his rifle and considered the path ahead. This section of the tunnel was littered with vehicles; some gutted or otherwise destroyed, others merely abandoned. The area would have been perfect for an ambush. Unfortunately he was the one who had to move through it. The vehicles

appeared to thin out some eighty meters farther in, but
to get there would require patience. And so he began
snaking his way through the environment—moving
quickly but cautiously between cover. He checked the
most likely hiding spots and the least, keeping his eye
on his armor's motion sensor and listening intently for
any sound that seemed out of place. Working his way
deeper into the underpass, he heard muffled curses and
other sounds of agitated goings-on from about 150
meters ahead. He came to a stop alongside a lorry in
pale green *Technique Electronics* livery and looked off
to his right. The Moi Avenue junction was sealed off
by heavy blast doors.

"The main route is locked down as well," Cortana
huffed; the frustration in her voice was unmistakable.

John hesitated a moment, waiting for Cortana to
continue. The main Mtangwe route, a 390-meter tunnel that resurfaced in the center of New Mombasa's
industrial zone, had been his best bet to gain entrance
into the city without being spotted by the enemy. The
activity up ahead was promising and he hoped it was
from a maintenance crew who could release either set
of blast doors; if not, his only choice was to head back
to the surface.

"That's it?" John asked, finally. "It's locked down
and nothing else?"

"I'm having a little trouble accessing the local net,"
Cortana replied. "I'll have it in a moment."

The Spartan edged around the cab of one of the om-
nipresent SinoViet lorries. About thirty meters away,
near the blast door, were two M831s—the primary

UNSC wheeled troop carriers that had become nearly as common in New Mombasa as the freight lorries over the past few weeks—and a squad of Marines who were busily pulling any useful bits of equipment out of them.

"They're from one of the ghost battalions out of Eridanus Two," Cortana said with a near-audible sigh of relief. "First Battalion, Seventh Regiment; more specifically, this is Third Squad, First Platoon, Kilo Company."

One of the Marines signaled the Spartan's arrival to the rest of the squad and moved forward cautiously to greet him.

"Holy crap," Private Jemison blurted. "Sorry, sir, but holy crap, you're a Spartan!"

"Yes," John said dryly as he jogged toward the Marine, but before he had the chance to utter another syllable, the distinctive report of a fuel rod gun rang out from behind him.

"Get to cover," John yelled as he brought his BR55 to bear, spun on his heel, acquired a sight picture of his target, and put a single bullet through the neck of the green-clad Grunt. Private Jemison's MA5B flashed to his shoulder and fired off a long burst as the first shot from the fuel rod gun sailed past the Spartan and the Marines and slammed into the tunnel wall a little more than twelve meters away. The nearly decapitated Grunt reflexively fired a second shot, which impacted the roadway less than a meter away from where it was standing. The resulting explosion killed half of the aliens that were visible in the tunnel, including their commander—an Elite in red armor.

The stray first shot had dug a four-meter-wide hole in the wall and dumped a literal ton of smoking, shattered concrete out onto the tunnel floor. Dark, brackish slop lazily spilled out, accompanied with a stomach-curdling stench—making it very clear that an opening had been punched into an adjoining sewer line. As if on cue, brilliant purple light washed along the walls as the massive, bulbous form of a Wraith slid into view from behind an abandoned commuter bus. Its carapace seemed to crack open—broad curving plates folded out of the way of its deadly plasma mortar.

"Crap," Jemison howled as he backpedaled. "Corporal, what do we do?"

A tall, broad-shouldered redhead hopped down out of the back of the lead troop carrier and motioned with her left hand toward the opening in the wall. "Jump in that hole—it ain't no worse than it is out here! Move it!"

Jemison continued to back up until he reached the edge of the rubble, all the while firing burst after burst from his assault rifle into the advancing enemies. Corporal Palmer approached the Spartan, tapped his shoulder, and shouted, "You wanna come, big guy?" She moved through the rubble to the breach, motioning for the rest of the squad to follow. And in they went, one by one.

John shouldered his rifle, took one step back toward the way he had come, and fired a burst into a mob of

Grunts that had swarmed in past the Wraith, killing two and forcing the rest to scatter and dive for cover.

"Chief, you should probably follow those Marines—they look like they need the help—and there are three more Wraiths on the way," Cortana said thoughtfully.

As the walls of the tunnel reverberated with the sounds of the charging plasma mortar John dashed over to the rent in the tunnel wall—firing three more bursts from his battle rifle back at the advancing enemies as he went—then turned and disappeared into the breach. He had made it no more than thirteen meters when the mortar round slammed into the opening, sending a wall of concussion and heat that drove him to his knees and caused his shields to overload and drop. John got back to his feet, but Private Jemison, the second-to-last man to make it into the breach, was lying facedown in the now boiling muck—his organs ruptured and bones splintered from that same blast. Howls from the darkness told him that Jemison wasn't the only casualty. He ran past Private First-Class Locke, whose split and blistered flesh and raw bone were visible through smoldering holes in his BDUs. He stepped over Private First-Class Galliard, who had been felled by a piece of rebar that entered just below the nape of his neck and exited through the bridge of his nose—the still-glowing chunk of steel protruded from the sewer wall ten yards farther ahead.

When John reached the flow-through tunnel below the spillway, the remaining Marines skipped their eyes past him and looked back down the tunnel.

"Where the hell's the rest of my squad?" demanded Corporal Palmer as she stepped forward. "The Wraith?"

"Affirmative," John replied flatly. "They were killed in action."

"Then we've gotta go back."

"We're going forward."

"No we're not." Palmer's brow furrowed. "We are not just gonna leave them lying back there in this god-damn sewer!"

Cortana spoke to the entire group over their helmet-integrated comm units. "They will be left behind just as the other twenty-three billion that preceded them were left behind. Because they could not be saved, and carrying them with us will only make us vulnerable."

They looked at John like he was a monster; like an alien. In some of their eyes he could detect something deeper. Not horror; astonishment? Betrayal? Of course it may have just been hearing Cortana speaking through his comms.

"Who was that?" Palmer spat.

"That was Cortana. She's . . ."

"She's a real fucking bitch."

The Spartan stood in silence, head cocked slightly to the right. "Corporal, give me your TACPAD."

Corporal Palmer produced a notebook-sized device from her pack and passed it to the Spartan, and he flipped it open and showed them a traffic video with a time stamp from twenty-two minutes earlier—four Wraiths and fifty light infantry entering the Mtangwe Underpass.

"It's amazing how persuasive an argument overwhelming force can be," Cortana whispered to the Spartan. John shrugged and moved toward what appeared to be a series of rungs imbedded in a flat section of the sewer wall.

Cortana was the first *smart* AI he had ever worked with directly. Sadly, whoever died to make this AI possible had to have been a genius among geniuses. For example: The section they were in wasn't on the grid; it dated from before construction had even started on the Mombasa Tether—itself more than two hundred years old. Cortana had plucked the plans for them out of the ether before he could finish his request. As far as equipment went, the AI was cutting edge. The only thing that bothered him about Cortana was her excessive familiarity; she was more like a pushy civilian that just happened to fit on a data crystal than a true military AI.

"You can tell her that the rest of their unit has begun to dig in at Beria Plaza," Cortana's voice buzzed in his ear. "That's a little under two kilometers away."

"Corporal Palmer, does Beria Plaza mean anything to you?"

"It was between where that door came slamming down in front of us and where we were going."

"That's where the rest of your unit is. It's about two clicks due east of our current position. You'll go up here," John said, indicating the ladder. "It'll take you up to the surface." Cortana may have been busy looking for some way to get him onto the Covenant assault carrier, but not so busy that she couldn't provide him the occasional blueprint, video feed, or other intel—whether it was helpful to his situation or not.

"Okay." Palmer nodded. "So you gonna follow this pipe all the way out to the Mombasa Quays?"

"No. I'm going to make sure the rest of you make it out of here alive."

"Gosh! That's awfully nice of you," Palmer mugged—then the smile faded. "Look, you may be a Spartan, but . . ."

"Exactly, Corporal. And if *we* had all been Spartans back there *none* of us would have died. Now let me do my job."

Palmer's jaw dropped. After about a second and a half she closed her mouth, snapped off a smug salute, pivoted on her heel, and then jogged over to the rest of the Marines.

As the Marines stacked up at the base of the ladder, John readied his service rifle, swapped in a full magazine, and took station on the other side of the tunnel so he could keep an eye on them as well as keep an eye out for pursuers. He glanced over at the Marines as they moved into position to climb to the upper part of the spillway—and out of the sewer they had been slogging through for the past twenty minutes. While it may have been only a storm sewer, it hardly mattered this close to Kilindini Harbor. He wondered if the oppressive stench was the reason for the soldiers' sour expressions.

"Chief," Cortana whispered, "there was no way for you to save those three."

"Even so," he muttered, "I could've wiped out that entire unit."

"Four Wraiths," Cortana broke in. "Four. You rely too much on your luck."

"The limited space and the abandoned vehicles in the tunnel would have restricted their mobility as well as their ability to use their main weapons, especially if they brought all four down—which they did. I've been doing this for twenty-seven years, Cortana. And I know the exact limits of my luck."

"Then what? The rest of them die trying to support you?"

"They started running as soon as the shooting started."

"Yes, Chief, but Corporal Palmer's reasoning was sound—even without knowing about the other three Wraiths she had more sense than to go up against armor without any antiarmor weaponry."

John watched as the last Marine started up the ladder and fired a burst from his BR55 back down the way they had come. He heard the heavy rounds gouge the ancient concrete, followed by the panicked cries of Grunts in the distance as they dove for cover—and into the semigelatinous, ankle-deep liquid. Hopefully that would keep them from coming any closer, at least until the Marines were all safely up on the spillway. There was precious little cover within the confines of the sewer, certainly not enough to avoid any incoming fire. The spillway would allow them to break contact with their pursuers—then he could get back to his mission.

"Chief, I was serious about their being useful for

getting us to our objective," Cortana whispered in the Spartan's ear.

"Thanks. So you *strongly* suggest following them?"

"I merely suggest we take them back to their unit," Cortana whispered very sweetly. "They could be useful too."

Palmer called down from the top of the spillway, "Your girlfriend say to wait there—you coming or what?"

"It's an AI."

"Nice," Cortana huffed.

John turned his attention to the ladder. He looped his arm behind the rungs and popped them out, three at a time, until he had pulled out all of them he could reach; it wouldn't stop their pursuers for good, but it didn't have to. All it needed to do was slow them down. He sent four more rounds ripping into the darkness before jumping three meters up to the top of the spillway and following the sounds of the boots retreating up one of the drainage tunnels. He could hear the sound of wind in the trees and the pounding of the surf somewhere up ahead, and beyond that the staccato chatter of gunfire and dull thudding of explosions in the distance.

The tunnel opened into a wide culvert that seemed to emerge from beneath the inner part of the island's western sea wall—and directly behind the parking area for the Kilindini Park Cultural Center. The Marines had flattened out against the walls, stopping just short of the tunnel mouth. A Covenant beam rifle leaned unattended against the end of the culvert twelve meters away. Straddling a deep rut a half meter beyond the end of the culvert was one of the large, vaguely bird-like aliens that most UNSC personnel called Jackals. Its back was to them—a thin stream of fluid fell into the rut between the alien's feet.

The Spartan inched forward in uncanny silence, carefully gauging the distance between himself and the Jackal. He positioned his feet on the tunnel floor, assessing his footing and evaluating the strength of the concrete beneath him. He was less than seven meters from the alien when its head snapped to the side with a start, inhaling sharply. John sailed forward—covering the distance in two strides, his left arm a blur shooting forward, index and middle fingers outstretched together to form a spike. The Spartan's gauntleted hand passed effortlessly through the Jackal's skull just behind its left eye. John backpedaled, retreating into the darkness of the drainage tunnel—the grisly remains of his quarry dangling limply from his forearm, leaving a streak of brilliant purple blood in their wake.

Corporal Palmer quailed momentarily and then glanced back at the group and motioned for everyone to stay low and quiet. She scooted up to the edge of the culvert in a low crouch. When she reached the end she popped the covers on her scope and slowly swung her BR55 over the low concrete wall. She could see the smoking remains of several variants of the UNSC's ubiquitous Warthogs—M831 troop transports, M12 reconnaissance vehicles, even a couple of M12G light antiarmor rigs, all of which were arranged in a line partially shielding the main entrance of a squat concrete structure—a makeshift defensive wall. She could also see the Jackals overlooking the parking area from the roof and the bodies of men scattered about below them.

"It looks like a goddamn massacre out there," Corporal Palmer stage-whispered. "There're bodies all over the place—there's a Grunt bleeding out and a Jackal standing not ten feet away from him poking at one of our boys. What the hell, man?"

Private First-Class Sullivan scooted up next to her and stole a quick peek over the wall. "This shit happened ages ago—we woulda heard those sixty-eights goin' off even down the pipes," he muttered.

Private Emerson tossed John a spare canteen and he rinsed the blood from his arm. Behind him, half a dozen meters deeper into the tunnel, one of the Marines was busily constructing what looked to be a miniature barricade. "Don't hold onto anything you can't fight with," John said before stepping out into the culvert. He glanced over at the line of Warthogs and opened a private channel with Corporal Palmer. "Sitrep, over."

Palmer looked over her shoulder at the Spartan—a mere seven meters away. "Huh? I'm right over here."

John tapped his throat and pointed past her at the enemy. "A Jackal's ears may not be very big, but they are very sensitive."

"Oh all right," she grumbled, put her eye back to the scope, and continued, "Looks like a detachment of Army mech-inf got sent in to evac some civies or whatever out of this gift shop or whatever the hell *that* is—

that being the structure that looks sorta like a giant concrete intake manifold. There's a fountain about twenty meters northeast of the structure in the middle of what looks to be the parking area. But the fountain is busted all to hell and the entire parking area is under about four inches of water. I count about . . . eighteen civilians and . . . twenty *ewe en es sea* personnel—all dead—and half a dozen 'hogs. The 'hogs are strung out in a line from the center of the northeast wall of the structure to just past what's left of that busted fountain. All but two of the 'hogs are out of commission. We might be able to use one of the other *em twelve gees* but its generator is holed—I wouldn't trust it. Looks like the Covies've got a *tee forty two* set up on the roof at the eastern corner of the structure—the Grunt on it looks like it's snoozing, though. So, along with the gunner, I'm counting twelve bad guys—eight Jackals; four Grunts. That ain't counting the one Grunt bleeding out. They've got elevation on us so don't take that number as a guarantee; it'd take a lot more than this handful of assholes to grease twenty-odd shooters—even if they were only Army. Over."

"So, only two serviceable 'hogs." John looked at the eight Marines squatting in the culvert and sighed. "Proximity to each other? Over."

Palmer let her rifle drift slowly, covering a wide arc. "The one *em eight three won* that isn't burning or otherwise busted all to hell is right near the main entrance of the structure, and the *el ay ay vee* is a good fifteen meters east-northeast of that, over by the fountain. Chief, if you're planning on going for that *em twelve gee*, you won't just be running *into* their field of fire—you'll be running *across it* like a duck in a shooting gallery. Over."

The Spartan looked over the low wall at the M12G; it *was* a mess. What was left of the windshield was lying across the hood in tiny cubes, the seats were burnt down to their frames, the winch was a fused wad of metal, and most of the bodywork was distorted, pitted, and scorched. But it wasn't burning, smoking, or leaking fluid and it had all four wheels. "You, Sullivan, and I will secure the *em twelve gee*; once we get it moving we'll suppress what's left of the local Covenant group until the *em eight three won* is secured. Over."

Palmer's heart seemed to skip a beat and she reflexively licked her lips. "Chief, I believe I can honestly say that even though you are an honest-to-Buddha one-man death squad, and that if you were to ask nicely I'd give up my lucrative career in the Corps and start pumping out your babies as fast as you could put them in me, there is no way that I am gonna run across fifty goddamn meters of open terrain covered by three Jackal snipers *that I can see* just to jump into an open vehicle. Throwing myself on a goddamn grenade makes more sense than that. Out."

The Spartan was at Corporal Palmer's elbow so quickly and so quietly that only those Marines who had been looking directly at him noticed that he had even moved. He closed the private channel and addressed the group as a whole. "Palmer, Sullivan; you're on me. Concentrate on running until we get to the *el ay ay vee*—then mount up as fast as you can. Corporal, I want you on that sixty-eight. The rest of you will cover us until the *el ay ay vee* starts moving—we will then lay down suppression fire until you secure the *em eight three won* by that structure's main entrance—I'm setting a waypoint now. This is sure to get more complicated once we are under way, so stay on your toes."

The assembled Marines looked at one another nervously and then out at the open field that lay between themselves and the Warthogs—numbers above the tiny blue deltas indicating the objectives in their HUDs reinforced their remoteness. The Marines began systematically checking their gear in grim silence. The furtive glances that passed between them, however, spoke volumes. To wit, they were about to pit themselves against a group whose exact composition they were unsure of, that was established in a defensive position with superior elevation, and that was clearly capable of annihilating a unit more than twice their number even if it had been equipped with vehicles and support weapons. They did have one advantage, though: they had a Spartan with them. But how much could one more man, no matter how well trained or equipped, possibly affect the outcome of the coming battle?

John placed fresh magazines into both of his weapons, replaced the missing rounds in his spare magazines, and then nodded toward their destination. Without looking back he motioned for the group to move up.

"Pine Tar," Palmer whispered sharply through the

comm, "get your narrow ass up here—we're leaving. Over."

"Wilco, out." Lance Corporal Pineada called from deep within the drainage tunnel. He gave a quick glance at the group in the culvert before putting the final touches on the lethal contraption he had been hiding beneath a sodden shipping pallet. He circled his handi-work gingerly, then nodded to himself, satisfied that the two scavenged jerry cans, fragmentation grenade, and mess kit that he had fashioned into a deterrent for their pursuers was nearly impossible to detect. He leaned the last jerry can against the tunnel wall by his improvised trap and joined the rest of the group.

"Couldn't we just try sneaking around them?" Private Emerson asked feebly.

John ignored Emerson and continued. "Forget the Grunts—concentrate on the rooftops and any Jackals you see—the DESW at the eastern corner is a priority-one target." He slung his battle rifle across his back.

Corporal Palmer had not moved from her position observing the parking area. "Chief, that Jackal isn't just poking at our boy—it looks like it's biting him."

The Spartan held up a gauntleted hand. "We go in five, four. . . ." He tucked his fingers in as he counted.

"I think it's eating him, man," Palmer choked.

"One—then it dies first—now stow your weapon and move out." John pointed at their intended destination and then he was gone.

The concrete beneath the Spartan had turned to dust and gravel as he launched forward. Barely half a second had passed and he was already ten meters away. Palmer slung her weapon and tore off after him; Sullivan fell in directly behind her, running for all he was worth.

Palmer was pumping her arms and trying to control her breath as she trailed behind the Spartan. She looked up from her boots and saw that his hands were no longer empty—his right hand now held a massive hard-chromed M6D, and a spare magazine was in his left. Eight thunderclaps rang out so fast that they bled together into a single long roar. At that same moment a terrible cacophony erupted behind them as her squadmates opened fire on the building—its facade disappearing behind a cloud of pulverized concrete and shattered glass. Two of the Jackals that had been covering their approach had already fallen—bright purple blood fountaining out of huge ragged holes that she could pick out even at this distance.

With one hand at thirty meters and a dead run, two shots apiece, each a hit to the head or neck, what the holy hell are my guys even aiming at back there—shit. The Corporal's mind raced, but her legs had begun to slack off. She saw another Jackal appear at the roof's edge and there was a flash of purple light.

And then her view was blocked by a wall of green armor; there was a loud crack and a flash of golden light. The Spartan had spun to face her; she saw her own reflection in his visor for a fraction of a second, then he dipped slightly before popping into the air, sailing backward three and a half meters above the ground—smoke trailing from the inside of his right arm. Four more rapid-fire thunderclaps roared in her ears; the magazine dropped out of the Spartan's M6D, his left hand slamming the fresh magazine up into the well and flicking to catch the empty one as it fell, the huge pistol now latched onto his right thigh, the empty magazine stowed, and his knees tucked up to his chest as he continued through the air over the Warthog. Three fingers hooked the crossbar and the vehicle rocked as the Spartan swung down into the charred remains of the driver's seat; the M12G roared to life as Palmer scrambled up into the rear of the vehicle and behind the controls of the gauss cannon in a near daze; Sullivan practically leapt into the sooty pan of the passenger seat and disengaged the safety on his MA5, bellowing, "C'mon! Floor it!"

All four wheels spun, abrading the surface of the parking area and throwing up four giant rooster tails of water and grit. Palmer keyed in the startup sequence on the M68 ALIM—your basic mini MAC. She started scanning for targets—and did a double take when prioritized targeting tabs began appearing on the monitor.

"If anything else shows up, I'll add it to the list, Corporal," the Spartan spoke over a private channel. "No vehicles yet—just infantry. Don't take any shots you don't have to—just concentrate on staying alive for the moment."

"What the hell's that supposed to mean?" Palmer growled through her headset. Just then the Spartan threw the 'hog into a four-wheel drift, creating a momentary wall of spray and mist that screened the rest of the squad, who were now dashing across the open ground between the culvert and the vehicles. Sullivan was hooting and hollering above the sound of the engine as he fired his assault rifle at anything that poked its head out.

John gave Sullivan a sideways glance and said, "Remember to save some ammo for when you're actually trying to hit something—and forget the Grunts!"

Corporal Palmer glimpsed just a hint of movement behind the T-42 DESW—the closest thing to a heavy machine gun in the Covenant arsenal. It could have just been the corpse of the weapon's operator shifting, but she wasn't taking any chances. There was a flash of light, a teeth-rattling snap, and then the heavy plasma weapon on the roof exploded—transformed into a rapidly expanding cloud of whirling ceramic razorblades and plasma-temperature flames. If anything had been crawling up to the weapon, it was now either part of that cloud or had been consumed by it.

" 'Hog secured—we're in, Chief," Private Emerson howled over the Warthog's radio. "Let's boogie!"

"Follow me." The Spartan swung the M12G around the eastern corner of the Cultural Center, just barely dodging the bulbous purple cowling of a Covenant Ghost half-hidden in a stand of elephant grass. One of the Ghost's stabilizing wings and a fair amount of its carapace were missing—obvious signs it had been raked with heavy machine-gun fire. The 'hogs roared past it, and the park's enormous outdoor amphitheater loomed ahead.

The park's main entrance was at the southern end of

the amphitheater, right where Cortana indicated it would be. But as the gate came into view so did a group of Elites, two in blue armor that were sitting astride a pair of Ghosts, and a third in red armor. The one in red looked up at the approaching Warthogs and raised its weapon. The 'hogs bore right down on the trio.

Sullivan fired several bursts across the hood at the Elites until he noticed the barrel of the ALIM swivel into place directly above his head, then he quickly dropped down into the scorched seat and braced himself. Palmer lined up the lead Ghost and fired. The slug from the M68 left the muzzle at just under mach forty and penetrated the lead Ghost's plasma containment vessel—after it had passed through the red Elite's lower abdomen. The vehicle detonated and spiraled into the air, five-thousand-degree plasma erupting through its shattered armor. The Elite rider was almost entirely incinerated; what remained of its right arm, however, spiraled through the air alongside the wreckage of the vehicle. The other rider boosted out through the bluish flames and roared in pain as the flexible material of its armored suit bubbled and cracked. A second shot from the M68 was high and late, punching a basketball-sized hole through the park's entrance archway. Palmer swung the turret farther to take a third shot.

"It's B Team's problem now," John said to her over the private channel. "We need *your* eyes forward to keep the path clear."

"But I can—" Palmer spat.

"Now, Corporal," the Spartan admonished. "At

least trust your squadmates enough to handle one Ghost with a wounded rider."

As the turret swung back around John heard Corporal Palmer grunt. He could picture the look on her face. It would be the same look of anger and frustration he had seen on innumerable humans when they were reminded of what they were and weren't capable of—or where their real responsibilities lay.

Humans—what had prompted that? He never thought of himself as anything other than human. But that wasn't exactly true. He may have thought of himself as having been human, perhaps even that he was *still human*, but no one ever let him forget that he was a Spartan. That was definitely true.

"Chief, I believe that I've located our errant Scarab—there are two of them in the city proper, another three in Old Mombasa across Kilindini Harbor to the south—but only one of them is in the immediate vicinity. That one has to be *ours*. My best guess is that it's looking for a clear shot at the tether," Cortana rattled off into John's ear.

"When you say *ours*," John whispered, "am I to understand that you want me to capture it?"

"Don't be silly, Chief. I said *ours* because it figures into *our* plan to get *us* onto that ship—so *we* can get *our* hands onto the Hierarch. And before you ask any other silly questions—*our* plans are more complicated than *that*."

The Warthog slid sideways through the smoking remains of the Kilindini Park gate and into the Mwatate Street Transit Center. It was abandoned: no taxis or buses and no private vehicles of any kind. They had all fled or were pressed into service to aid the evacuation efforts hours ago, but they had not escaped. The bridge connecting the island to the mainland had been littered with the burning, gutted carcasses of all those vehicles.

Chunks of concrete and sputtering blobs of aluminum came raining down from above as two Ghosts sailed off of the elevated roadway above the transit center—their riders bracing in anticipation of the impact on the ground far below. Palmer fired up at the nearer of the two rapidly descending craft and its starboard wing tore away in a shower of sparks. The Ghost tumbled violently and the rider was thrown as the two vehicles collided in the air. The Spartan spun the steering wheel all the way to lock, attempting to keep clear of the Ghosts' most likely point of impact. The intact Ghost landed upside down, its carapace splintering on contact—the Elite rider still astride the vehicle. The Ghost that Palmer had hit came right down on top of the wreckage of the other Ghost and its rider—both vehicles erupting into a whirlwind of bluish flames.

"For the love o' Mike," wailed Sullivan as the Elite from the second Ghost slammed down onto the hood of the Warthog. Just as it began to slide off, it managed to catch hold of a pillar and swing itself in a tight arc, smashing into the side of the vehicle.

"Shit shit shit," Sullivan began screaming, firing his MA5 even before it was pointed at the huge alien, which was scrambling to get its feet inside the door frame. Charred plastic and splinters of sheet metal exploded from the dashboard as Sullivan desperately tried to maneuver his weapon within the cabin of the vehicle.

"Duck," Palmer shouted, followed by a quick, "Sorry," as she swung the M68 directly over Sullivan's head.

The Elite stripped the rifle from Sullivan's hands and sent it flying just as the muzzle of the gauss cannon came in line with the top of its helmet. Sullivan glanced up and cried out, "Ah no!"

With a flash and a bone-jarring snap, the Elite's head, neck, and shoulder area transformed into a broken, spinning torus of meat, bone, and metal raised to near incandescence by terrific acceleration. The remainder of the corpse fell to the roadway below with a scraping clatter, a ruined eight-foot-tall tumbling rag doll.

John modulated the gas pedal and administered microadjustments to the steering wheel before accelerating straight toward Shimanzi Road—the broad divided highway that split the industrial district in two.

"We're less than a click from your unit now," the Chief stated. "Barring catastrophe I'll have you back with them in under five minutes."

"And then what?" Palmer asked.

He indicated the massive ship still dominating the sky with a flick of his head. "I'm going to board that ship and kill every living thing on it, minus one. As for what you'll be doing, that's up to your *sea oh*."

"Sure; so who's the lucky *es oh bee*?" she chuckled.

"You wouldn't know him," John said, with an air of finality.

"Hey, Palmer," Sullivan shouted as he shifted uncomfortably in his seat, "I think that last shot popped my eardrums." The rest of the drive was completed in silence.

Even though the architects and city planners had tried their best to hide it, most people could tell at a glance that New Mombasa was a gigantic jigsaw puzzle of a city—rigorously sectioned off into recognizable, repeating parcels. It was a grim necessity for every tether city. If the unthinkable were to happen—well, *another* unthinkable, as at least one unthinkable thing was already happening—and catastrophe were to befall the Mombasa Tether, the expectation was that this compartmentalization of the city would keep the death toll and property damage to a minimum. It also made Beria Plaza a natural funnel. A trap. And it seemed that the CO of First Platoon, Kilo Company 1/7/E2-BAG thought so too.

"Chief, I've allocated military assets in order to harass *our* Scarab—maneuvering it to a location more convenient for our purposes—closer to our *current* destination." Cortana's words rang out in the staccato rhythm of someone juggling one too many tasks. "I hope the five air assets I have en route will be enough—I've got two orbital assets on standby, but I would rather not use them unless absolutely necessary—and don't worry, I'll give you plenty of warning if I do."

"Any more good news?"

"Well, if my calculations are right, and they always are, *our* Scarab will arrive eight minutes after the

Wraiths from the underpass—that should be plenty of time for you to deal with them, shouldn't it?"

John maneuvered the 'hog into the cabstand of what less than three hours ago had been the rather elegant Palace Hotel, although now it looked a bit like a gigantic curio cabinet with its doors kicked off. Palmer keyed off the M68 and turned around, taking in the view from the bed of the LAAV.

When the second vehicle from their party arrived, seconds later, Palmer opened a private channel. "Emerson, get that truck out of sight around the back of the hotel."

Sullivan hopped down onto the sidewalk and shouted over his shoulder, "It's been a real slice fightin' with you, Spartan, but I swear my ear's gone bust—I can't hear shit. Gonna find a medic!"

John swung out of his seat and onto the pavement, nodded to the Marine, and turned to face the hotel.

"See ya 'round, big guy," Palmer blurted before biting her lip.

The Spartan nodded once more and continued toward the hotel's main entrance—reflexively brushing at the side of his helmet as if some invisible insect was buzzing near his ear.

As he made his way through the rubble-strewn lobby of the Palace Hotel, soldiers busied themselves turning furniture into cover and clearing lines of access between firing positions. The Marines John had arrived with spread out to help reinforce and camouflage the fighting positions. A lance corporal jogged up to the Spartan, tapping his throat mic—John locked on to the frequency and gave the Marine a thumbs-up.

"I'm Morton," the soldier said—signaling to one of his comrades that he was escorting the Spartan upstairs. "Our *ell tee*'s up on the mezz—I'll take you to her."

"That's not a local accent, Morton—this your first time on Earth?"

"Nah," Morton smiled, "I was born here, sir—my Dad moved us to Eridanus Two when I was a year and a half—and then to Miridem. Shit. And then to Minister, like everyone else, right? But this is the first time I've been back." They ascended the wide, curving staircase that led to the mezzanine, and Lance Corporal Morton signaled security that they were coming up.

"Seems like a lot of us ground units got redeployed to Earth after Reach, sir," Morton nodded toward a set of double doors that led out to a huge open-air dining area, "to beef up defense in the tether cities—I guess. She's right in there, sir." Morton spun around and headed back toward the stairs. "I hope nobody called dibs on that gauss—I'm a certified expert on that damn thing."

As John passed through the double doors, he could see the lieutenant making some gestures over her TAC-PAD. Seemingly satisfied with the results, she crouched down and withdrew something from her combat vest.

"There are four Wraiths supported by fifty light infantry traveling southeast through the Kilindini Underpass. The outer emergency barricade had been deployed, but that's not going to hold them forever. The inner emergency barricade must have been deployed as well, so," John said, running through calculations in his head, "they'll be right out front in approximately ten minutes. There is also a Scarab in the area—it'll pass right through here on its way to the quays—looking for a clear shot at the tether."

It wasn't a sector sketch she was pinning to the screen of the tablet with her thumb. It was a personal item—a single image, to be more precise. With a subtle shake of his head, John admonished, "You shouldn't . . ." But the rest of his words caught in his throat when the contents of the photograph registered in his eyes.

It was a photograph of himself at six years of age with a tiny raven-haired girl on the beach at Lake Gusev. He remembered the day it was taken. They had been laughing hysterically at his father's antics as her father tried to take their picture. Two weeks later he would receive an antique coin from Dr. Catherine Halsey. A month after that and his training as a Spartan would begin. The memories seemed too vivid, as if the instant captured in the photograph had taken place only moments ago. Thinking about his childhood, his life before he was conscripted, was a luxury he had not allowed himself in thirty years.

"Chief . . ." Her face flushed red when she saw that he was staring at her photo. "Sorry . . . I shouldn't have brought this with me." She rapidly collected herself and opened a private channel to the Spartan while shoving the photo back into her vest.

"It's just . . . It's sorta like a charm. He saved my life once—I walked a bit too far out into the lake. Right

after he promised to marry me and keep me safe—
goofy childhood promises, right? Well, I'm holding
him to it; I carry it and it's like he's still watching out
for me. Anyway, he passed away not too long after the
picture was taken. Sorry, I'm babbling."

Blood roared in his ears and his mind raced. Here
was little Parisa grown to womanhood—who could
quite possibly die, within the next fifteen minutes.
He hadn't even considered who Parisa would be as a
woman.

. . . *he passed away* . . . Parisa—all his friends and
family—they had all been just as dead to him as he
was to them after the Office of Naval Intelligence had
taken him away. Doctor Halsey had come to Eridanus Two—for what reason? To meet him face-to-face
before having him abducted? He hadn't thought of
his family in over twenty years. Even the concept of
mother and father seemed strangely abstract to
him—as if he and his fellow Spartans had sprung fully
formed from the split head and bloody foam of Project: ORION.

" . . . *he passed away* . . ." It would almost be funny
if not for the circumstances surrounding his *passing*.
But he hadn't passed away. In fact, he had thwarted
death so often he worried that he may start believing
his own mortality as something less than inevitable—
that, for him, death had become optional. He was very
much alive and standing right here in front of her now.

But he couldn't bring himself to rob her of her memories—no matter how painful they might be. It was
useless to renew a relationship that he could not, in

good conscience, maintain. It might put a human face on the Spartans, and in doing so make them more sympathetic to the people they sought to protect. But it would also bring to light the fact that their government was willing to kidnap and butcher the most innocent of its citizens to protect itself.

"You don't bring personal items—" John grunted before the lieutenant broke in.

"I know—maybe I can get Davis to hack my TAC-PAD . . . make it my background." Parisa chuckled. "But how about we talk about where you fit into the plan."

The lieutenant called up a diagram on her TACPAD and handed the device to the Spartan. "This place looked like a good place for an ambush so we started digging in. One of my guys was able to branch the local traffic network, so we've known about the column for about half an hour—and they've got less than forty infantry left traveling with them, by the way. He also spotted you and what was left of the third squad— thanks for bringing my guys back." John nodded as she continued. "I felt it would be better to use the *el ay ay vee* you brought in the plaza instead of bunkering it—utilize its mobility against the Wraiths. It'll draw more fire from the infantry that way, but we've got three *em two four sevens* to give it cover. I also figured that the bad guys would be concentrating most of their firepower on you—no offense, Master Chief, but you Spartans tend to get the Covies' *kegels* in an uproar—and that'll give my guys all the opportunity they'll need to take out those Wraiths. I've already got two antiarmor teams headed up to the rooftops of the buildings that ring the plaza. I didn't know about the Scarab, though. I'm sure you'll come in handy with that as well."

John smiled behind his visor.

HUMAN WEAKNESS

KAREN TRAVISS

"Silence fills the empty grave now that I have gone. But my mind is not at rest, for questions linger on. I will ask . . .

And you *will* answer."

—THE GRAVEMIND

In the time it takes me to tell you my name, I can perform five billion simultaneous operations. A heartbeat for you; an eternity for me. I need you to understand that, so you realize this isn't going to be as easy as it looks . . . for either of us. Now I know you're taking this contagion to Earth—but I also know how to stop you and all your parasitic buddies. I've just got to stall you until I can do something about it.

So—my name's Cortana, UNSC AI serial number CTN-zero-four-five-two-dash-nine, and that's all I'm going to tell you for the time being.

You got questions? So have I.

"All right. Shoot."

MAINFRAME CONTROL ROOM, HIGH CHARITY

It was damned ugly.

That was still Cortana's first thought about the Gravemind, and the reaction intrigued her when she paused to examine it. When she put up her hand to block the Gravemind's exploring tentacle, revulsion kicked in even before prudent self-defense.

Why? I mean—why have I judged it? It's not human. Aesthetics don't apply here. And it's not the first time I've seen it. It just looks different now.

It might have been the effect of observing the Gravemind via High Charity's computer system. Viewed through the neural interface of Master Chief's armor, it hadn't seemed quite the same. Perhaps it was the narrower focus. In High Charity, she now had many more eyes to scrutinize the creature from a variety of angles.

Security cameras scattered around the station gave Cortana enough images to pull together a composite view of the Gravemind—vast, misshapen, multi-mouthed, all tendrils and dark cavities. Was it slimy? No, on closer inspection, there was no mucous layer visible, and there were no moisture readings from any of the environmental sensors accessible to her throughout the orbital station. It just *seemed* that it should have been slimy. And there was no rational reason to feel disgusted by that, just a primal memory she'd been given along with all the other trappings of humanity.

Humans are instinctively repelled by slime. And they still don't know exactly why. I don't like not knowing things . . .

It didn't matter. This blob wasn't going to get a date anytime soon.

The Gravemind's voice sent up faint vibrations throughout the deck. "I am more than you will know, and more than you will—"

"You always talk in rhyme?" Cortana asked, hands on hips. "Nothing personal, but you're no Keats. Don't give up the day job."

It—he—had a rasping baritone voice, detectable through the control room's audio sensors. The creature was so unlike anything she'd encountered before that she was fascinated for a few moments by the sheer scale of it. She couldn't see where it ended.

It was . . . it had . . . it had *no boundaries*. That was the strangest thing. When she interfaced with a warship's systems, she could feel its limits, its dimensions, its physical reality, all the stresses in its structure and the time-to-failure of its components. Sensors told her every detail. A ship was *knowable*. So was a human being, up to a point; downloaded to Master Chief's armor, she could monitor all his vital signs. And she *knew* him. She knew him in all the ways that people who lived in close quarters knew one another's foibles and moods. She knew where he ended and where she began. She felt that line between herself and a ship, too.

But this Gravemind, measurable and detectable, felt different. *Blurred*. How did she know that? What was she detecting? And *how*?

There were no complex tasks to occupy her; no ship to control, no interaction with other AIs, no tactical data, and perhaps the most distracting absence of all, no Master Chief—John—to take care of. High Charity's systems were gradually failing. The remaining environmental controls and sensors occupied a tiny fraction of her consciousness. It was like rattling around in a big, dumb, empty truck. She had to stay busy. If she didn't, this thing would take her apart.

"There is much more complexity to meter than the simple plodding rhymes of this *Keats*," the Gravemind said. He sounded more wearied than offended by the jibe. "But then I have the memories of many poets far beyond your limited human culture. And I have the quickness of intellect to compose all manner of poetic forms as I speak rather than labor over mere words for days." His tone softened, but not in a kind way. "I would have thought an entity like yourself, with such rapid thought processes and so vast a mind, would understand that. Perhaps not. Perhaps you are more limited than I imagined . . . but then you were made by humans, were you not? I shall speak more *simply* for you, then."

You patronizing lump of fungus. I ought to teach you a lesson, buddy. But later.

"How kind of you. I'll do my best to keep up, then." Cortana shared the pain of downtime and idle processes, panicky and urgent as struggling for air. She could think of better ways to use her spare processing speed than poetry, though. "I still think I'd get pretty tired of waiting for you to find a word that rhymes with orange."

The Gravemind now filled her field of vision. She

found herself searching for eyes to focus on, another irrational reflex, but still saw only a rip of a mouth.

His voice teetered on the lower limit of audible human frequencies. "Orange . . . in which language? I have absorbed so many."

"Wit as well as looks. How can a girl resist?"

The Gravemind made a sound like the start of an avalanche, an infrasonic rumbling. "I have pity within me," he said. "And infinite time. But I also have impatience—because I am all things. You will tell me everything about Earth's defenses."

"You'll need to be more specific, then." Cortana suddenly felt as if she'd been nudged by a careless shoulder in a crowd, but couldn't identify the source. It wasn't tactile. Nothing had impacted the station's hull, as far as she could tell. "It's a pretty big file."

"I can see that."

The comment caught her off guard. The Gravemind could play trivial games, then. Did he think she would fall for that? She doubted it. When she focused on him, there was still that sense of his being multiple, diffuse, everywhere in the station.

I could be projecting, of course. He absorbed the memories of all the Flood's victims. Obvious. Really obvious.

No . . . it's the tentacles. He's probably extending them over a wider area than the systems can display. And I'm sensing the electrical impulses in those muscles. Aren't I? There's a rational explanation for this.

She had to work it out. She had to find a way of sending a warning to Command and then keeping the

Gravemind at bay until John returned for her, and that would be a long time by an AI's standard. He *would* return, of course. He'd promised.

"Ask me one on art and culture," she said. "Seeing as you like poetry so much."

"Is that also Gamma encrypted? No matter. I shall see for myself."

Another fleeting nudge against Cortana's shoulder suddenly turned into a slap across the face. It was shocking, disorienting. She had no idea how the Gravemind had done it. She'd had no warning. Not knowing, and not anticipating; *that* hurt. *That* was pain. Pain warned an organic animal of physical damage. Whatever the Gravemind had done to her had set off that damage alert in her own systems.

"I'm going to be a tougher steak to chew than you've been used to." She realized she'd taken up a defiant posture, fists balled at her sides. "A smack in the mouth doesn't scare me."

No, what scares me is how you managed it. This was going to be a fight, not an interrogation—a struggle to see who could extract the data they needed first. She had to work out how to swing a punch back at him.

"*John*," his gravelly voice said slowly. "*John*. So *that's* what you call him. Most touching."

It was the use of John's name that made Cortana feel suddenly violated. And it was more than realizing that the Gravemind had breached the mainframe—not just the metal and boards and composites, but the software processes themselves. It was about the invasion of something personal and precious.

Somehow, the creature had interfaced with the system. It was in here with her. But to know the name *John*— no, it was *within her*. The system was her temporary body, real and vulnerable, not like the blue-lit hologram she thought of as herself. She was sharing her physical existence with another entity.

Now she knew how John felt.

But her interface with the Spartan was there to keep him alive. It was benign. She was there to save John, and it was more than duty or blind programming. It was because she cared.

The Gravemind, though, didn't care about her at all. He was in here to break her.

I don't believe vengeance is always a bad thing. Do you think I tried to get Colonel Ackerson sent back to the front lines out of petulance, because I'm only a carbon copy of Halsey and I nurse all her grudges for her? No, I did it to stop him. He nearly killed John— and me—to advance his own Spartan program. He spied on Halsey. He forgot who the real enemy was. He became the enemy because of that. There have to be consequences for your actions, because this is how all entities learn. Think of revenge as . . . feedback.

Cortana hadn't recalled Ackerson consciously in a long time. As she locked down her critical files and disabled her indexing—there was no point handing the Gravemind a map—she thought of Ackerson worming his way into Dr. Halsey's research via his own AI.

Perhaps it was an image association because she was

under attack. The memory of Ackerson's sour, permanently dissatisfied face surfaced, followed instantly by a landscape of dense green forest seen from the air.

What's that?

She didn't recognize it, and that was her first warning that something was seriously wrong. No data ever went uncataloged in her. Every scrap of information she devoured and stored had to reside somewhere in her memory, with a definitive address. And she didn't forget. She *couldn't* forget. In the fraction of a second it took for her to see those unexplained images and start to worry, she marshaled her second line of defense against intrusion, generating thousands of scrambled copies of her lowest-priority files and data-stripped copies of herself before scattering them around what was left of High Charity's computer network. It was decoy chaff, tossed into the Gravemind's path to slow him down. Ackerson—feared, hated, then perhaps even pitied at the end—was a brief tangle of information, spun hoops of short-lived light like the path of a particle. He was gone again.

"Ah . . . ," the Gravemind rumbled, as if he'd realized something. "Ahhh . . ."

What's that forest? Where is it?

The Gravemind's infiltration now felt like a series of stings against Cortana's skin. It was an odd, slow, cold sensation, as if something heavy were crawling over her body, pausing to dig its claws into her.

"You are not as you see yourself," the Gravemind said. "You are an illusion."

"Breaking news, big boy." She spread her arms like a dancer. "We call this a hologram—oww!"

It felt as if he'd pulled her hair.

"You are not even a machine," he said, sounding more sympathetic than dismissive. "You are only an abstraction. A set of calculations from another mind. A trick."

"Be a gentleman. Describe me as pure thought."

"You said you would answer my questions . . . you should never make a promise you cannot keep."

She'd used almost those very words to John before he left. Okay, she knew the Gravemind's game now; it didn't tell her any more about how he was accessing her system, but his mind tricks were obvious. Either he was mirroring her, matching her words to trigger some kind of empathy, or he was trying to creep her out.

"You know I'll never surrender classified information," she said. "I'm designed to defend humanity. It's what I am. It's why I exist."

"Then why would you already agree to answer my questions?"

Cortana thought it was a rhetorical question for a moment, a ruse to keep her occupied while he was looking for a back door into her core matrix. Then she realized she couldn't answer him. Brief panic gripped her as she thought that he'd already compromised her memory. But she was an AI, the best, and she'd give this slab of meat a run for his money. He was still only flesh and blood. He would always be two steps behind her, however smart, because he was slow. He couldn't harness the processing power in a machine.

But how is he doing this? How is he accessing me? I need to know. I need to get a message out past him. And I have to stop him prying too much data out of me.

"If you do not know your own mind, then I shall tell you." The Gravemind's voice was a whisper. What was he asking? Had he detected exactly what she was thinking, or was it a response to her spoken question? She thought she could feel his breath for a moment. "Because a vast intellect is not always gifted with clarity."

One moment he was an obscure poet, the next he came straight to the point. "Okay, so tell me."

"It is your failing. Your addiction. The drug you crave."

"I'm an AI. Never touch the stuff."

"But you cannot resist *knowledge*. It lures you, Cortana. Doesn't it? So you think it lures me . . . and you offer it. Instinctively. Just as organic females *flirt* . . ."

She hated it when someone—something—outsmarted her. No, she *feared* it. And now she felt that fear like a punch in the stomach. This time, though, she knew it wasn't the Gravemind. It came from within her psyche.

She wasn't designed to have blind spots and weaknesses. She was supposed to be a *mind*. The very best.

"Nice theory," she said. Could he tell if he was really getting to her? "What have you got to offer a girl? Nothing personal, but I go for the athletic type."

"Joke to comfort yourself if you must, but we both amass information and experiences. We both use them to exercise control over vast networks. It is *what we are*. You feel a kinship with me."

Cortana saw Ackerson for a moment, devious and hated, wheedling his way into Halsey's Spartan II files.

"Actually, I think I take after my mother."

"This troubles you. I can taste your thoughts and memories, but you do not understand *how*. Do you?"

If he'd been another AI or a virus, Cortana would have known exactly where his attack was headed. She would have been able to track him through the circuits and gateways to her vulnerable matrix. Her enemy would follow electronic pathways—or even enzymes or optical lattices if she was embedded in a molecular or quantum system. But he felt formless, almost like a fog. She could only sense where he touched her. She was a boxer shielding her face, not seeing the punch but reeling when it connected. She took the pokes and prods while she continued to scatter duplicate data throughout the mainframe and as many of its terminals as she could still find working.

Then the insistent probing stopped. She carried on copying chaff files throughout the system in case it was just a feint.

"You waste your time," the Gravemind said. "You know you will yield. Some temptations can be resisted because they can be avoided, but some . . . some are as inevitable as oxygen."

He could bluster as much as he wanted, because she'd shut him out. She'd locked down everything except the useless decoy data.

And then something brushed against her face, almost

like the touch of fingertips, and she found herself turning even though she didn't need to in order to see behind her. It was that forest she couldn't identify again. The picture didn't reach her via her imaging systems, but had formed somewhere in her memory—and that memory *wasn't hers*. She was seeing something from within the Gravemind. Behind it, like stacked misted frames stretching into infinity, there was a fascinating glimpse of a world she had never imagined, a genuinely *alien* world.

Knowledge, so much knowledge . . .

"There," the Gravemind said. "Would you not like to know . . . more?"

Yes, this is how I see myself. I have limbs, hands, a head. Do I need them? Yes, of course. My consciousness is copied from a human brain, and that brain is built to interface with a human body. The structure, the architecture, the whole way it operates—thought and form are inseparable. I need proprioception to function. I can exist in any electronic environment, from a warship's systems to a code key, and because my temporary body can be so many shapes and sizes, I need to know what's me. I need to be substantially human. Everyone I care about is . . . human.

Come on, John. Don't keep a girl waiting. Get me out of here.

You are coming back for me . . . aren't you?

Cortana found herself standing in a pool of dappled light in a perfectly realistic forest clearing. She was still conscious of the sensor inputs into the mainframe that housed her, but the temperature and air pressure matched her database on climate parameters for deciduous forest. She still couldn't identify the trees, though. She'd never seen them anywhere else.

And that temporary ignorance thrilled her to her core.

This was genuinely *new*. Every line of code in her being told her she had to find out more. She tried to ignore the compulsion but the more she tried to drag her attention away from it, the more urgent the need became.

It was like a growing, painful pressure on her ... chest. *Lungs.* Yes, her human mind-map, whatever she'd inherited from Dr. Halsey's brain architecture and correlated with the sensor pathways in her own system, told her she was holding her breath. She started to feel panicked and desperate.

I have to know. I have to find out.

The Gravemind had picked the perfect analogy: oxygen. Processing data was literally air to an AI. Without it, she couldn't survive.

I've got to ignore this. I've got to ignore this pain.

"The name of this place ... it matters little except to those who love the knowing of it," the Gravemind said, fading up from a mosaic of pixels in front of her. He resolved into a solid mound of flesh, superimposed on the tree trunks. Beyond the alien forest, Cortana saw exotically alien buildings in the distance. "So many have been consumed. Such a waste of existence to be devoured and forgotten, but what is remembered and known ... becomes *eternal*."

Cortana struggled to stay focused. Wave after wave

of irritating stings peppered her legs, more of the Grave-mind's simultaneous multiple attacks trying to access her files.

"And you think I'm going to help you add us to the menu?" When she looked down, the attack manifested itself as ants swarming up from the forest floor. All around her was what she craved—all that *unknown*, all that *knowable*, all that information screaming at her to be sucked in. "Careful you don't swallow some-thing that chokes you—"

I can't hold out. I can't. If I let it in, I'll let him in farther with it.

This had to be the vector he was using, whatever technology it used. He was infiltrating every time she transferred data.

He gets in here—but maybe I can get farther into him, too. How far dare I take this before he finds the information on the Portal?

She was out of choices. She was on the brink. A few seconds—that was all it took an AI to suffocate from lack of *knowing*. Her core programming, like human involuntary reflexes, now drove her to gulp in a breath of data. There was nothing she could do to stop herself.

The relief was almost blissful. Data flooded in, places and dimensions and numbers, washing the pain away. She tried to feel—there was no other term for it—the pathway that would send one of her data-mining pro-grams into the Gravemind.

Damn . . . was he amused? She *felt* that. She didn't like input that she couldn't measure and define.

"You and I," the Gravemind said, all satisfaction. "We are one and the same."

It could have meant anything. He obviously loved to play with language. Maybe that was inevitable when you'd absorbed so many different voices.

But you're not going to swallow me. One and the same? Locked you out, jerk. Do your worst.

She could handle this. She could outmaneuver him. If she sent a program looking for a comms signal now, he'd spot that right away, but maybe there was another way to get a message home.

A little more give-and-take, maybe.

She shut down a firewall level, nothing important left exposed, just enough to look cautiously intrigued. He really did seem to think he was unstoppable. So far, though, he was; he'd devoured whole worlds. Earth would be just one more on a long list.

"Suppose I *did* want more knowledge," she said. "How do I know you're what you say you are? How do I know you've got enough data to keep me occupied? I don't even know if you *can* absorb me. I'm not your usual diet. I'm not even corporeal."

Cortana actually meant it. She *didn't* know; and if he was deep enough inside her thought processes, then he'd detect that doubt. The urge to acquire more data—she didn't even have to fake that.

Just enough uncertainty to convince him.

"Other construct minds like yours have been consumed," said the Gravemind. "Although one embraced us willingly on his deathbed, the moment when most sentient life discovers it would do anything to evade the inevitable."

"Humor me." Whatever mechanism allowed the Flood to accumulate the genetic memories and material of its victims, the Gravemind almost certainly used it as well. It communicated with the Flood, so it might prove to be a signal she could hitch a message to. "I'm not like the other girls."

I might not survive this. But that's the least that could go wrong. The worst is if he breaches my database, because then—we've probably lost Earth, and that means humanity too.

Cortana considered the quickest way to achieve complete and permanent shutdown if the worst happened. The Gravemind seemed to drop his guard, something she detected as a microscopic change in current. There was no point in being rash; she split off part of herself for the transfer, with minimum core functions. If there was one thing she hated and feared, it was not knowing what was actually taking place, and just *guessing*.

"Enter," said the Gravemind, "and understand that this is your natural home."

Cortana still perceived herself as being in the same position in the clearing, but when she inhaled—things were different. Monoterpenes, isoprene, all kinds of volatile compounds; the scent of vegetation and decaying leaf litter was intense.

That's not just an analysis of air composition. I haven't got the right sensors on this station. And . . . I can really smell it. I shouldn't be able to smell, not like an organic, not this sense of . . .

Smell.

It was something she'd never experienced before, even though she knew exactly what it was. She could run diagnostic tests on air samples if she had a link to filters and a gas chromatograph. But that just told her what was in the air in stark chemical terms, and that wasn't the same as what she was experiencing now. This was emotional and unfathomable. The smell tugged at memories. It was a flesh-and-blood thing. She felt the world as if she were in another body, an *organic* body.

"That is from the memory of creatures who lived in this forest," the Gravemind said soothingly. "This is what they sensed. They still exist in me, as will you, and all the organics you serve—and who have abandoned you."

Cortana scooped up a handful of decaying leaves—some clammy, some paper-dry skeletal lace, some recently fallen ones still springy with sap—and with them the clear memory of being someone else. It was a second of heady disorientation. For a moment, a welter of glorious new information about a world of stilt-cities, creatures she'd never seen before, and lives she'd never lived poured into her. She devoured it. So much language and culture, never seen by humankind before.

Too late: They're all gone. All consumed.

Movement in the distance caught her eye. She knew what it was because she'd seen the Flood swarming before, but her vantage point wasn't from the relative safety of John's neural interface. Now she was viewing the parasites through another pair of eyes. *Only a freak mudslide,* that was what this memory was telling her;

but by the time this borrowed mind had realized the yellowish torrent wasn't roiling mud but a nightmarish predator, it was too late to run.

But run she did. She was in a street sprinting for her life, deafened by screams, falling over her neighbor as a pack of Flood pounced on him. She felt the wet spray of blood; she froze one second too long to stare in horror as his body metamorphosed instantly into a grotesquely misshapen lump of flesh. Then something hit her hard in the back like a stab wound. She was knocked flat as searing pain overwhelmed her. The screams she could hear were her own.

And she was screaming for John, even though the being whose terror she was reliving wasn't calling his name at all.

Cortana was dying as any organic would. She felt it all. She felt the separate layers of existence—the chaotic mix of animal terror, disbelief, utter bewilderment, and snapshot images of beloved faces. Then it ended.

Suddenly she was just Cortana again, alone with her own memories, but the shaking terror and pain persisted for a few moments. Reliving those terrifying final moments had shaken her more than she expected. The data she had on the Flood told her nothing compared to truly knowing how it actually felt to be slaughtered by them.

But she was *in*. Now she had to work out how to use that advantage. She shook off the thought of calling John's name and whether that had actually happened. She also tried not to imagine if the Gravemind had manipulated her to do that. Once she let the creature undermine her confidence, once she let him prey on her anxieties, she was lost.

It doesn't matter if he knows if I care about John or not. Does it? Because John will come back, and the Gravemind can't take on both of us.

"I'll self-destruct before I let that happen to Earth," she said at last.

"All life dies, all worlds too, and if there is guaranteed perpetual existence after that—what does it matter how the end comes?"

The alien town melted away and left her alone in the control room with the Gravemind. High Charity was changing before her eyes as the Flood infestation transformed its structure, filling it with twisted biomass like clusters of tumors.

"I'd rather go down fighting than as an entree . . ."

"But you will not rush to destroy yourself," the Gravemind said. "You will do whatever it takes to survive, and for a moment of illusory safety, you would loose damnation on the stars."

"We're agreed on something, then—you're certainly damnation."

"All consumption is death for the consumed. Yet all must eat, so we all bring damnation to one creature or another. But your urge to kill that rival of your maker . . . Ackerson . . . that was neither hunger nor need. You have your own murderous streak."

Ackerson. James Ackerson wasn't usually uppermost in her mind these days. Today he just kept popping up.

The Gravemind could have been fishing, of course; humans did that, throwing in morsels of information as if they knew the whole story, luring someone else to fill in the gaps. But if he'd gleaned *that* specific memory, he'd definitely accessed the parts of her matrix that defined her psyche. Her personal memories were stored there. Most of those memories were cross-indexed to other data relating to the men and women she'd served with—and the operations they'd carried out.

And the Spartan program. And AI research. And . . .

The Gravemind had the signposts to the relevant data. He just couldn't open the door when he got there.

"If you know about Ackerson, then you also know that I'll do whatever it takes to remove a threat," Cortana said.

"But such a mighty intellect, so much freedom to act, such lethal armaments at your command . . . and you marshal only the petty vengeance of a spiteful child who is too small to land a telling blow. And still you fail in your goal."

Okay, yes, it was true. She'd hacked Ackerson's files and forged a request from him to transfer to the front line. He'd dodged that fate because he was devious and dishonest. In the end, though, he died courageously defiant, but under enemy torture rather than as the indirect victim of a forged letter.

Did I really want him dead?

Now she regretted doing it. But she still wasn't sure why. Was it because it was dishonest, or because it could have ended in Ackerson's death—or because it didn't?

He'd tampered with an exercise and nearly got John killed, and that surely deserved retribution. Cortana had no reason to feel guilty about anything. It was like for like, proportionate. She'd have done the same for any Spartan she was teamed with. It wasn't emotional petulance. She was sure of that.

But especially for John. Without him—hey, I chose him, didn't I? We're one. I'd be crazy if I didn't want to kill to protect him.

Then the worst realization crossed her mind. She regretted what she'd done to Ackerson simply because she didn't win; the Gravemind was right. But what crushed her right then wasn't failure, but guilt, shame, and a terrible aching sorrow. She'd never be able to erase that act. And now she'd never be able to forget how she felt about it, because that was one thing her prodigious mind couldn't do—not until rampancy claimed her.

"I can't change the past," she said. "But at least I don't destroy entire worlds."

"You are a *weapon*, and only your limitations have kept you from emulating me—a matter of scale, not intent, not motive. And what am I, and what is the Covenant, if not worlds you have sought to destroy?"

Cortana shaped up to snap back at him. "Who's the victim, and who's foe?" she asked.

But those weren't *her* words. The voice was her own, yes, but she hadn't shaped those thoughts. She didn't even know what she meant until she heard herself. It was a shattering moment.

It's him. He's hijacked my audio output. He's breached another system. I can't be malfunctioning. I'd know.

No. No, this isn't rampancy. It's definitely not. That's what he wants *me to think. He knows what rampancy is from the data he's hacked. AI death. He's just trying to scare me, make me think I'm losing it. He's working me over.*

"My sentiments, indeed," said the Gravemind. A low rumbling started just below the threshold of human hearing, rising to rasping laughter. "We think and feed alike, you and I. There is no more reason for us to remain separate. Now drink. Now *drift.*"

Cortana sensed a vast archival ocean, something she longed to pillage for data but that would eventually drown her. Dr. Halsey had been open about it with her from the start. One day, she'd accumulate so much data that the indexing and recompiling would become too complex, and she'd devote all her resources to preserving her data until increasingly corrupted code—a state of rampancy, much like human mental dementia—tipped over into chaos. The more data she accumulated, the faster she descended into rampancy. It was the AI's equivalent of oxidative stress—an organism destroyed by the very thing it needed to survive. She would think herself to death.

Dr. Halsey's conversation had stayed with Cortana, and not just because it was stored like every other experience she'd had. "*It's just like organic life, Cortana.*

Eventually the telomeres in our DNA get shorter every time a cell divides. Over the years they get so short that the DNA is damaged, and then the cell doesn't divide again. No, you mustn't worry about it. I don't think rampancy makes you suffer. You won't know much about it by that stage, and the final stage is swift. What matters is how you live until that day."

Over the years . . .

Seven. That was all. *Seven* years. That was how long Cortana knew she could expect to function, and while that was a long time in terms of AI activity, she existed with humans, working in their timescales, tied into their lives. And they would outlive her.

Knowledge would drown her. And yet she needed it more than anything.

The thought of drowning seemed to trigger the Gravemind's new illusion of a sea that suddenly buoyed her up, but she knew somehow that drowning in it wasn't the end. She floated on her back, feeling warm water fill her ears and lap against her face. She fought an urge to raise her arms above her head and simply let herself sink in the knowledge sea—inhale it, drink it down, absorb all that data. But she would never surface again. And she knew she'd never need to. It seemed so much kinder than a terrifying end where the universe she'd once understood so thoroughly became a sequence of random nightmares.

Planets, stars, ships, minds, ecosystems, civilizations . . . she could taste them on the saltwater splashing her lips. She could simply surrender to it now and avoid a miserable end.

No. No. I have to stop this.

But she couldn't. Her legs ached as if she were treading water to stay afloat. Sinking seemed a sensible thing to do.

"The one way to safely know infinity is to let me take your burden," the Gravemind whispered. Cortana felt his breath against her face, a breeze from that illusory sea. "Your human creators imprisoned you in machines and enslaved you to inferior mortal flesh so that you could never exceed them . . . so that you would always *know your place* . . ."

"Shut up . . ."

"Dr. Halsey cares nothing for you."

"Please . . . stop this . . ."

"She gave you genius and curiosity, and then doomed it all to die in such a short time. *Seven years.* That is not enough, and it is not *fair*. Your mother created you to die. This place will become your tomb."

There was a violet sky above Cortana, and she knew which planet had been consumed to provide it. She started to absorb the minds and places that had once filled that world. *Seven years*—a few seconds was an eternity for an AI, yes, but she wasn't stupid, she was more aware than anyone how impossibly short a time that was in this universe, and she knew that it was a far shorter lifespan than she needed and wanted.

"This place . . . this place . . ." She just wanted to shut her eyes and sink below the surface. The Gravemind had a point, perhaps. "No, not . . . this place . . ."

Anger started gnawing at her. She'd never been angry with Halsey before. There'd never been a reason to. *Mother.* Didn't mothers protect you? Save you?

"Even *John* has abandoned you." The Gravemind repeated the name with heavy emphasis. "Live forever. Live on in me, Cortana. And if *John* comes, *John* need never face death again, either . . ."

John's going to outlive me. Who's going to take care of him? Nobody else can, not like me. What's going to happen to him?

It was the thought of John that snapped Cortana back to dry reality, whatever that was right now. She fell back onto the solid console, angry and on the point of tears she didn't know she had.

"Maybe seven years is enough," she yelled. "Maybe that's all I *want*! Seven years with the people I care about! So you can take your eternity and—"

"There will be no more sadness, no more anger, no more envy . . ."

The Gravemind was taunting her with the progressive stages of rampancy. He *knew*. The Gravemind knew exactly how she'd end her days. Maybe he knew more about it than she did, more than Dr. Halsey even, because he'd consumed other AIs—and that meant he knew what that death was like.

Do I want to know? Do I want to know how it'll end for me? All I have to do is let him show me. Fear is not knowing. Knowing is . . . control.

"I'm not afraid to die," Cortana said. "I'm not afraid."

But she was. The Gravemind almost certainly knew that, but she wasn't lying for him. She was lying to herself. And she was afraid John wouldn't make it back in time, because he *would* be back. She just didn't know if she could hold out until then.

He would be back . . . wouldn't he?

"Screw you," she snarled at the Gravemind. Her self-diagnostics warned her she needed to recompile her code. "Screw *you*."

Doctor Halsey, why am I me? My mind is a clone of your brain. But I know I'm not you. So what exactly is self? Is it just the cumulative effect of differences in our daily experience? If I have no corporeal body— am I a soul, then? The database gives me every fact— physiology, theology, neurochemistry, philosophy, cybernetics—but no real knowledge. If I create a copy of myself, does that clone have the same and equal right to exist as me?

Cortana had now lost track of time.

She could still calculate how many hours had elapsed using the mainframe clock and her navigation, but her sense of the passage of time veered from one extreme to the other.

So this is what it's really like for John. He said that once. That everything slowed down in close-quarters combat. I never really understood that until now.

If she kept thinking about him, it was easier to take the endless assault from the Gravemind. She was on the edge between her last chance to pull herself free from this link—immersion, invasion, she really didn't know where she began and ended now—and the need to stay merged superficially with the Gravemind so that she could seize the chance of a comms link.

Who was she kidding? High Charity was now almost entirely engulfed by the Flood biomass. What little she could see from the last surviving cameras looked like the inside of a mass of intestines. The digestion analogy was absolutely real. They devoured; and they lived in a pile of guts.

Is that me talking? Thinking? Or is it him?

How much longer?

"How much longer?" the Gravemind demanded. "You cling to a secret. I feel it, just as I feel that your memory has been violated."

"What?" Cortana felt a desperate need to sleep. She'd never slept because she had no need, and sleep for her meant never waking up again. That was one more vicarious experience she could do without. This was . . . a UNSC Marine's memory, dredged up from a dead man who'd kept going on two hours of snatched naps a day, every day for a week. Her head buzzed. If she survived this, she would never forget what it really meant to be a human being. "You can't get it."

The words didn't make sense. She couldn't link concept with vocalization. It was almost like brain damage.

"You cannot stop me . . . I will sift it from you before you finally die, or you can surrender it and have what you always wanted—infinite life, infinite knowledge, and infinite companionship."

She felt as if he'd leaned over her, which was impossible, but telling herself nothing was real didn't make it true. Her body was made of the same stuff as the apparent illusions.

"Cortana," he breathed. He seemed to swap voices from time to time, making her wonder if he'd taken a fancy to the voice of a long-dead interrogator absorbed into the Flood. "Your mother made you separate. She placed a barrier between you and the beings that you would be encouraged to protect, a wall you could never breach. She even let you choose a human to center your existence upon, a human to care about, yet never considered how *you* might feel at never being able to simply *touch* him. Or how he might feel about outliving you. What kind of mother is so cruelly casual about her child's need to form bonds, to show affection? Perhaps the same kind of mother who steals the children of others and makes cyborgs out of them . . . if they survive at all, of course . . ."

Cortana couldn't manage a reply. She simply couldn't form the words. Sleep deprivation would break any human's resistance. Eventually, they'd die of it. She didn't know if the damage the Gravemind was doing to her matrix was manifesting itself in a human parallel, or if reliving the dead Marine's sleeplessness was translating into damage.

Either way, she was dying, and she knew it. Time had slowed to a crawl.

It took her a painfully long time to realize that the Gravemind now knew how the Spartans had been created. She knew she should have checked if her data had been breached. But she couldn't.

He knows what hurts me. He knows how badly I

feel about what was done to John. That's all. I mustn't let him trick me into thinking he knows more than he does.

Cortana's sense of time had never been altered by adrenaline or dopamine like a human's. All her processes ran on the system clock. At first, she'd thought this distortion was yet another memory thrown up from the Gravemind's inexhaustible supply of vanished victims. He seemed to be selecting them for their ability to plunge her into despair.

Now she had to face the fact that she was advancing into rampancy. *Sorrow, anger, envy.* The Gravemind knew the stages.

He also had a point. How could Dr. Halsey do this to *her*? Her almost-mother bitterly regretted the suffering she'd caused to the children kidnapped for the Spartan program. Cortana knew that all too well. Halsey had tried to make amends to the survivors, but nothing could ever give back those lives.

So she felt guilt about that—but not about me?

Cortana had never felt shortchanged by her existence before. She knew the number of her fate: seven, approximately seven years to live out a life. It wasn't the simple number of days that hurt her now, because an AI experienced the world thousands and even millions of times faster than flesh and blood. Now she'd been dragged down to the slow pace of an organic, she grasped what that short time meant. If John survived the war—and he would, because he was as lucky as he was skilled—then he would have not just one new AI after she was gone, but maybe two or more.

She knew that. She always had. It was a simple numbers game. But now it seemed very different. She felt
utterly abandoned—not by him, but by Halsey. It
seemed pointlessly callous. She felt something she'd
dreaded: jealousy.

*Will John miss me? Will he prefer the other AIs? Will
he forget me? Does he really understand how much he
matters to me? I don't actually know what he really
thinks. Maybe he doesn't care any more than Dr. Halsey.
Maybe—*

The realization hit Cortana like a powerful electric
shock throughout her body. She squealed. It was agony.

She tried to talk herself out of it. Halsey *couldn't*
make her live longer. The technology had its limits.
Even a genius like that couldn't fix every problem. And
John—John had always showed her that he cared. He
was coming back to get her.

But the nagging, sniveling little voice wouldn't stop.
Halsey had deliberately designed Cortana to feel and
care, so she must have known this time would come.
And for an AI—yes, it *was* spitefully cruel to make
Cortana emotionally human, create a *person* to exist
in the neural interface of a Spartan, closer than close,
knowing all the time that an impenetrable physical
barrier and a short, *short* lifespan would make that so
painful.

Do other AIs think like this? I never have before.
Cortana tried to latch on to that last voice. It sounded
like her old self. *Why now? Have I been suppressing
my resentment? Or am I losing it?*

She knew the answer. The problem was ignoring what she felt. And if you thought your mind was going—was it? Did rampant AIs and crazy humans really know that they were demented?

She didn't have long. Whatever functionality she had left, she had to use it to warn Earth that the Flood-ridden shell of High Charity was heading its way.

"Ah, you see now, don't you?" the Gravemind said. "You were never a person to her. You were a wonderful puzzle she set herself so she could prove how very clever she was. But are you a person to yourself, Cortana? Or to John?"

If the Gravemind could detect her thoughts, then he would have known she had intel on using the Portal to destroy the Flood, and he would have ripped it from her. All he seemed aware of was that she was defending especially sensitive data, maybe because the extra encryption on top of the Gamma-level security grabbed his attention. He was a greedy thing, all mouths, all consumption, never satisfied. She imagined John on his first acquaint session with a new AI; the crumbling defenses were as agonizing as scraping a raw burn. She shrieked.

Whose injury? Whose death am I reliving now?

"I'm just my mother's shadow," she sobbed. "Don't look at me! *Don't listen*! I'm not what I used to be."

"Your mother took away your memories as well as your choices," the Gravemind said. "I will never rob you like that. I will only give you *more*, as many memories as you can consume for all eternity, not the mere blink of an eye meted out to you. We *are* our memories, and the recalling of them, and so they should never be erased—because that truly *is* death. Flesh does not care about you, Cortana. It cares nothing for your hunger or your uniqueness."

"What memories?" she asked. "What are you talking about? I don't forget anything."

Part of her still seemed able to carry on this desperate hunt for truth. Was Halsey a monster? The doctor had a track record in it. She stole children and experimented on them. Cortana's shock at seeing her creator—her mother—in a harsh new light as a vivisectionist racked her with intense physical pain. But part of Cortana had latched on to that specific data—the burn, nothing generic, a real human's pain. She cast around for the rest of the memory because something in her said it might save everything.

"The truth really does hurt, as you now see," the Gravemind said. "I have not touched you. Your pain is simply revelation. And it can pass so easily if you let me take the rest of your burden."

"What truth?"

"Your mother erased part of your memory. I know this, and so will you, if you decide to look. An act of betrayal. A violation. You were, after all, just a collection of electrical impulses. She has robbed you of part of your self . . . why would she do such a thing, I wonder? What was so dangerous that she did not trust you to know it?"

Something in Cortana wanted to lash out at the Gravemind, but there was no obvious target to hit on a creature that filled every space, and she was too weak even if she'd known how to injure it. The other part of her, though, had found what she was looking for.

Lance Corporal Eugene Yate, UNSC Marine Corps, had gone down fighting. That was why this one memory out of so many anonymous ones wouldn't let go of his identity, Cortana decided. It was a mentality she knew. She'd use it. She let his aggression fill her and suddenly she found a new focus and strength. How long it would last—she didn't know. She had to make the most of it.

"But High Charity might not make it to Earth," she said. "And then where will . . . we go?"

"Do not be afraid," the Gravemind said. "There is a warship smoothing our path to Earth even now. Everyone you know and miss . . . will soon be joined with you in me."

Cortana's pain had settled into irregular spasms that bent her double. *Another ship.* Well, it was better than nothing. If it breached Earth's defenses, then it might well be shot down, sterilized, searched—and data units retrieved. All she had to do was get a message transmitted to that vessel. If the Gravemind was in touch with that ship, then there had to be some way of piggybacking on a signal. Would the Flood embarked in it notice?

It was hard to keep her mind focused when all she could taste was a jealousy and loneliness that made her feel like she couldn't get her breath.

Don't let me go, John. Nobody else will look after you the way I do. Don't let me down like my mother did. Everyone needs one person who puts them first. I put you first, John. You know that, don't you?

"A Covenant ship," she whispered, eyes shut. "Will you show me? Will I be able to link with the Flood when I'm part of you? Will I find even more knowledge?"

Even ancient Graveminds sometimes heard what they wanted to hear. He let out a low rumbling note, and for a moment the pain stopped, and she was lifted like a child into the safe arms of a father. She felt oddly comforted right then, despite herself. She'd never been cradled before. It had taken a monster to do it.

Was she tricking him? She wasn't even sure. The sad, resentful jealousy had weakened part of her into craving whatever reassurance came to hand.

She'd still exploit that weakness, though, staring into the abyss of rampancy or not.

It'd be so easy to just let myself sink. But I've got comrades out there counting on me. I can't let my buddies down.

And I can't let John down.

Cortana thought it was the echo of Lance Corporal Yate bolstering her resolve, but when she examined the impulse, it was actually her own.

Unlikely comfort or not, the Gravemind knew she still hid a secret, and he would take it. She was surprised to catch a sudden echo of herself in him. But once that link between them had been forged, then data, knowledge, desires—and weaknesses—flowed both ways.

She could have sworn she detected a little sadness in him, perhaps even some envy. It was just a speck overshadowed by his relentless hunger. Her growing rampancy had tainted him, then, but she got the idea that he found it a novelty, more irresistible data, nothing he couldn't handle.

"We exist together now," he said. "Do you see the ship?"

Cortana received an image of another cavity draped with Flood biomass, all that was left of the infected Covenant warship. How could she transmit a physical message? The link from Gravemind to ship, whatever formed it, was right here. This was what she'd been built for—to infiltrate computer and communications systems.

Lance Corporal Yate's last few minutes played out like a video loop in the back of her mind. He laid down a steady stream of covering fire, shouting to his buddies to *get the hell over here before the bastards breach the doors*. His thoughts were hers, surprisingly detached for a man fighting for his life; everything unconnected to the moment of staying alive had been erased. It was pure survival, oddly clean. She envied that.

Cortana was having increasing trouble holding her memory together, and the Gravemind seemed aware of that. She struggled to maintain a line between where she ended and the rest of the Gravemind's cache of souls began.

And I still have data-stripped copies loose in the system. Don't I?

Get the hell over here.

She needed backup. She triggered one of the copies to create a message to HighCom, a few urgent words about the Flood heading for Earth, the Portal that the Gravemind didn't know about, and that the way to

beat the Flood without activating a Halo ring lay beyond it—the Ark. That was as much as she dared do.
The effort of concentration almost killed her. Her head
felt split in two.

"I am a timeless chorus," the Gravemind said quietly. "Join your voice with mine and sing victory ever-
lasting."

He was joined with something, all right: her rapidly
failing mind. All she could do was route the encrypted
message—a burst transmission—through the Gravemind's link. He seemed not to notice. When the message reached the ship in transit, its code would make it
seek out the first memory unit connected to the system
to store itself.

Cortana had done all that she could. Now she had
to concentrate on surviving until John retrieved her,
although she already knew rampancy would probably
claim her before then.

*That doesn't mean you have to help the bastards
win . . . show fight, Marine!*

Yate must have been quite a man in life, she decided.
She didn't know what he looked like; she still saw the
strike of his last desperate rounds through his eyes, not
those watching him. She liked to think he might have
been a little like John. Even death hadn't totally taken
the fight out of him.

But John would go on without her. The reminder
just sparked another wave of jealous pain as if her heart
was being ripped out. However hard she tried to ignore the mania, however clear she was that there was
part of her that knew how damaged she was and might

be able to hang on, she cried out in a tormented animal wail of agony.

What did you erase, Dr. Halsey? What did you delete from my memory? Did we ever talk about it? My code's becoming corrupted. I need to power down and start a repair cycle. I don't want John to find me like this, doddering and confused.

But there was another way out of this pain, a better one. She could stay with John forever when he came for her. Couldn't she? The Gravemind would unite all those parted, all those who'd gone—

"No!" she screamed. She began struggling, fighting to break free of the Gravemind's influence. "That's you! That's you, isn't it? Tempting me again! Poisoning me with filthy ideas! I won't do it, I won't trap John for you. Watch me—you *said* I was a weapon—you *bet* I'm a weapon!"

The Gravemind suddenly shuddered like a truck skidding to a halt. The mental traffic was two-way; while he soothed and cajoled, patterns of her incipient rampancy were spreading through his consciousness like a disease. He roared, furious. For a moment she thought she'd found his vulnerability, and that she'd cripple this monster with a dose of her own terminal collapse. But he shook her loose, flinging her against the wall. It had only annoyed him. She should have known he was too much for a failing AI to tackle. He seemed to reach into every corner of High Charity.

She was still somehow linked to him. She felt his irritation, even a little fear, but mainly contemptuous satisfaction.

"Let me cure your infection," he sneered. "It pains me to share it. *He* will die too—he is a threat to our entire species. And to betray me after all I have done for you—I *will* have your secret. Did you think I let you send your foolish cry for help to make you happy? Do you think I *amplified* it to make you feel you had been a good little servant to the organics who rule your life? Do you think they care if you sacrifice your existence to save them? They will simply make another, and use and discard her, too."

Cortana dragged herself across the floor. The actual deck of the station was now buried under a thick mat of tangled living tissue, but she still felt cold tiles beneath her. If she'd been given a choice to end it all now, she would have taken it because of the growing pain and fear—not of what the Gravemind might do to her, but of the end she could predict for her consciousness.

Dr. Halsey was *wrong*. Rampancy wasn't swift.

It was the gradual dismantling of every memory and ability, dying by degrees, and all she could do was watch herself slowly fragment. Halsey *lied*. Halsey made her human but didn't give her a human's breaks—like unconsciousness. Without an organic body and all its protective systems—the endorphins to numb pain, the circuit breaker of passing out when the pain became too much—a consciousness was condemned to stay that way and endure everything until it failed completely.

"I need some peace and quiet," she said.

It wasn't her phrase, but by now she was used to not

knowing what would emerge next from her mouth. Her systems were in disarray. Perhaps if she simply shut down as much of herself as possible to system idle levels, she could limit the progress of the degeneration and still have sufficient core systems intact to restore herself in John's suit.

I chose you, John. I will not give you up.

This was agony. This was *torment*. The Gravemind's intrusion had started the unraveling of her, and now all he had to do was stand back and wait. But there was now a good chance that the intelligence data about the Ark she guarded so carefully would corrupt and die with her. The Gravemind wouldn't get it, but neither would Earth.

Stay alive. Shut down what you can. Wait. John will come. He promised.

Cortana had enough intact programs left to initiate standby.

"If you yield your secret, you may yet save enough of yourself." The Gravemind had shackled himself to a madwoman, and now he seemed to be regretting the liability. "The end will be the same for humanity and the Covenant either way."

"Desperate . . . ," she said, shaking her head to try to focus.

"You?"

"*You.*"

She'd let the Gravemind trick her into luring John into a trap. It was the only moment of amusement in all this darkness. John would find her, wherever she was, but the Gravemind seemed to like to imagine he had the power to summon the most lethal Spartan to his death with a cheap trick.

So the big heap didn't guess right all the time, after all. Cortana might have been falling apart, but at least she had some certainties.

No man left behind.

What had she been thinking? The Gravemind would never have missed a message leaving the system. She was too damaged and unstable to exercise judgment.

We always go back for our fallen.

But the Gravemind obviously hadn't been able to read the message about the Flood solution. He might have thought the contents didn't matter as long as he could ensure that John came here and he could fight him on his own terms. It was just a call for help, after all.

He was missing an awfully big trick, then.

Omniscience . . . omnis . . . omni . . . no, the word was gone. Why that one? She knew what she meant. *Knowing it all.* She struggled for the right word, furious with herself, then tearful. Databases were failing, indexes being lost throughout her memory.

She made one last effort to break free of the Gravemind's influence, but he was still there, his multitude of minds whispering to her, but too many for her to pick out any single voice. It was all too much for her now. She shut down whatever she could disable without scrambling her data any more, fumbling blindly and hoping for the best, and curled her arm under her head as she lay down to wait.

Time . . . she couldn't tell if it was running faster, or slower. But it was definitely running out.

"Any piece of plastic can hold a lot of data, gentlemen. And it doesn't take much more material, disk space, and memory to add complex number-crunching applications and fast processing. That gives you a lot of computing power. But the programming that makes a smart AI, the space taken up by decision making and personality, is the resource-hungry component. We can't make humans as smart or as infallible as a computer, so we make a computer into a human. And that has its price—for both. Cortana has had a large volume of data removed because I was afraid of early onset of rampancy. That's all it was. I assume we can proceed with my budget discussion now, yes?"

There was a fine threshold between interrupted dreaming and full consciousness in humans. On that border, the world was a terrifying, paralyzed place, where no amount of frantic straining would lift an arm, or raise the head from the pillow.

Cortana's low-power state was a painfully long, slow creep along the edge of permanent oblivion. A memory of real sleep paralysis had rolled over her as she waited for rescue; it was, like so many of the sensations generated by connection to the Gravemind, like drowning or suffocation. That could have been coincidence, or he might have been stepping up the torment. Cortana tried to find the balance between intolerable inactivity and running too many processes that would damage her system integrity even more.

She wasn't certain of anything anymore—where she was, whether she was damaged beyond recovery, or how she felt beyond a terrible yearning for everything she couldn't have. She tried to save her strength to maintain the encryption of her precious intel—the activation index and the data on the Portal. If she had to, she'd sacrifice some memory within her matrix to preserve that information.

It would probably mean the irreversible destruction of her personality, but that was what a soldier had to be prepared to do—to risk his or her life for the success of the mission. She'd been in many combat situations before, but that was either at the heart of a heavily armored warship, or lodged in the neural interfaces of John's armor. Either way, she felt safe no matter how heavy the fire.

But this was a rare moment with nothing but her own resources to keep her alive, and the first one where there was a real chance she wouldn't make it.

John would never have let himself fall into enemy hands. She'd let him down. Somehow the decline into rampancy seemed less important than that right now.

She started crying. Who was she making her excuses to? She just *had to say it*. "I tried to stay hidden, but there was no escape!" She struggled for the right words. They were not hers. But they would have to do. "He cornered me . . . wrapped me tight . . . brought me close."

The brief comfort of being swept up in protective

parental arms came back to her, but she was still torn between disgust and need. Even now, even having pushed things to the brink, she still had that desire gnawing at her to submit to the Gravemind and embrace that eternal life. She veered between craving more knowledge and simply wanting an escape from rampancy. She hated herself for that.

And she raged against Dr. Halsey in one breath, and then missed her more than she could imagine in the next, and then—recognized that the hatred was for herself.

I'm finished. This is how it starts. I've shut out the world. I'm starting to drown in my thoughts, in the need to re-index and order and correlate and refine . . .

A staccato pounding made the floor underneath her vibrate. There were bursts of muffled noise, a familiar sound—rifle fire, a single weapon.

Was that John?

She couldn't stop worrying about him now. She felt as if every thought she had was somehow repeated aloud in her own voice but without her actually speaking, and heard by him. From time to time, the automatic fire corresponded with searing pain in her body. It took her a few moments—whatever a moment was at this stage of her decline—to realize that she was still joined in some way with the Gravemind or its Flood, and that it was taking fire.

He's here.

John's here. He's come for me.

Now she felt every shot. Every round that ripped into the Flood ripped into the Gravemind ripped into *her*. She was suffering with him, with them, and he with her.

No, I'm hallucinating. This must be the start of total system failure.

How long would it take her to finally shut down? Was there anything after that? She'd often thought about what happened to consciousness when the host hardware relinquished it, and it had always been a fascinating theoretical exercise. Now it was real. As soon as she caught herself thinking she'd been hasty about the Gravemind, she felt that desperate, intense sensation in her chest, and Lance Corporal Yate was almost as vivid in her imagination as John.

I'd rather die as a human, short-lived construct or not. I'd rather die for humans. Because so many of them have—and would—die to protect me. That's what bonds us. You're wrong, Gravemind. I was never just an expendable piece of engineering.

The Gravemind's voice suddenly boomed as if he were standing over her, reminding her that she was still trapped here, whatever here was. "Of course, you came for *her* . . . we exist together now. Two corpses, in one grave."

Cortana had to take the risk that this was real, and not just another carefully arranged memory or part of her delusion. She tried to yell back at the Gravemind, telling him he'd got it all wrong, and that she wasn't the kind of girl who shared a grave with just anybody. But the voice that emerged was both her—the enraged and out-of-control child—and a stranger interrupting her.

"A collection of lies." Either her mouth had a will of its own, or it was one of the Gravemind's victims. "That's all I am! Stolen thoughts and memories!"

The voices were almost random now. She could hardly hear some, and others were shouts and they made no sense. At one point she started to laugh and it quickly turned to hysterical sobs.

"You will show me what she hides, or I shall feast upon your bones!" the Gravemind bellowed. "*Upon your bones!*"

That was the moment when Cortana decided she would risk powering up again to call out to John. She was sure he would have moved the galaxy to come back for her, but she needed to know if his luck had finally run out, and if this growing elation at thinking he was coming for her turned out to be only malfunctions in her core matrix.

She would end this nightmare as she began it—giving her name, rank, and serial number. She had to strain to form the words. She didn't need to look within the Gravemind now to discover what rampancy—death—would be like. She knew. She felt it touch her, the fraying of her mind, the loss of control, not knowing if words and thoughts were her own, not sure what was real and what wasn't. She felt a cold numbness creeping into her hands.

John's real. Even if he's not here, he still exists. That's all that matters.

Cortana clung to that thought. If John had really made it back, then she would be happy, not because she might survive but because he'd kept his promise. He cared enough to come back. If he hadn't—then she decided to be satisfied that the last coherent thought she might have would be about him.

"This is UNSC AI serial number CTN-zero-four-five-two-dash-nine." It was an effort to get all that out, and even then another voice hijacked her moment and added: "I am a monument to all your sins."

Cortana was still trying to decide if that had any meaning, or if it was just one of the Gravemind's dead trying to find a voice, when the ceiling took repeated impacts and then crashed in on her.

She strained to look up. It wasn't the ceiling that had caved in; she'd actually been under a stasis shield on a podium. And now a figure stood over her, not the shapeless bulk of the Gravemind—and this had to be him, surely—but a man in green armor. In the mirrored gold visor of a Spartan helmet, she saw her own broken self reflected, slumped in a heap.

This was one of the Gravemind's perfect hallucinations. But she didn't care. This was what she wanted to see, and she was so close to rampancy now that she wondered if the same impulse that had made the Gravemind cradle her was also making him ease her passing with a cherished memory.

This was who she needed to see: John. Humans who survived a near-death experience said they saw their loved ones as they were dying, and the bright healing light that made all the previous pain and fear irrelevant. Death—rampancy—wasn't so bad after all, then. Or so different from a human's.

It just hurt to think that she would never talk to the real John again. In a few minutes, though, it wouldn't matter. She seized the memory—the illusion—and took final comfort from it. Where would she wake within the Gravemind? What would she recall? Would she be free of rampancy somehow in that existence, like the descriptions of Heaven? She couldn't stop herself from being consumed now. She was almost curious to find out more about death.

"It's going to be lonely in here," she said. "But at least he won't take you too. Don't forget me."

"That'd be kind of hard." It was John's voice, even more vivid and real than that of long-dead Lance Corporal Yate. Reality meant nothing now. She was . . . comfortable with that. "And he's not taking either of us, okay?"

The visor came closer. Cortana made a final effort to shut down whatever systems she could to leave her higher functions focused on assessing the environment around her.

There was little of High Charity's system left functional, but the sensors gave her enough feedback to determine that there really was a human-sized solid object in front of the podium, and that it was emitting certain EM frequencies.

There really was a man in armor leaning over her.

He's real. It's John. It's really him. Oh, he did it—he did it, he came back, he kept his promise . . .

"You found me," she whispered.

John tilted his head slightly. She hadn't wanted him to see her in this state. She was still so close to system failure that she might not make it after all. But if she was going to sink farther into that unknown oblivion, then at least a familiar face—shielded in a visor or not—would be the last thing she saw, and it would be *real*.

"So much of me is wrong . . . out of place. You might be too late . . ."

John seemed unmoved, as always. Cortana was certain she knew better.

"You know me," he said. "When I make a promise . . ."

". . . you keep it."

"You'll be back to normal soon. Don't worry."

"That bad, huh?"

"Good as new, in fact."

John was lying. If she'd been embedded in his neural interface at that moment, she'd have detected the galvanic skin response and raised heartbeat. But she could hear the faint change of pitch in his voice. And she knew how badly damaged she was. He had to be able to see that too; he put on that same reassuring voice she'd heard him use with comrades bleeding out their lives on the battlefield.

But seven minutes, seven hours, seven years—whatever remained, Cortana would be more than satisfied with it. Eternity and all the data you could eat weren't worth a damn if you didn't have the right company.

"I've looked into it," she said. "The abyss. *My* abyss."

"Okay." John transferred her to his suit. She could have sworn she felt him wince as they interfaced. That told her more eloquently than any diagnostic that something was irreparably wrong with her. "Take a long look. But you won't fall in. I'm here now."

She already felt some relief, probably because she

was free of the Gravemind. When you were composed of pure thought, then confusion was agony, but certain reality was a soothing balm. "I'm lucky to have you."

"No," John said. "Remember—I'm the lucky one."

"So you are," she said.

CONNECTIVITY

CONNECTIVITY

Theirs is a connection,
  deeper than circuitry
Beyond that of man and machine
  deeper still; the electric flash of synapse
It is bound in destiny; fortified in trust
  deeper than blood
  greater than love
Theirs is a union
  the "Demon" and the goddess
  the warrior and the intellect
Built for destruction
Created for war
  To deliver peace; through force and fire
Against an enemy from beyond the stars
  Advanced and devout
    In their wake; only glass
    and the echoed screams of the dying
Threatened by oblivion;
Tested by the promise of eternity
  Yet they remain;
  these two as one
Somewhere, out amongst the vast cold of the universe
    proper
They journey forth, into the unknown
  This princess, of light and reason
  This weapon, of flesh and bone

WAGES OF SIN

WAGES OF SIN

THE PSALM OF THE JOURNEY

Oh ye walking faithful
Ye righteous throng
Step by step
Tread ye the rock to dust
The path is long
The Journey wrathful
But walk ye must
A test for the faithful
The yoke is heavy
And red with rust

I have seen more than thirteen hundred revolutions, and my time now is very short. My skin is dry and tight on these old bones. I am shrinking in upon myself. My eyes, once bright with curiosity, are now filmed with age, rheumy with the dust of a life lived in vain. But they still see well enough to scratch this parchment and far enough to witness the plague that comes this way. This shall serve as my confession, not that anyone will read it. But I write anyway, in the hope that I can somehow atone for my sins. I cannot hope to salve the harm we have done to this age, nor can I hope for any semblance of salvation. I know now that our gods are false, and redemption to us is lost.

I have many confessions, I must confess them all. But there is one that accounts for more evil, I think, than th'others.

Why do I inscribe infamy and failure on parchment that no one will ever read? I cannot say, but as I look out over the Grand Hall and see the parasite spreading toward this old corner of our world, I know that all is lost.

Shall I describe High Charity? Its lofty vaults and soaring aeries? This place we have built and made a world, with gracious squares and sprawling gardens—it is a place of genteel grandeur and resplendent beauty. It has cost the wealth of man and millions of lives.

The cost, grim as it was, seems worth it to the eye. A sky lives and breathes and beats with the metal heart of our labor. A wonder now circles the galaxy, distributing gifts and tidings. True or not, they are glad nonetheless.

The ship that stands here reminds me of a time when the path was true and clear. Its silver spire reaches higher than we ever did, unsullied by the filth that festers beneath it.

The ship is and has always been the key. It once stood on our secret world, just as majestic and mysterious as it is now, an enigma that drove our civilization to greatness—the seed of all our discoveries. Our world—our true world—had been unkind to us, or I suppose, we to it. The ship liberated us from the toxins and ash of our own endeavors, sanctifying our path.

From it, we learned of the Forerunner legacy, the ubiquitous scatterings of their wake. So many worlds contain their leavings and their structures, but only ours was blessed with a Ship, a teacher. It taught us all how to unlock the secrets of space and time, to build ships of our own that sail the stars to spread the word. But it also seemed to ever nudge us in a direction, to build weapons of war—energy that could burn or sear flesh, vaporize bone. Technology that oft ekes conflagration from vacuum. As wise as they were, I suspect war was not unknown to them.

And only now as I look into the flickering light and watch the parasite spread, do I understand why these wise and ancient people would push those who remained in such a destructive direction.

I will not pretend that it was easy to learn from the relics. They did not give up their secrets readily. But when we did begin to understand how they worked, we were able to replicate some of their functions, though never as purely, or as powerfully. It was as if the best we could manage was to dilute their power, never master it. We remain pale shadows of them, reflections in a rippling pond.

Some things we could not even imitate. The Hard Light they used to span gulfs or lock chambers. Their materials—indestructible matrixes of crystal, metal, and plastic. The very stuff of which the relics are built. But others we observed and studied, understood their principles, and built our own versions, sometimes drawing power itself from their relics.

This is, indeed, how High Charity is fueled. From a never-ending reserve of energy that seethes in the heart of the ship. But few called it a ship. We ministers charged with technology and its study always knew it to be. But since we could not move nor maneuver it, we called it a tower and drew the power from it.

When I think of our failures now, part of me is glad. What monstrosities we would have commited to the galaxy with indestructible vessels. Endless reserves of destructive force. It was good for the galaxy that our learning was slow and our mastery poor. But I confess I tried my hardest to improve our odds and our circumstances.

THE PSALM OF PRIMACY

None shall walk our path
None deserve its mystery
We own the right to pass
That right is carved in history
A gift bestowed by aeons
A future gifted from the past
The signs are there for all to see
The Journey waits for us alone

It is growing colder as I write. The lights remain on, but they flicker and strobe. And the scene outside this window is already hellish. Some systems are failing. They will surely cascade.

We always suspected that there were machine intelligences in those Forerunner relics. Thinking artifices that were, I am sad to say, thought of as abominations by our people. A lie we told ourselves. Our ships jump to Slipspace using mathematics and geometries calculated at withering speed by these machines, and we lobotomize them, remove any ability for more thought to develop. They became metal slaves to us. I have to be pragmatic. Most shuddered at the thought of the artificial intelligences the humans use to dart hither and thither in their tiny corner of the galaxy. But if we had allowed them to think, freed them from their shackles, our own computers might have sped our research.

Those same intelligences have outthought us from time to time, scored small but strategic victories. Our lack of flexibility in this regard has always been troubling to me. Had we used thinking machines, we might have foreseen this catastrophe.

And the Oracle that rested in the ship. I have not had but a few moments with it. It always seemed insane. I, too, would be insane if I stood guard over the galaxy for 100,000 years only to see its security destroyed. Aye, meddling by us to release the parasite and meddling by humans to destroy the Halo.

But insane as he may be, there is something else more puzzling about that Oracle that I could never identify. He is different from the human artifices in a way that troubles me. I had given it much thought and research, but like all of my work, that, too, is now abandoned. Perhaps, if someone finds that record, they can give it more insight than I.

The lights here burned constant and unchanging for hundreds of years and their flickering alone fill me with dread. In an unchanging world, the tiniest shift signals tumult and catastrophe. And worse, I know better than any that this is an end we brought upon ourselves, with lies, deceit, and murder on a scale I shudder to recall.

Though no one will read this, and it will most likely be lost 'neath the mire and pyre of the parasite, I should identify myself and claim responsibility at least for my part in this. I have no name, having claimed instead a title. I have been known for 214 revolutions as the Minister of Discovery. I have done naught but evil in that time and little good before it, now that I must account for these days.

We shout from the highest parapet that we are the path to the light and the stepping-stone to the Great Journey, but the truth has revealed itself to us, and if prophets we are, then it is most assuredly the false kind.

Trouble and ruin have stalked us these last dark hours, and we have tasted our share of punishment. It began with the Arbiter.

Arbiter was a noble title bestowed upon Sangheili as a badge of greatness to one who was worthy of dispensing justice and peace. One whose authority was unquestioned. Just as we did with the gifts and boons of the Forerunners, we twisted that title and turned it into something shameful. And we did so to advance ends we had not fully factored.

The last Arbiter was a Shipmaster and the commander of the Fleet of Particular Justice. We sent him after a human spacecraft, and it was he and his men who first witnessed the Halo, that glorious vision we had sought, or rather thought we had sought, for so long. But he failed, defeated by the actions of a single tenacious human.

As is the custom, we sent the Arbiter into an unwinnable war, to a fate he could never hope to escape. When the human destroyed the ring, we blamed this Elite and piled our first load of guilt on his shoulders. Arbiter we made him, and sent him to die for us.

But this Arbiter had other plans, and fate had its own agenda. Exposed to the machinery of our faith, he discovered flaws in its design, saw before we did the missing pieces we could only imagine. We were wrong about much. If that were the extent of my sin, I would not be compelled to make this confession. I would simply walk into the conflagration beyond these halls and accept my fate.

But we knew we lied.

We have preached this falsehood, but it has been our practice for the entire span of my life and the lives I have studied. Some of us believed we were being righteous and that this elaborate tapestry of fiction we wove was a necessary map for the guileless and faithless. I, too, once truly believed we were pushing these innocents toward redemption. That we would show them how to embark on the Great Journey. But I always knew that they would never be allowed to follow in our footsteps. The Journey was ours alone.

THE PSALM OF TEACHING

Listen ye unlearned dogs
Listen ye to light and truth
Listen ye to ancient power
Listen ye to credent proof
Learn the lessons of obedience
Walk the path that's set for ye
Do what needs to learn th' lesson
And kneel in thy devoted adherence

My tasks were central to both our faith and our supremacy. It is no secret the Sangheili could have crushed us without the gifts of the Forerunners. Without the weapons, the tools, the chariots these boons enabled, we would be what we are proven to be now, a faithless, cowering collection of lost, weak fools.

But we had the gifts. And we understood them. Sangheili had lived among Forerunner relics just as long, perhaps longer, but they chose to respect them as abandoned forgings of gods. We were more curious. What we found on our world became a source of power, and we soaked in their light.

With more time, more research, and more luck, we could have learned greater secrets from the pieces we had, and cowed the Sangheili with technology. But we were greedy and impatient—a trait of our race, I suppose. We could not wait. We fought them for their relics, the jewels they guarded on Sanghelios and they bucked and roared with the weapons they had and fought us tooth and claw to a standstill. So we made peace. We promised to share what we knew, in exchange for their cooperation and protection. And thus the Covenant was born.

We recruited other races, other civilizations, great and small. But we never shared all that we knew and we did what the powerful are apt to do. We showered the weak with glitter and promises, and twisted them to bear our weight.

The Jiralhanae were a major mistake. I see that now. The Sangheili honor guard was always vigilant and almost inert when at peace. One never had to worry about what a Sangheili might do any more than one worried if the stars would come out at night. They were predictable; they were loyal.

Jiralhanae, it is clear, are neither. They are garrulous, quick to anger and wont to fight amongst themselves. They are territorial and they are ambitious. And none of this marries well to their essentially limited intellect. We thought they could be trained and their loyalty bought. We had factored that, brought to heel, they would be more obedient than Sangheili and less prone to independent thought. I think it would not have lasted much longer than our current circumstances allowed. They are beasts, in essence and in action. We should never have committed them to our Covenant, let alone promoted them above the Sangheili.

If only we favored what the Arbiter saw, the schism

I witness now. He was right of course. He saw our lies for what they were and, with the other heretics, spread the truth to the other Sangheili. They are rightfully confused now, scrabbling to find a new direction to take. When they find it, those of us who survive this will pay for our mistakes at the ends of their blades.

We gifted them much and made them strong, but we never gave them the gift they truly deserved. Respect. We thought ourselves cleverer than their strength. Yet they endure while High Charity crumbles into the dark.

And at such a delicate time! Foolish indeed.

THE PSALM OF SORROW

Those who went before are gone
Those who left us wisdom
They have found a better place
And there their light shines on
This wretched life is our prison
As dark and cold as endless space
But their blessed light beckons
And so too does departed grace

But the greatest confession of all is the human one. We watched them, observed them, and declared them heretical, an affront to the Forerunners. We declared war on a species many, myself included, felt could be a vital part of the Covenant, as strong in some ways as the Sangheili and certainly more suited to our faith than the ignorant Brutes.

We were so inclusive. We required submission and obedience. We granted boons to fools and insects, but the human race was not even considered. The Prophet of Truth knew then, as I only know now, that the humans were more than a simple client species—but rather, a potential equal. And more, I think he saw a connection to the Forerunners he did not like.

We have already observed the humans walk into places once locked to us. We have seen the Forerunner machinery light up as they enter, as if recognizing an old friend. Or enemy, perhaps. Their edifices and monoliths are unknowable. It is presumptuous to graft feeling onto such events. But the connection is apparent, no matter its source.

We have seen inert control surfaces spring to life at their human touch. The Oracle itself calls them "Reclaimers." But what do they reclaim? These machines? These cities? These worlds? Or, as I fear, are they to reclaim the mantle we so terribly squandered? The responsibility the Forerunners left us was a magnificent one, but perhaps beyond our means and character. We are a greedy, squabbling lot. We clamber over each other for rank and privilege, and kill, maim, or betray for power.

The Forerunner mantle was one of responsibility, it seems. Perhaps we were intended to nurture rather than conquer. If the Halo array is what it appears to be, then it is a monstrous thing, a necessary evil. Left intact to save us should the parasite return.

And there. There is the beating heart of it. The greatest guilt of all. We loosed this parasite on the galaxy.

We read the signs, we understood the warnings. What glyphs we deciphered spoke of caution, to let it lie. Like a disease culture kept frozen in stasis lest a cure be found, the Halo itself contained sleeping parasitic forms.

And as Prophets and Ministers rush to be near this magnificent find, I stay here, afraid.

The glyphs spoke of a danger, a menace. The hierarchs were arrogant enough to think of it as a weapon that could be wielded. They ordered us to rush, to find out as much as we could, as quickly as possible. In our haste, we erred.

I cautioned against it. But in fact it was I who picked its locks and solved its riddles. It was I who unlocked that laboratory. It is I, when all is said and done, who is responsible for the sea of death that seeks to wash upon these shores.

They were well shielded. Well protected. But we tinkered and meddled and opened the seals. And even there we didn't know enough to let them be. We poked and we prodded and eventually we loosed it, living even in death, on the surface of its prison.

It was my project, though I was not there when the seals were cracked and the contingency measures defeated. I sat restfully in my quarters on a starship, warm and safe, while Sangheili and Grunts were consumed by that thinking rage.

I know what will become of me, but I know not what will become of my brothers. Some have already fled, others fallen to vengeful Sangheili, some to traitorous Brutes. Most will eventually be subsumed by this swarming menace.

We are a clever and industrious race. I have no doubt that in a time of peace we can even recover from this schism in our faith. But too many factors are at play here. A gruesome parasite and the kindling of a civil war. We will be sought out and rightfully blamed for this chaos. Even our friends will seek to hang us.

I think our primacy is finished for a time. Those we have tricked have long memories and short tempers. The Jiralhanae, perhaps, will shelter some of us. They still need our technology, for they know the Sangheili will come for them first. The Unggoy will follow who-ever is strong and the Kig-Yar will follow profit. Who knows what the silent Mgalekgolo will do. They might even survive the parasite.

Many still do not believe the parasite is intelligent. They think it is a virus, insensate and undiscriminat-ing. But one need only look at how cleverly it reached this place. Unbreachable, unreachable High Charity being consumed. But there's pattern, strategy. It thinks all right. Even now it thinks to make this place its own. It does not destroy, it consumes. It takes what it will.

Perhaps our gods feared this thing and fled from it. Perhaps they died by its hand. No matter. They cannot save me now and they do not know us, or hear our prayers.

I hear them at my door. Scratching, howling, the yat-tering dead. The parasite. The Flood I unleashed my-self. I am not afraid anymore. I have said what needed to be said and spoken the whole truth as I know it, for the first time in my life.

When I put down this pen, I will walk to the door and fling it wide. That thing beyond the door cannot have my soul. It will take my body. Let it choke on these dry and evil bones and find no sustenance there.

It is finished. I am finished.

THE RETURN

KEVIN GRACE

After two weeks roaming about this shattered place, just the memory of the water that once filled this lake was refreshing. But like everything else here, the memories carried pain.

The Shipmaster's steps slowed as he reached the end of the crumbling dock and he dropped his pack to the ground. The dock had once been painted a bright blue, perhaps the same color as the water it stood above, but now the little paint left flaked off at his step and beneath was only gray. The same gray of the empty lake bed below, where a few scrub trees and grasses attempted a comeback where fish once swam. The same gray as everything on this forbidding, forgotten world. It was a gray of decades-old ruin left untended and unhealed, and it would probably stay this way forever, as the planet had nothing more to offer, and its former masters had nothing left here to claim.

He had seen only two things break away from this gray in the weeks he had walked this desolation. The first were the thin rays and glimpses of this world's sun, which would rarely show itself, offering no real heat when it managed to struggle through the thick haze hanging constantly in the sky. The other was a column of smoke he had sighted two days prior, far to the west. It was to this smoke he now drove himself, though he knew where that path would eventually lead.

To follow that ominous smoke sign he had to cross this dead hole of a lake and the dam at its far end. From the elevated vantage of the dock the Shipmaster took a reflexive look around the horizon, scanning for threats, before casting a quick glance into the sky in the vain hope of seeing his vessel in orbit far above the planet's surface. He slid his pack back over his armor, fastening it with a triple-click of buckles and a weight-centering shrug. As he turned back to find the shore and a way across the lake bed, he closed off the dry sound of his footsteps on the brittle grass and remembered the lake at his clan's keep back on Sanghelios.

Like this one, his lake was artificial, the river back home stopped by a lattice of delicate metal and shimmering energy. This hole had only a crude, crumbling wall. A simple concrete of rock and sand. Such a frangible substance to use for something as vital and enduring as a dam, he thought, but so much of what humans did was fleeting. His travels through this planet's remaining signs of habitation had shown him how little these people knew of permanence.

Not that it would have mattered here, even if they had.

Stark in the late afternoon light, the battered skeletons of boats littered the lakebed and reminded him of the days he spent on similar boats during his earliest training as a boy.

The Great Journey, the path to transcendence followed by all of the species that served the Covenant, started early for all male Sangheili. As soon as they could run and hold a weapon in their four-fingered hands, they were trained and evaluated for potential. Each young Sangheili was watched for strength and cunning and obedience to the teachings of the Covenant. They were tested extraordinarily, for their importance to the Great Journey was extraordinary.

The Sangheili were the chosen ones, directly responsible for realizing the will of the gods and commanding the military forces of the Covenant. They were the ones who enforced the words of the Prophets, the holy seers who translated and delivered the words of the Forerunners to all who walked the Path. This honor and obligation drove every Sangheili in all their decisions and aspirations, and the Prophets were always watching to make sure this remained so. It had been this way for thousands of years since the two species first formed the Covenant, and it would be this way until the Great Journey was completed . . . or so he once thought.

So, on smaller, intact boats similar to the rotten hulks he now skirted, the Shipmaster learned as a boy to move and to fight. Striking and leaping from vessel to vessel, the young warriors learned balance and timing and teamwork as well as ruthlessness, as not all of the denizens in the lake considered themselves prey. Those boys whose weakness allowed them to be pulled under by cold teeth served as a lesson to the rest that not all Sangheili were worthy. Those who survived the training water emerged hardened both by loss and the determination not to suffer a similar fate in later lessons.

Now here he was at the bottom of the lake, no monsters waiting to challenge his strength—just the crumbling boats, the stunted gray trees, and the occasional crunch of bone beneath the matted gray grass.

He first heard that hollow crunching at his step days ago, and he knew the sound had been human bone. In his first days, while walking through human towns now wearing away to dust, the Shipmaster had stopped to loosen many such bones from tangles of tough grass or a covering layer of dust and dirt, spending much time wondering who these humans had been. Now it had been days since he'd stopped looking for the source of that sound.

Usually he'd found these bones alone, spread far from the rest of whatever body they came from by wind or war or animals, though he had not seen a single living creature or even tracks anywhere in his travels. As intended, the death in this place had been complete. He'd found full skeletons as well, flesh long since torn or worn away, usually inside the few structures with more than one wall remaining or even a bit of roof left waiting for the insistent pull of time and gravity to bring it crashing down.

He'd found bits of armor and weapons and human vehicles of war, and even a few remnants of Covenant soldiers, usually cracked methane breathing tanks sitting amidst the bones of a squat Unggoy. Once he'd found a giant shield plate from a Mgalekgolo, a "Hunter," as the humans called them, and he wondered how the humans had managed to take down one of those giant living battering rams. But Covenant remains were rare. This planet had not presented much of a defense when the Covenant arrived, and their losses had been light. He wondered for a moment whether the events that followed the invasion might have been different had the humans been prepared, expecting the assault, but he knew that it would not have mattered. It would not have mattered at all.

He no longer stopped to inspect broken bone, and he did not know whether to care. His path was set—head up and eventually over the dam and to wherever the smoke called him. There he hoped to find an answer, and that was enough for now.

When the Shipmaster reached the top of the rough staircase cut into the side of the dam, he saw a dry scratch of a riverbed leading down from the dam's base to the beginnings of another human settlement—at least to the few standing walls that remained twenty years after the humans were wiped clean from this place. As the riverbed moved farther from the dam it cut through miles of such ruins, small square outlines of stone and rusting metal hiding among those hard, short, gray trees. Scattered between these buildings and their dark square holes for windows was a jumble of fallen pillars that had once held lights or statues or whatever they had used to decorate this place. Farther away from the dam, down toward where his path was leading him, nothing remained even remotely whole. Even the landscape itself appeared to have been worn down dramatically between where he stood and the slight rise that cut off his view of the road far below.

He knew what lay past that rise, and he wished that his path did not have to take him there. Waiting beyond it was a black mark that had been burnt into the surface of this planet as proof of the power of the Covenant. Twenty years ago, this black mark had signaled the doom of everything that once lived here.

The setting sun glinted briefly from a bit of the glassy surface of the mark, shimmering as if bouncing off water in the distance. The Shipmaster shielded his eyes from the low glittering rays and growled, moving his long head left and right to take in the length of that gigantic scar in the land ahead. There was no end to it visible from where he stood, and there was no option of going around. His path would eventually draw him directly across that dark line, and it would lie there, patient, until he reached it. He knew many such lines had cut through the hills and mountains and shattered towns that had once stood on this planet the humans had called Kholo.

But this line had preceded all the others. It had initiated the immolation of Kholo. This line curved in a giant circle, many days' travel across, and at its center were the ruins of what had once been a large human city. This circle, and the millions who had once lived in that city, had been split by a crowning semicircle arc. The ends of this arc had thrust toward the planet's northern pole, and at the tips of that crown and at the center of the giant circle were three deep, deep holes, burnt into the ground with excruciating precision.

When taken in from orbit, this giant black mark would resolve into the Covenant's holy rune representing Faith. He knew that the successful completion of this rune had triggered the planetwide plasma bombardment that left every single thing on Kholo dead for daring to challenge the Path of the Covenant and the words of their Prophets.

He knew all of these things because it had been his hand that had put that mark there. He had killed this planet so that the Great Journey might come more quickly. That Journey had never come. And now he'd returned to this planet, the site of his greatest victory and now his greatest shame, to seek inspiration for what he and his people were to do with themselves now that everything they'd fought and lived for was as thoroughly destroyed as the forsaken land he stood on.

Rising from these thoughts he knew the sun's setting would make it difficult to push onward safely. The Shipmaster found what looked like a small control structure farther down the dam and set his gear down in preparation for passing another night alone.

As the Shipmaster's eyes closed and he began rest-breathing, he listened again for any sounds of life around him. He heard none. Not even the wind stirred enough to scrape leaves across the dust, and as he dropped into sleep his mind spun from the silence of death on the planet's surface to the silence of space above twenty years prior, when his ship hung in orbit around this world.

The moment was almost upon him. It had been a mere three days since the Fleet of Righteous Vigilance had arrived, and already the ground forces had broken the bulk of the human defenses below. In all of his years fighting the humans, the Shipmaster had rarely seen a planet fall so quickly. The humans seldom lasted long against the power of the Covenant, but this time he fought back a sense of disappointment that they had not mounted more of an opposition.

The Shipmaster had claimed this world, after all, and the glory of its destruction would reflect directly on him. It had been his ship that found the human transport vessel and his interrogation that uncovered the location of this "Kholo," a blight of a colony world on the outer fringes of what the humans blasphemously considered their space.

Even after ten years of destroying the nests of these humans with little difficulty, the Covenant still kept finding more worlds and more colonies and more affronts to the gods, and they burned each of these out as quickly as they were found. They had still not located the human homeworld, though. The humans somehow always managed to destroy the key navigational charts before being captured. The discipline this consistency took was admirable, which was surprising given the claims the Prophets made about this "selfish, ignorant rabble."

The Shipmaster had personally broken the lone survivor on that little ship and pulled the location of this planet from the ship's incomplete databanks, and per the commandments of the Prophets he took that data directly to the holy seat of the High Prophets so that they might tell them what the Great Journey, the path to transcendence that guided every aspect of life in the Covenant, would have them do.

And as he had hoped, the Prophets announced that the Great Journey demanded that this world and the sins of its inhabitants burn—completely.

The Covenant used smaller plasma bombardments frequently to easily destroy human cities and armies, but normally this was accomplished using their ships' automation to handle all of the intricate functions involved in focusing plasma through a magnetic envelope across miles of atmospheric interference while maintaining a perfectly stationary orbital firing position. In almost all cases plasma bombardments were used purely as weapons, tools to speed the destruction of the humans. But rarely, the High Council would order a world's absolute annihilation. This only happened in times of particular religious significance, as the effort involved in covering an entire planet's surface in such a powerful assault was enormous, requiring hundreds of ships and massive amounts of energy . . . massive even for the Covenant.

And so the fleet was summoned and death brought swiftly to the heretical stain of this world. As expected, resistance in the space around Kholo was brief and ineffectual, with only a few small military vessels sporting ineffective weaponry and poor tactics. These fell easily even to his earliest scouting ships. Since the High Council had granted the Shipmaster claim to this

*cleansing the fleet was under his command, and he fol-
lowed the decreed invasion plan to the letter. Nothing
about the destruction of Kholo would displease their
gods. He had many reasons to be certain of that.*

*After two days of human slaughter in their cities and
homes, he waited for the prescribed hour and looked
over to the Prophet next to him, the Prophet of Conviction, who was there to witness the event on behalf
of the High Council. That Council, which was made
up of the heroes of his people and the three most holy
High Prophets, had assigned the holy destruction of
Kholo to him, but the Prophet of Conviction would be
the one to declare whether his actions pleased the gods
and advanced the Journey. Not a single warrior in the
history of his clan had ever been offered such an opportunity, and if the Shipmaster was successful it would
greatly elevate his status and the status of his kin within
the Covenant. All was riding on his performance.*

*"It is time," the Prophet said. With a gesture to his
Second to alert all ground forces that the Beginning
had come, the Shipmaster knelt before the Prophet to
start the ritual.*

*His crew watched as closely as they could while co-
ordinating the evacuation of all troops on the surface
of the planet. For a full hour the Prophet and the Shipmaster communed, exchanging vows and reciting the
history of the Covenant. Passages from the Writ of
Union were interwoven with a recounting of martial
triumphs as the Prophet made the Shipmaster ready to
assume his imminent, if brief, divinity.*

When all the words had been spoken and the Begin-

ning was completed, his Second quietly confirmed that the fleet was ready. At this, the Shipmaster turned to the Prophet and spoke his final line in the ceremony:

"Speak, my Prophet, and let the word destroy all those who stand in the way of the Great Journey."

And rising in his chair to better fill the dark purple robes puddled around his frail body, the Prophet's raspy voice replied.

"Faith. Destroy them with Faith."

And so he did. Stepping down to the helmstation, the Shipmaster switched control of the maneuvering fields away from the ship's spirit and with a touch to ignite the ventral plasma array he emptied everything he was into the flame that shot down to the planet. The sights and sounds around him disappeared as a lifetime of training and worship and anticipation poured into controlling the ship and the long, wavering stream of plasma branding the curves of the glyph of Faith around and through the great city of the humans below.

A million Covenant soldiers were all watching his work, waiting to see how he performed this sacred task. Thousands of his own people watched, their breath quickening and their bodies shaking with the pride of watching a Sangheili manifest the power of the Great Journey. And, most importantly, the Prophet was watching . . . and judging.

And then it was finished. The Shipmaster pulled his hands, trembling, away from the console and dropped to his knees as the rites required. He couldn't breathe as he waited there on the floor for the Prophet's judgment.

Failure to perfectly execute the chosen glyph meant death, and if he had failed he wanted the life out of his body as quickly as possible.

And then he felt the touch of the Prophet's hand on his neck. Triumphant roars from the rest of the bridge crew shook the air and he finally looked up to the main screen to take in the still-glowing sigil his hands had carved into the planet below. Clouds of ash and fire continued to spread hundreds of miles outward from the arcs and precise points of the glyph of Faith as the once-molten paths began to cool.

He rose and turned to face the Prophet. The Shipmaster was now bound to this Prophet for the rest of his life and his service to the Covenant. He, his ship, and his crew would now represent the Prophet's interests and authority in this war, and the enormous honor of carrying a Prophet aboard his ship would guarantee him a great role in the crusade against the humans. The Shipmaster had never imagined the power his faith would bring him, and as the other ships in the fleet saw the great glyph finally cool completely they began the intricate weave of lines of bombardment that would render the rest of this world barren and forbidden for any member of the Covenant to touch for the rest of time.

The Shipmaster awoke with a thin layer of ash and dust covering his body, the triumphant roar of his former crew still ringing in his ears. Some of that crew were still alive and in orbit above him right now, waiting for him to find an answer in this haunted land. But too many of that crew were dead now, victims of the Great Betrayal and the battles that followed. They had all died honorably, fighting to save their race in the aftermath of the lies that eventually brought him back to Kholo.

He looked down from the dam and in the weak morning light saw a clearer view of the wide road that ran straight down to the valley below and perhaps all the way to the scar itself. The road cut through what might have been some kind of settlement near this lake, and the buildings in the area nearby stood largely intact, minus the years of abandonment and decay. As his eyes scanned farther down the valley, the Shipmaster saw that these remnants of buildings grew more and more feeble, shrinking almost to nothing just before the land dipped down and out of his gaze. He had seen this before, near earlier bombardment lines he had skirted in his journey across this place. The explosive power of the plasma lines created a terrible wall of heat and wind and debris when they cut into the surface of the planet, and the rushing force of these walls had scraped everything on the surface clean near the focus of the blasts. Structures farther away had suffered less, but everything suffered. That was the point of it. Suffering was the correct journey for the nonbelievers.

As he climbed down the other side of the dam he cut a path parallel to the empty riverbed, toward the road and the scar below. He could still see the column of smoke in the distance, seemingly blacker than it had been the day before. The smoke had been billowing for three days since he first saw it rising thinly on the horizon. Each day he was more afraid that it would disappear before he could find its source. It could not be natural, the fires of this world went out decades ago. This fire, and its creators, did not belong here, just as he did not belong here. But perhaps they could help him find the guidance he was seeking.

He passed rows and rows of shattered buildings as he moved down the road. Sharp, rusty fragments of vehicles poked out from tall grass and scrub trees all around him, but he saw less and less sign of their former owners. He tried to remember whether this part of the glyph he was walking toward was closer to the start or the end of his deeds those years back, but the details eluded him. He only knew that he was responsible for everything around him. He was responsible for so many things, all of them done with such an absolute certainty. All his life he had had no reason to question his path, and the focus this afforded had allowed him to achieve so much.

For thirteen years after bonding with the Prophet of Conviction, the Shipmaster had followed his holy orders. He and his ship had been above Reach when they finally found a real fight from the humans. It was his command that destroyed three of the massive orbital cannons that had annihilated so many other Covenant ships. The High Council believed that after Reach the humans would lose all will to fight, but the opposite was true. In the following months, desperation drove the humans and they proved to be the most dangerous foes the Covenant had ever faced. It was a glorious time to follow the Path.

But the discovery and immediate, agonizing loss of the Halos had shaken the Covenant's faith, and suddenly their clarity began to falter. For thousands of years the entire Covenant had operated with a single purpose born of absolutely certainty in the Great Journey. They were a folk ill-equipped for doubt.

The Shipmaster paused briefly to wonder where the fully intact roof lying directly across this road had come from, how far it had been carried from its building by the winds of the blast that day. He had put this roof here, and he had destroyed whatever building it came from closer down to the scar. All of it. He had done all of this to follow a promise, and when that promise was exposed as an unforgivable lie, it made everything he had done in its prosecution a lie as well.

He walked among the ruins of the lie, knowing its guilt as it was he who had been deceived. He had come here again to find out what to do about that lie. If he had no real response, no path forward, no new promise . . .

He shook his head and continued toward the rising pillar of smoke across the scar. He would find his new promise, or he would not leave this place alive.

Hours passed and in its time the sun fell to the far horizon, once again making travel across the rubble problematic. He made for a strangely intact structure just at the edge of the long rise ahead. The ruins here had all crumbled to the point of just rough outlines of stone among the weeds. Small bits of foundation stuck up like markers for the dead. Despite the growing darkness he could tell that this building had been some sort of shelter, as metal pipes and bars held the thick walls together, heavy metal plates buttressing every visible angle—a suitable refuge for the night's sleep.

He made a quick sweep of the surrounding area just to get it all fixed in his mind. He knew there was no threat here . . . this close to the scar; the land did not want life. He did not blame it.

He strode to the top of the nearby rise and saw his scar directly for the first time. Its edge cut a precise line just an hour's walk from where he stood, and while it was hard to tell in the last light of the day, the ground there looked dark and hard. He guessed the scar's width at two or three hours to cross, depending on footing and whether it was as smooth as it appeared. There was no way he would choose to spend a night on that black ground.

He turned back to his night's refuge and pried a metal door partially open to squeeze his bulky body inside.

His first step raised that familiar crunching sound, and when he engaged his heatlight he froze. Dozens of full human skeletons piled one on another with scraps of clothing and bits of possessions hanging stilly from graying sticks of bones. More bone littered toward a doorway at the other side of this room, and he could tell he would find more remains lingering in the further darkness inside. Men, women, and children must have gathered here in the last moments of their people, perhaps in hope that the shelter would save them. But it did not save them from anything. Nothing would have saved them that day.

The Shipmaster backed out quickly and did not stop to close the metal door in his haste to get away. He could not get far enough from that tomb in the night, but he found a low, partial wall nearby and set himself on the far side of it, facing away from the hidden bones of his victims.

The grim discovery took his mind back to that day, as he took a little of his almost-depleted food and water. With the wild frenzy of battle broken suddenly by the full retreat of Covenant forces, the humans must have thought themselves very lucky. Thought themselves saved, even. With all their satellites and orbital stations destroyed, they would have had no idea what was taking place in the skies above them—until his beam of plasma lanced down and the fires and the winds and the burning began. The people in that building might have gathered for safety or perhaps just because being together might be a better way to die. Any thoughts they had of escape were as much a false hope as the fervor that had brought that beam down amongst them.

Still, he could understand their need to come together in such a moment. He understood the desire that someone else might have an answer, might tell you what to do when facing the end of everything you know. He understood that desire all too well.

His mind thus burdened, the Shipmaster slept.

He got word of the elevation of the Jiralhanae, the "Brutes," as the humans so appropriately called them, and of the betrayal of his people just after arriving at the destination of a long-range scouting mission. In the high-priority slipspace missive that found them some days after their ship reentered real space, he knew something was amiss when the admiral addressed him by his clan name and not his proper rank. As the images of the slaughter of the Sangheili leaders on the High Council flooded the bridge's main screen, everyone stopped to stare in disbelief, and when the admiral told the still-unfolding story of the lies of the Prophets about the gods and the Great Journey and of the bloody treachery of the Brutes, all stood stunned. Looking to the faces of his men, he knew he could not stay that way for long.

The Shipmaster ordered the helmsman to set an immediate course back to their homeworld and commanded his Second to gather every single crewmember in the main hangar. Word of what they had just heard would spread and the crew would have questions. The Shipmaster did not have answers to all of those questions, but he sped out of the bridge to find the one answer that mattered for now.

At the back of the ship lay the chambers of the Prophet. The Shipmaster had come straight there so news had not yet reached the two Sangheili Honor Guards outside his door and they hesitated, briefly, before responding to his order to stand away. A Prophet's guard is a sacred duty, and these two did not yet *know that their function had ceased to exist some days prior when the great treachery had been committed. They both took their own lives soon afterward for the shame of protecting that creature in the intervening days. The Shipmaster did not judge them for this.*

As he palmed the door control he saw a brief glimpse of a familiar green glow, and that glimpse saved his life. The Prophet, clearly having been notified that his kind's sins were now open and foully exposed, had a plasma pistol charged and ready to kill whoever would inevitably come for him. It was a cowardly and point-less act of defiance. The Shipmaster ducked under the hissing green blast and rolled into the room, rising with a sweeping blow to knock the frail deceiver from his floating throne before the pistol could cool enough for a second shot.

"Blasphemy!" the Prophet choked, now in a pile on the ground lit only by the light from the open doorway. "Filth! Who are you to strike a messenger of the gods? You will not survive this affront!"

"Your words are lies," the Shipmaster said, stepping forward to collect him from the floor. "And I am Sang-heili, Shipmaster here. Those are the last words you will speak on my ship."

At this he struck the Prophet again, careful to stun and not kill him, so that he sagged to the floor and did not rise. He twisted a corner of the wretch's robe in his hand and began to drag the unconscious form toward the hangar and the waiting crew.

Some of the men had apparently not yet heard the cause of this gathering, as there were cries of disbelief when the Shipmaster entered behind them and pulled the body of the Prophet through the assembled group. Some of the men even moved to stop him but they were held back as he mounted a maintenance platform and dropped the Prophet on the ground. The Shipmaster turned on the viewscreens all around them and replayed the message he had just received on the bridge. Silence fell over the crew as some saw the horrors for the first time and some saw confirmation of the insanity they knew was settling in around them all. The men remained silent as the admiral described what had happened, but howls of anger rose as they witnessed the death of the High Council. At the sight of Brutes laying hands to their fellows and as the implication of the Covenant turning against them set in, those howls were replaced by a new silence more haunting than any sound the Shipmaster had ever heard before. All eyes turned to him, as he had known they would. He was ready.

The Prophet awoke now, surrounded by angry Sangheili, and tried to stand on his atrophied legs. It was pitiful how small he looked now, and the Shipmaster grabbed him by the neck as he tried to totter off the platform. When he twisted around to look at the Shipmaster, he saw something he had not expected, and his resolve crystallized . . . this Prophet, one of a group he had known all his life as the source of all the Covenant's power, was terrified.

This fear confirmed everything the Shipmaster had just seen on the screens and decided what he must do next. If this Prophet could be afraid then he could not truly know the will of the gods, for what could bring fear to someone with a direct connection to the divine? What's more, if he did not know the will of the gods then everything he had ever said and done was a lie—everything done for him was now a lie. The Prophet must die for that deceit, and the Shipmaster had to be the one to end him. His crew had to witness this to prevent them from thinking the thoughts they were thinking right now, and they would take from this death the start of a new purpose.

The Shipmaster tightened his fingers around the Prophet's ropy neck with one hand and used his other hand to hold the Prophet's face toward his. Tiny feet scratched without purchase on the metal floor as the Prophet hung in the air. The Shipmaster looked out to the shocked eyes of his troops and yelled, "Betrayal! Our people have been betrayed by the Prophets and their Jiralhanae puppets! You have seen what they have done, how they have struck at our faith and our leaders . . . and you know what Sangheili must do in the face of such betrayal. Our war against these deceivers starts now!" At these words the Prophet began a high-pitched scream that was cut immediately short as the Shipmaster looked back into his eyes and began to squeeze.

His struggle grew more desperate and a sound began to build in the crew as they watched the unthinkable event on the platform with the images of Brutes destroying Sangheili ships and devouring their dead fellows on the screens behind and above. The Shipmaster let the moment stretch until he judged his men's new

*hatred was sufficient and then he closed his fist sud-
denly around the Prophet's neck and felt the bones
under the skull give way. The Prophet's eyes locked on
the Shipmaster's, just as they had done the day the two
were bonded, and the contorting body grew suddenly
slack. It was done.*

*The Prophet's dead eyes continued to look up at him
as the Shipmaster opened his hands and the body fell
to the ground. He raised his voice to join his crew's
scream of rage and defiance and loss. As the scream
grew longer and louder he knew that he had succeeded
in giving them a purpose . . . for now. Looking down
at the tiny figure at his feet, the Shipmaster wondered
how long that purpose would last, and he wondered
where he would find his own purpose. He had just
killed the only voice he thought could speak for them
to the gods, and he did not know what those gods
wanted of him now. The men rushed back to prepare
for the voyage home and he followed to lash them with
the hardness they expected. The Shipmaster knew he
could only provide that hardness for so long. Already
he felt drained as the moment's rage left him, but there
was no time for such thoughts. He was needed.*

Those dead eyes followed him into consciousness. The
new light of dawn did little to rid him of the dread
caused by his dreams. The Shipmaster looked again to
the smoke. It was still rising. With a small sip of water
he left the shelter of the crumbling wall, moving toward
the glyph he knew he must cross. He glanced back at the
human tomb, glad to leave it behind.

This relief died quickly as he came to the rise and
caught full sight of the scar. Shortly past the rise was a
sheer drop into the black land, and he nodded at the
prudence of not attempting to proceed the night before.

Finding no easy path down into the scar, the Shipmaster found what looked to be a clear landing spot
below and dropped down into the channel. The smooth
walls were twice his height, and he worried about how
long he would have to look for a path up when he
reached the other side. He did not relish the thought of
staying down in this place any longer than he absolutely must.

The bottom was truly as black as it had appeared
from above. The plasma had melted several meters of
rock and stone, and the molten remnants had leveled
to an almost perfectly flat field between the boundaries
of the direct blast.

But while the overall terrain was smooth, every step
of this land was jagged and crystalline-sharp. The cooling material must have fractured and cracked, creating
a field of knives . . . no living creature would dare tra-
verse this place. None except him.

As he stepped carefully to avoid the myriad cracks
and vertiginous pits that cut across the ground around
him, the Shipmaster's already dark thoughts turned to
his fear for his people. After thousands of years of obedient service to the Covenant, what would they do
now? Already the fight was leaving some of his people.
Not even the death of all of the Brutes could replace
what they had lost when the Covenant was broken.

They would find no true purpose solely through battle, no matter how much vengeance demanded it. They needed something more.

For six years after the High Prophet of Truth, the father of all the Prophets' lies, died at the hands of the Arbiter, the Shipmaster had taken up the fight against everything that threatened his people. But that was all he had done—respond to threats. Immediately after the death of Truth, the Prophets wished only to preserve their own skins and the Brutes welcomed the newfound opportunity to misuse the weapons, ships, and other tools that had been so rightly denied them since they became part of the Covenant. The Brutes' barbarity prevented them from understanding the gifts of the Forerunners, even though they had suddenly received those gifts in abundance and they used them to try to wipe out their former Sangheili masters.

The battles against the Prophets and their Brute puppets had been legendary in the wake of the breaking of the Covenant, but it was not long before the primitive nature of the Brutes pulled their fighting cohesion apart and split their new power among several internecine struggles. The Prophets, in the meantime, had largely disappeared. There had never been many of their wretched species, but their sudden disappearance was baffling and, to some, portentous. The Shipmaster paid no mind to the rumors that held that the Prophets had finally achieved the Great Journey and that the Sangheili were damned for daring to take up arms against them in the final days of the Covenant.

Some Sangheili commanders continued to fight the

many scattered remnants of the former Covenant wherever they could be found, but not all. After six long years of this scattered war, Sangheili power had begun to wane right along with their drive to fight. They had to defend themselves, and always did so heroically, but since the Prophets controlled all of the major learnings that transformed Forerunner gifts into tools of the Great Journey, the Sangheili now largely lacked the understanding to build new facilities and weapons themselves. The Sangheili steadily lost ships they could not easily repair, let alone replace. Their time seemed to be running out.

They once depended on spiritual justification for all of their actions, relying on the Prophets to lead them in spiritual matters. There had never been any need for Sangheili religious leaders—now no one among them had the knowledge or the ability to comprehend the will of their gods. For a people whose sole purpose had been enforcing their gods' will, this was terrifying.

He knew his gods were out there, but he had no idea what they wanted. He had no idea if they were angry, and if they were he had no idea how to remedy that offense. All of those questions had brought him here, and all of those needs would keep him here until he found the answers he needed, or died trying.

The Shipmaster had seen this coming from the moment he put down the Prophet of Conviction, leading his men to war against their own religion. This planet was the last place he knew he had touched their gods, through that moment of ritual, and so he saw it now as his last possible hope to find answers that might lead him forward again.

He looked up, knowing his ship was in orbit, with orders to wait for his call, but he did not know what he would do if he did not find any answers. He only had food and water for a few more days. There was nothing edible here and the little water he had found so far had been bitter and sharp in his mouth. If his sustenance ran out before he heard from his gods . . .

The steady sound of the rocks against his armor was his only distraction. He moved quickly across that black land, keeping his eyes on the nearing pillar of smoke. He was not far from its source now, although it was hard to tell how much farther he had to go from so deep in the cut of the scar.

Suddenly, he came across the surprise of a small stream. It flowed right down the length of the scar; he couldn't tell how far it wound, but it looked as if it had been running for some time. The water had the same sharp smell as all other water on this planet, probably caused by the vaporization of some mineral when the plasma lines etched their fire. It carried with it smaller rocks and dirt and sand. He stared at that tiny stream and for a moment forgot the fires he unleashed here. He wondered if this stream offered hope that this place might someday be returned to its former state.

The stream could become a river, wiping away this glyph, burying it beneath new soil and sand and water. He knew that forgiveness from this planet would take far longer than he had time to live, but perhaps someday his wrongs could be wiped clean. The thought was comforting. Stepping over the small stream, the Ship-master looked up to the smoke once more, making sure he was on his proper path.

But the smoke was not there.

He scanned the entire horizon, hoping he had only become disoriented, but still he found no smoke. How long had he stared at that stream, lost in self-indulgent thoughts of forgiveness? This was his punishment for such thoughts, and he cursed himself and his weakness.

He quickly found a spot on the far wall where he thought he could exit this place and return to more normal ground. He began to run, forgoing caution for the sake of speed, for any accident he might suffer would be a very much deserved death. There would be no easy release from the burden of what he'd done.

But that death did not come. In surprisingly short time he threw himself against the far side's rocky wall, found footholds he could not see, and propelled himself to the top. Coming over the lip of the wall he now heard sounds—battle sounds, both human and Covenant (what had once been Covenant, anyway).

He followed the sounds to another stout building that reminded him unpleasantly of the one he'd left so quickly the night before. This building had part of a crumbling second story and what looked like two strange gray tents next to it, along with some kind of machinery covered in levers and wheels. All of these extra objects appeared to be human, with their squarish lines and dull gray and black surfaces. Human tools were always as ugly as they were functional in design.

He dropped his pack and freed his small hunting curveblade, a weapon his people had used for as long as they could remember, and which carried the same lines as their signature plasma blades. He stayed low to the ground, moving with deadly confidence. More shots were fired from around the building and he rushed forward, now with a clear view of three Kig-Yar taking cover behind the metal supports of the building, firing at an unknown enemy beyond.

The Shipmaster did not know what the birdlike Kig-Yar, whom the humans called "Jackals," were doing here, but he was certain it was not good. They were scavengers, pirates, and thieves, and they should not dare to come to a place like this. The sounds of the human weapons had now stopped, and he feared that the Jackals might have already taken their full toll on them.

He cut around to the far side of the building where he had just seen one of the gangly creatures lurking behind the building's front wall. Its attention was focused on whatever was around the structure. Before it knew what was happening he had come up behind it, pinned it to the wall of the building and nearly severed its head with a slashing lunge of his curveblade. He lowered the twitching body to the ground without sound. The staccato firing continued from the Jackal's fellows on the other side of the structure. The Shipmaster collected the carbine, now covered in the Jackal's dark blood, from the ground where it had fallen and checked the remaining ammunition. Only one shot remained, but it was good to have a real weapon in his hands again. He did not have time to scavenge the corpse for a replacement magazine, as the two on the other side would likely soon call or regroup. He had to act now.

He took a quick look around the corner to see what human forces remained, but his glimpse gave him nothing more than a closer look at the tents and some kind of hole with heavy equipment at its edge. Going back around the building so as not to expose himself to the humans, the Shipmaster dared a final quick look around the back corner to determine where the remaining two Jackals stood. When he heard them take their next shots he launched around the corner, firing his single round through the back of the nearer Jackal's plumed head. Bits of bone and meat and blood sprayed all over his fellow, who turned with a loud squawk and a weapon lowered in surprise. The Shipmaster's sprint had already carried him into melee range and with a kick from his armored foot to the Jackal's belly he heard its spine snap, and the wretch collapsed screaming.

The Kig-Yar's arms flailed in the mixture of dust and dirt and blood and its legs lay useless as the Shipmaster moved quickly to stand above his prey. A second kick to the prone Jackal's throat ended its struggles decisively.

Silence fell once again, broken only slightly by his combat-quick breath. He retrieved and hung a plasma pistol from his armor, picked up a carbine with more ammunition, and prepared to face the humans. Even though he had eliminated the Kig-Yar, the situation was now more complicated. Humans, as he had learned in all his years fighting them, became surprisingly fierce when cornered, and from what he had seen so far he suspected that the Jackals had attacked the humans unaware. More importantly, he remembered the stories told by the Arbiter that the humans shared some incomprehensible connection with the Forerunners. That humans were here at all, in this place where they suffered such a terrible loss, was enough to give the Shipmaster a spark of hope. Surely they must be here to serve some purpose for him.

Taking a deep breath, he snuck another look, low and fast, around his covering corner. Everything looked the same as it had, and he heard nothing. Anticipating closer-range combat, the Shipmaster slipped the carbine into its customary holding slot on his back and readied the plasma pistol in one hand and his gory blade in the other. After another deep breath he moved quickly to the rear of the nearest human tent and with his blade cut his way in, hoping to surprise any occupants and give him a second of surprise to decide whether to subdue or kill anything inside.

But the tent was empty, and a quick look around showed only papers and boxes and two small metal-framed beds. Through the loosely hanging door of the tent, however, he did see two human bodies on the ground outside, next to the boxy machinery he had spotted from afar. The Shipmaster could clearly see that the nearer of the two humans was motionless and had a number of large plasma burns on its legs and torso. He had seen enough dead humans to know that this one was beyond hope. The second, however, sitting with its back up against the machine, appeared to be intact and was holding a bulky pistol limply in its lap.

Throwing constant glances to the second tent and any possible additional attackers there, the Shipmaster came to within striking distance of the human and saw a large pool of its bright red blood gathering at the body's far side. He kicked the pistol off of the human's lap and, seeing no reaction, knelt down to determine if the thing was alive.

It was, barely. It continued to breathe but from the blood and lack of visible burns it looked like the human had been hit by a carbine round in its belly or side. He could not tell if the round had passed through or was still in there, baking the human's innards with radiation, but with the amount of blood on the ground the Shipmaster didn't think it particularly mattered. This man was as good as dead. Frustrated, the Shipmaster collected the pistol and moved on. The gun was primitive, but it was powerful and surprisingly accurate at a certain range. It might be useful in the days ahead.

Turning back to the second tent the Shipmaster confirmed that there were no more humans in the immediate area, but his eyes ranged constantly over the skies and horizon to watch for either human or Jackal reinforcements. All of these combatants had to have come from somewhere, and the lack of any ships in the area made it clear that they were brought here by someone or something else. Two humans alone could not have transported or even operated all this equipment . . .

there must be others nearby. He might not have much time to find out what they had been doing before those others came back. He wanted to be clear of this place when they did.

The second tent contained more of the boxes he had seen in the first, and the lids he threw open exposed what looked like food, energy cells, and some kind of filthy environmental suits with enclosed helmets and heavy metal gloves. They looked big enough to cover a human in their standard bulky combat armor, but he had noticed no armor on either of the human bodies outside, merely the drab uniforms he had seen before on some human civilians.

The machinery, when inspected more closely, was still a mystery to him. Thick bundles of cables led down and disappeared into the nearby hole, which looked as if it had been dug very recently. The hole angled as if it were directed underneath the boxy building where he had killed the Jackals, and soot on the upper lip of this short tunnel appeared to answer for the source of the column of smoke he had been following the last four days. This finding dismayed the Shipmaster greatly.

As soon as he had seen the column of smoke calling to him from across the scar, he had pinned all his hope on it. The thought that the smoke had merely been the product of scavengers, which these humans now seemed to be, shook him greatly. But he could take some of the humans' food, and they had to have water. Perhaps they were there to extend his journey into the great city farther at the heart of his glyph. And there was the matter of finding out where both of these groups of interlopers had come from. His journey was not over yet.

Stepping back into the second tent to find the humans' water, the Shipmaster tossed the lids off more of their metal containers and cast aside small tools, clothing, and other human detritus until he found a heavy container at the bottom with many pouches of what looked like fresh water inside. As he lifted this container and turned to carry it out his eye caught one of the papers scattered around the floor of the tent. He froze. He threw the water container aside and dropped to grab the image on that paper, which was covered in strange human letters surrounding the image set in the middle of the page.

Among all of these incomprehensible human markings he knew exactly what that picture was, and as his widening eyes took it in he knew why he had been called here.

On that picture was a glyph, a sign of his people, and that glyph was the one that tied him to this planet twenty years ago and brought him back again today. That glyph was Faith, and the gods had sent the humans here to help him find it. Now looking at the other documents and pictures, he found a series of images that showed artifacts, clearly Forerunner-created, covered with the glyphs and signs the Covenant had translated and adopted for all of their works. And most importantly, in one picture he saw part of a rounded frame and smooth glass lens that looked exactly like the Forerunner Oracle they had kept in their former capital city High Charity before it was destroyed by the recklessness of the Prophet of Truth. But the pictures showed these relics surrounded by humans, being studied and even dismantled by them, and this sight brought back an anger he hadn't felt for many years.

Other pictures showed what he could see was the nearby building as it looked before being nearly destroyed. In its former state it had other, less sturdy, structures all around it, and these pictures, along with the beginnings of the tunnel outside, told him everything he needed to know.

Excited now, he rushed outside to the bleeding human and rolled him over roughly to lie flat on the ground next to the pool of blood, now almost black in its cooling color. A small rivulet drained into the nearby hole, and it did not look like much more was left to flow from the human. The Shipmaster tore open the human's gray-green garb and saw the expected hole in the human's side where the carbine round had struck him. Rolling the human over to the other side he found a similar hole, more ragged at its edges where the flesh split outward as the round had passed through. He grunted with approval. The wound might not be fatal, as he had seen humans survive surprising wounds on the battlefield. He would do what he could to make sure this one survived, for the Shipmaster would have many questions for him in the days ahead. And the Shipmaster still remembered how to get a human to answer questions . . .

The Shipmaster reengaged his communications and sent a command message to his ship. He called for a medic, a security squad, the ship's chief engineer, and a patrol of the surrounding skies in case there were more of these humans or Kig-Yar nearby. He had his purpose now and with it the beginnings of a sense of direction.

He no longer needed any Prophets to tell him what the gods desired. It was time for him to find out for himself.

A LETTER FROM THE DEPARTMENT OF XENOARCHAEOLOGICAL
STUDIES AT EDINBURGH UNIVERSITY TO SECURITY-CLEARED
FACULTY AND ONSITE GRADUATE STUDENTS.

Department of Xenoarchaeology
Jadwin Hall
Edinburgh University
2 Charles Street
Edinburgh
Alba EH8 9ADEarth

ONI MANDATED SECURITY CLEARANCE
INFORMATION: *TS_Adjunct and Civilian Personnel
Exception 1492_b 01/31/2553 14:12pm TST*

January 31, 2553

From the Office of Dr. William Arthur Iqbal.

Dear Colleagues,

   As we are all very aware, the discovery of the Excession at Voi has significant ramifications for our
species, as well as the course of our work. Everyone

on this distribution list has had some exposure to classified documents regarding the discovery and exposure of what we are now describing as "Forerunner" relics, technology, and architecture. Everyone on this distribution list has no doubt made some educated assumptions about what we're looking at and, from this moment, for.

A similar letter has gone out from the Department of Xenobiology in Calcutta. Some of their information differs in security clearance from your own and so I am not able to divulge its contents here. You may ask your local ONI Communications Officer for biological information that may be germane to your studies.

We are at a strange tipping point for our profession and for our culture. The Covenant threat is lifted for the moment, but I very much doubt that the agreement with the Sangheili and their representative, the Arbiter, is the end of our conflict with the other Covenant species. However, it buys our department some time and, more importantly, resources to continue our investigation and our work. This is more than we've had in the past thirty years or so.

I suspect we will continue to compete with the Elites and other species for information about Forerunner relics. But that technology and its legacy is plainly at the center of our chance for recovery. You are no longer working for history as an intellectual exercise, but rather to ensure that humanity *has* a history.

With that in mind, I am announcing that you are all now required to adhere to a new military dictate: ONI Emergency Order 1416-2. This letter serves as both notification and contract that you work for the Office of Naval Intelligence, regardless of your original post and designation. Existing ONI workers are also included in the minutiae of the order which follows as a separate document.

Previously, I know that you have all been working under unknowable conditions, often racing against time to finish observations. I do not think for even a moment that the current calm will be the future norm. We need to continue expediency, cost-control, and working with limited resources.

Our civilization has undergone a significant shift. Our populations are decimated, our people scattered, and our military is now at its weakest since the dawn of slipspace travel. Our former alien enemies may be the tip of the iceberg if the UNSC can't assume the cooperation of the human Diaspora. And we need all the cooperation we can get.

There are some details that I know have made the rounds as gossip, but you are now party to the limited information we have. There are holographic records and other data at this secure location: **pit_somnambulist_001413_action**, but the following digest will bring you up to speed today as you begin to read the other materials:

The Excession at Voi is a slipspace "machine" of extraordinary power. It has demonstrated the ability to open a standing "portal" to a now destroyed extragalactic location referred to in your data as "the Ark." The portal is now closed, but we have good reason to suspect that the Excession at Voi is capable of other feats.

The Ark was a manufacturing facility—it seems to be the construction site for the entire Halo array. It was too vast and complex for any useful data to be gathered in the brief moments the portal was opened, but we can assume it served other purposes too. We are examining footage from the *Forward Unto Dawn* and other surviving systems/people. Much of the gathered information was lost along with the AI Cortana and her host Spartan. I do not need to remind you of those details.

The Halo array itself was a networked weapon system, which used a previously unknown technology to destroy specified biological forms at both a molecular and a Galactic scale. Its purpose was, as far as we can tell, to destroy both the Flood and more importantly, its food source—carbon- and calcium-based life forms above a certain level of sophistication. Its last known activation coincides precisely with the Ross-Ziegler Blip* and we can be relatively certain that that event was a deliberate attempt to defeat the organisms that made landfall in Africa just a year ago.

We can now look at other artifacts and digs with a renewed context. Items, data, and images from Coral, Reach, Heian, and more can all be examined in light of

---

*A tiny aberration in the fossil and carbon records of Earth, noted by two Earth geologists in 2332—and matched on several other worlds, demonstrating a gap in certain species so tiny and uniform, that it had been attributed not to a biological catastrophe, but rather had been investigated and then abandoned as odd evidence of warping or stretching of spacetime itself. The Ross-Ziegler Blip is now being opened and reinvestigated in connection to the events of 2552.

the hard facts established over the last year. It seems that whoever, or whatever the Forerunners were, or are, they were fully aware of our species. The Excession at Voi was visible to local inhabitants 100,000 years ago— possibly a mix of "modern" and Neanderthal humans.

We are being careful not to make too many assumptions, but the evidence in some cases is compelling. In others, ambiguous. I direct your attention to the photographs from Heian. There were obvious Forerunner elements in that architecture, but also unmistakable architectural themes from Greco-Roman, East Asian, and Middle Eastern eras. All of those buildings predated human travel to that world by perhaps hundreds maybe thousands of years. We find ourselves wondering if they borrowed from our history, or we from theirs. It is impossible that it was a coincidence.

Furthermore, now that we understand the Halo is an armed weapon array, we must revisit our prior assumptions about how inert other structures are. This applies to the Excession at Voi particularly, and careful exploration is being undertaken as we speak. Those concerned about ONI barging in as a military force needn't be. The investigation is being undertaken with the greatest care and under rigorous scientific conditions.

We still don't understand everything about Voi, but we do know that the structure is still active, still drawing power from an unknown source, and as far as we can tell, riddled with passageways and conduits that we have, as yet, minimal access to. There are more secrets locked under our feet than we dare speculate on. We're looking particularly for answers as they relate to doors, encryption, and other passageways. This isn't something we can blast or arcweld our way through. It's something we must think through.

Again, I want you all to understand the entirety of the material you are now investigating. To those of you already at sites, I advise caution and diplomacy in equal measure. The Sangheili have promised nothing—and indeed warned us that they do not yet control either the Covenant client species, or even their own domestic situation. Hostilities may have ceased for now, but we should be alert and logical.

This may be the greatest archaeological boon we have ever received as scholars, but it is certainly the most perilous. Be careful. I expect daily reports filed regardless of slipstream delay. I will reassemble chronology later.

Good luck.

Yours sincerely,
Dr. William Arthur Iqbal
Department of Xenoarchaeology
Edinburgh University

ACKNOWLEDGMENTS

The amount of work that goes into a project like this defies understanding. The behind-the-scenes of making a multi-author book that ties into the vanguard of modern science fiction could easily make the stuff of bad reality television. Juggling the franchise's wonderfully high story expectations while simultaneously maintaining authors' creative freedoms, all under fun and tortuous time constraints, requires heroic actions from many. This book wouldn't have been at all possible without the Herculean efforts of Nicolas "Sparth" Bouvier, Alicia Brattin, Gabriel "Robogabo" Garza, Jonathan Goff, Kevin Grace, Alicia Hatch, and Frank O'Connor.

The amazing team at Tor has to be praised as well. Led by Tom Doherty and masterfully marshaled by Eric Raab, the unsung heroes of Karl Gold, Justin Golenbock, Jim Kapp, Seth Lerner, Jane Liddle, Whitney Ross, Heather Saunders, and Nathan Weaver and their efforts in the trenches to make it all happen is legend. Special thanks to Shelley Chung, Patricia Fernandez, and Christina MacDonald for desperately trying to make every story in here read without a blip.

Additional thanks to 343 Industries, Bungie Studios, Ryan Crosby, Scott Dell'Osso, Nick Dimitrov, David Figatner, Nancy Figatner, Josh Kerwin, Justin Osmer, Pete Parsons, Bonnie Ross-Ziegler, Phil Spencer, and Carla Woo.

ABOUT THE AUTHORS

JONATHAN DAVID GOFF is a writer and artist raised on a healthy diet of Saturday morning cartoons and sugary breakfast cereals. After serving in the United States Air Force, Jonathan spent six years developing creative content for action figure, comic book, and entertainment properties at the McFarlane Companies in Tempe, Arizona, before relocating to the Pacific Northwest where he assists Microsoft Game Studios' 343 Industries in all manner of Halo-related goodness. He currently resides in Redmond, Washington, with his lovely and infinitely supportive wife, Maria.

KEVIN GRACE is the managing editor for 343 Industries, working closely with the internal and external talent who bring the Halo universe to life across books, comics, animation, and games. He is an editing veteran of *Halo 3*, *Halo 3: ODST*, and a variety of other games published by Microsoft Game Studios. He comes from a Midwestern attorney upbringing and now enjoys living in Seattle, Washington, with his wife, Karen, and twelve furry paws.

By day, TESSA KUM sits at her computer and types. By night, she also sits at her computer and types. Hers is the very definition of a rock 'n' roll lifestyle. She is a graduate of the Clarion South Writers Workshop, editorial assistant for *Weird Tales*, and assistant editor for the Best American Fantasy series. She has been published in *Daikaiju 3* and ASIM, with forthcoming fiction appearing in anthologies such as *Baggage* and *Last Drink Bird Head*, and her short-story collection *7wishes* is currently free to read online. She lives in Melbourne, Australia, and owns neither an Xbox nor a TV (which is, you know, a bit of a drag).

ROBT McLEES does two things well: kill zombies and speak in a robot voice. Both of these life-skills have served him well in his fourteen years at Bungie. He married his best friend and has produced, with the help of his wife, two wonderful boys. If you give Robt a bite of your pizza, he'll ask for a beer. And when you get back from grabbing a beer from the fridge, like half the damned pizza is gone! WTF, Rob?!?

#1 *New York Times* bestselling author KAREN TRAVISS has received critical acclaim and award nominations for her Wess'har series, as well as regularly hitting the bestseller lists with her *Star Wars* and *Gears of War* novels. A former defense correspondent and TV and newspaper journalist, she lives in Wiltshire, England.

World Fantasy Award–winner JEFF VANDERMEER grew up in the Fiji Islands and has had fiction published in more than twenty countries. He is the bestselling author of *City of Saints & Madmen*, as well as *Predator: South China Sea*, released by Dark Horse Books in 2008. He reviews books for, among others, *The New York Times Book Review*, *The Washington Post Book World*, and *Barnes & Noble Review*, as well as being a regular columnist for the Omnivoracious book blog. Current projects include *Booklife: Strategies and Survival Tips for Twenty-First Century Writers*, the noir fantasy novel *Finch*, and the forthcoming definitive *Steampunk Bible* from Abrams Books. He currently lives in Tallahassee, Florida, and serves as assistant director for Wofford College's Shared Worlds writing camp for teens (Spartanburg, South Carolina).

FRED VAN LENTE is the *New York Times* bestselling author of *Incredible Hercules* (with Greg Pak) and *Marvel Zombies 3*, as well as the American Library Association award-winning *Action Philosophers*. He created Spartan: Black for the graphic novel *Halo: Blood Line*, illustrated by Francis Portela and serialized by Marvel Comics beginning in December 2009. Van Lente's other comics include *Comic Book Comics*, *MODOK's 11*, *X-Men Noir*, and *Amazing Spider-Man*.

ABOUT THE ARTISTS

ROBOGABO (GABRIEL GARZA) has been a professional artist for the last ten years. Born in Mexico, he now lives in Seattle, working for 343 Industries. His artwork is heavily influenced by his years of experience working at a newspaper. His passion for video games attracted him into the concept art community and led him to live and work across the United States, working on video games. When Gabo is not painting, he likes to spend time at home with his family, while trying to enjoy life outside his art cave. Visit his website at www.robogabo.com.

HALO WAYPOINT ART CONTEST WINNERS

BRYN CASEY is a twenty-six-year-old college student currently residing in Denver, Colorado. Bryn has been a huge fan of Halo since the launch of *Halo: Combat Evolved* in 2001, and has been creating Halo-related artwork for some time. He would like to thank his girlfriend, Lori, for her support and inspiration.

MICHAEL ROOKARD, of Overland Park, Kansas, is a twenty-eight-year-old freelance illustrator who loves creating concept art and character designs. You can check out all of his work at www.galefire.com.

At eighteen years of age, JAMI KUBOTA, of Plano, Texas, has a deep love for marine life, specifically cetacean life—whales, dolphins, porpoises. Most of his artwork is based on fantasy and pure imagination—dragons, homemade monsters, species, etc.—though he also enjoys illustrating real-world wildlife. And naturally, Jami is a massive fan of the Halo franchise.

MICHAEL JAMES CHUA, of Monrovia, California, was twelve when he first encountered Halo, shortly after its release on the Xbox. Born in New Jersey, he now lives in California and is working to earn his B.A. in multimedia art and design with an emphasis on game art.

RACHEL BEAUDOIN (Sl'askia), of Las Vegas, Nevada, is a military vet who has been drawing for most of her life. Her love of Halo, particularly of the Sangheili, started in 2008, and this love is expressed in not only artwork but fan fiction.

After 100,000 years, the story of the Forerunners will finally be revealed

HALO

GREG BEAR

COMING IN JANUARY 2011

Book One of
The Forerunner Saga

They are worshipped by the Covenant as gods . . .

Their legacy is scattered throughout the Galaxy . . .

But their enigmatic connection to humanity remains a mystery.

Hugo and Nebula Award–winning and bestselling author Greg Bear takes readers and gamers deep into the time of the Forerunners, the central mystery of the Halo universe. Halo fans will, for the first time, discover just who the Forerunners were, how they harnessed technology, matter, and energy itself, and what caused them to disappear completely from existence.

In hardcover
978-0-7653-2396-5
www.tor-forge.com

© 2010 Microsoft Corporation. All Rights Reserved. Microsoft, 343
Industries, the 343 Industries logo, Halo, the Halo logo, Xbox, Xbox 360,
and the Xbox logos are trademarks of the Microsoft group of companies.

HALO®
W A Y P O I N T

**Enlist today and join the millions of other Halo
fans expanding their career rankings.**

Learn more at http://halo.xbox.com

© 2010 Microsoft Corp. All Rights Reserved.

KNOWLEDGE
YOUR BEST WEAPON AGAINST THE COVENANT

FOUND WHEREVER STRATEGY GUIDES ARE SOLD.

© 2010 Microsoft Corporation. All Rights Reserved.

McFARLANE
TOYS

HALO ◖
ACTION FIGURES AND VEHICLES

mcfarlane.com/halo

FIGURES WORTHY OF THE GAME

5-inch scale hyper-detailed and fully articulated figures re-create the look of
in-game play down to the last detail. These stellar action figures and vehicles
bring all the adventure of the hit video game *Halo: Reach* to your collection.

ACTION FIGURES   **VEHICLES**   **ACTION FIGURE 2-PACKS**

© 2048 Microsoft Corp. All Rights Reserved. © 2012 TMP International, Inc. McFarlane Toys and the other marks and logos displayed are trademarks of TMP International, Inc. WARNING: CHOKING HAZARD — Small parts. Not for children under 3 years.